The Adventures of Poppy and Lord Ted

and Lord Ted

The First Summer

T.M Jorden

**Grosvenor House
Publishing Limited**

The right of T.M Jorden to be identified as the author of this
work has been asserted in accordance with Section 78
of the Copyright, Designs and Patents Act 1988

The book cover is copyright to Tim Millward
Cover illustrations by Ruth Palmer.

This book is published by
Grosvenor House Publishing Ltd
Link House
140 The Broadway, Tolworth, Surrey, KT6 7HT.
www.grosvenorhousepublishing.co.uk

A CIP record for this book
is available from the British Library

ISBN 978-1-83975-590-3

With thanks to:

Rachel for her unconditional love and support,
Katharine at Island Meadow,
Sally for bringing a vision to life
and Lord Ted
who sits proudly in his rightful place,
on the bed,
at home,
in Derbyshire.

For Rachel, Poppy, James, Charlie and Oliver

"adventures fill your soul."

1

Lord Ted is Grandpa's bear. He lives on the big bed in the sunny back bedroom at Nanny and Grandpa's house.

Lord Ted, or to use his full name Lord Teddington of Bearshire, has been Grandpa's bear since Grandpa was a young boy and he is an exceptional bear.

Poppy visits her nanny and grandpa one night each week after school and she stays for tea. *Somehow it's different here*, she always thinks to herself, and Nanny and Grandpa are always so happy to see her.

Snuggling up to Grandpa in his chair and listening to his adventures from when he was a small boy with his very remarkable teddy bear, are memories she would keep forever.

Little did Poppy know what was in store over the summer.

"I think it's about time you met Lord Ted," said Grandpa one fine spring day, after a story about Lord Ted and a fairy house.

"Can I?" said Poppy excitedly, "do you still have him?"

"Yes, of course I still have him, I'm not that old," said Grandpa, laughing. "He's a very special bear and I think it's time you met him now," continued Grandpa with a wink. "What do you think Nanny?"

"Yes," said Nanny, already looking up from her book at Poppy's reaction. "I think it's the perfect time."

Grandpa went upstairs and fetched his bear. "Hello old boy, it's been a while since you've had any real adventures hasn't it? But if you are still up for it, I'd like you to meet Poppy," said Grandpa as he scooped him up in his arms and returned downstairs.

"This is Lord Teddington, Poppy," said Grandpa with a smile nearly as wide as his face. "Lord Teddington of Bearshire, I'll leave him with you for a while to get acquainted," he said, placing Lord Ted on the settee next to Poppy and stroking his ear as he turned to leave.

"I'll go and help Nanny with the tea."

"Thank you, Grandpa."

Poppy looked at Lord Ted. He was just as Grandpa had described in his adventure stories. Slightly creamy grey in colour and oh so fluffy, with a podgy tummy and a little brown nose. He looked so cuddly it made Poppy smile; *what a good-looking bear* she thought, and so proud, after all he is a lord.

"Hello Lord Teddington."

Poppy picked him up and sat him on her knee facing her. "You are a very handsome bear," she said, admiring Lord Ted for a while.

She stood up. "Let's go and sit in the garden." As she did so Poppy instinctively cuddled Lord Ted, squeezing him to her chest.

"Wwwmmppfff, mppff, mmppffw," said Lord Ted, with a muffled voice. Poppy threw her arms out in shock and Lord Ted bounced off the small low table in the centre of the room and on to the floor.

"Ouch," he said, rubbing his chin with his paw as he sat up.

Poppy looked stunned, mouth and eyes wide open. "Oh my, you can t-t-talk," she stuttered still in shock.

"Yes, I can if you hug me, but not so hard next time please," he replied gently. "So, you must be Poppy?"

"Yes, I am, and sorry about that – are you, err, OK?"

"Yes, I'm fine thank you," replied Lord Ted still rubbing his chin. "Your nanny and grandpa talk about you all the time you know."

Poppy smiled. Lord Ted paused for a while then said, "How old are you Poppy, if I may ask?"

"Nanny told me you should never ask a lady her age," said Poppy, laughing.

"Yes, you're right," he said, smiling at the pretty girl in front of him. Poppy was tall for her age with long blonde hair and a smile that would melt any heart.

"But, as you asked so nicely, I'm nearly eight," she responded.

Poppy picked up Lord Ted and sat him back on her knee. "May I call you Lord Ted, Lord Ted?"

"Yes, I think you can, and I think we will be friends for a long time," he said.

"Me too," replied a very smiley Poppy.

"Shall we go into the garden then?" asked Lord Ted, "it's been a while since I was outside."

"Yes, let's." Poppy picked up Lord Ted and carried him outside, he blinked as the spring sunlight hit his eyes.

2

Nanny and Grandpa's cottage garden was full of colourful flowers. At the end of the long garden were several trees, one rather large oak tree with an old tree house high in the branches which had seen better days, created shade. Beyond the trees was Grandpa's vegetable garden, then a hedge with a small gate that led to barley fields sloping down to old barns on the edge of Dave 'Jonny' Johnson's farm. Jonny Johnson, who had been at school with Grandpa, was Grandpa's closest friend. Beyond the barns were some old oak woods and more fields, all planted and ready for harvesting later in the year.

The smell of the garden made Poppy's nostrils tingle as she breathed in the sweet-smelling air, and the low hum of the working bees made it sound like a plane was passing in the distance.

"It's beautiful isn't it, Lord Ted?"

"As beautiful as I remember," said Lord Ted, "and look at all the bees!"

"I know bees are very important for the garden, Grandpa told me, and I have read about them, but they are a little scary."

"Bees are OK, they're not bothered about us really, it's the nectar they want, to make honey. Bears love honey, and I'm a bear," said Lord Ted very proudly.

"You look very young to be Grandpa's bear though Lord Ted."

"Grandpa looks after me. It's important to look after all your things so they'll last longer."

"Then I'll look after you too Lord Ted," said Poppy. Lord Ted was rather pleased with that idea.

Poppy sat on the garden chair and squeezed Lord Ted in beside her, just as she squeezes in next to Grandpa in his chair. As she did so Nanny appeared with a glass of Poppy's favourite homemade raspberry lemonade.

"Here you are Poppy," she said kindly, placing the drink on a small table beside her, "tea won't be long. Who were you talking to?"

"Oh, thank you Nanny, just Lord Ted," she said as if having a conversation with a teddy bear was an everyday thing.

"Lovely," said Nanny smiling as she turned to return to the kitchen, "won't be long now, it's your favourite tonight," her voice drifted down the garden.

Back in the kitchen Nanny stood next to Grandpa who was staring out of the window towards the garden.

"Poppy was talking to Ted," she said, placing her hand gently on his shoulder.

Grandpa continued to stare out of the window and after a few seconds softly said, "Good. Good, I knew they would. That didn't take too long did it – I'll lay the table my love."

In the garden Poppy smiled to herself, *what a wonderful day,* she thought and closed her eyes as the sun warmed her face and made her blonde hair sparkle. Lord Ted snuggled into Poppy's side.

As Poppy drifted away with thoughts of the adventures Grandpa had spoken about, the silence was broken by Grandpa himself.

"I can see you have made friends already," he said, "rub a bit of this sun cream into your face and arms please Popsicle. It's important to cover up in the sunshine."

Grandpa handed the tube to Poppy who secretly loved being called Popsicle but sometimes wrinkled her nose at the name.

They sat in the sunshine for a while longer watching the bees hard at work.

Eventually Poppy got up, kissed Lord Ted's forehead, sat him back down and went to return the sun cream and help Grandpa prepare for tea.

Lord Ted sat and contemplated; *what a wonderful day* he thought and closed his eyes as the sun warmed his face.

"Can I help you Grandpa?" asked Poppy, as she placed the sun cream back on the table.

"Yes, that would be lovely thank you, I think Nanny may have a bowl of salad to bring out. She has made pizzas tonight and the salad is from the garden, your favourite."

She skipped down the hallway to the kitchen where Nanny was waiting with the bowl of salad for Poppy to collect.

"Thank you Poppy, please take this, then wash your hands and sit at the table. The pizzas are ready."

Poppy placed the bowl on the table then quickly ran to wash her hands, then into the garden to fetch Lord Ted. From now on Lord Ted would be permanently at her side when she was at Nanny and Grandpa's house.

As Poppy sat, Lord Ted by her side at the table, Nanny appeared with the tea.

On the table were placed two of the most colourful pizzas. Fresh green salad with the ripest shiniest red tomatoes, long green cucumbers and a bowl of homemade mayonnaise already lay on a white tablecloth.

Poppy waited to be asked to help herself. She carefully chopped the cucumber and tomato as Grandpa cut the pizza into slices and helped with the salad leaves.

"Your table manners are lovely Poppy," said Nanny, "I think it will be time to go to The Greedy Duckling restaurant in the village together one day soon – what do you think?"

Poppy finished her mouthful, took a sip of lemonade and nodded her head. "That would be just lovely Nanny, thank you. Do you think Lord Ted could come too?"

"What do you think Grandpa?" enquired Nanny

"Yes, I think that would just be fine," he said.

Poppy smiled at Grandpa as he winked at her and everyone ate their tea, chatted about the week ahead and Poppy talked about school and her friends. After the pizzas and salad were all gone, Nanny brought out a homemade trifle as a treat.

This is truly a magical place, Poppy thought to herself as she stared at the trifle, then down at Lord Ted.

Nanny served the trifle, which did not last very long, and after they had all finished Poppy helped clear away so they could all sit back out in the sunshine before Poppy had to go home.

"It's been a lovely afternoon hasn't it Poppy," said Grandpa with his eyes closed and face in the sun, his short white beard glinting every so often.

"Yes. Another lovely tea thanks Nanny and a big surprise meeting Lord Ted, Grandpa."

"Yes," said Grandpa slightly distracted, "I think we might mend that tree house one day soon too – what do you think?"

"I think that might be a great idea," replied Poppy bouncing Lord Ted on her knee.

"Maybe you could stay sometimes now you are a bit older too Poppy," said Nanny.

"Yes please Nanny," said Poppy excitedly.

"Grandpa or I could take you to school the next day."

"And maybe we could go on a little holiday to Meadow Island over the spring holiday too." suggested Grandpa.

"Is that where the fairies live in the story you told before tea Grandpa?" Poppy asked.

"Maybe," smiled Grandpa.

"Daddy will be here soon to take you home so go and put Lord Ted back on the bed in the back bedroom. He will be waiting for you there next week," said Nanny, "I'll speak to your mummy and daddy about staying sometimes and coming on holiday with us."

"OK, Nanny."

Poppy picked up Lord Ted and walked upstairs smiling. As she entered the back bedroom she looked around; the sun was streaming through the window, lighting up the room which was painted all white. A huge pine wardrobe with boxes on top was to her left with a pine dresser to the side, and there was a slightly out of place crooked panelled door with a gleaming brass doorknob on her right.

A big brass framed bed with crisp white cotton sheets, that looked so inviting, was opposite the window. This was the bed where Lord Ted lived. It had a few different coloured cushions neatly placed against the white pillows and she could see the imprint where Lord Ted sat. As she walked past the bed across to the window, which had a low windowsill almost like a seat, she looked out at the pretty garden with the fields and barn roofs beyond and could see Nanny and Grandpa sitting and talking; how she loved spending time with them.

Although Nanny and Grandpa had lived here for many years, this is where Grandpa slept when he was a boy as the house used to belong to his grandparents.

She climbed up and sat on the side of the bed and spoke to Lord Ted again.

"It's been lovely to meet you Lord Ted. I can't wait to see you next week," she said. Lord Ted sat motionless.

"What shall we do next week do you think?" Lord Ted did not move.

Poppy waited for a response.

"Oh, I forgot," Poppy picked him up and gave him a loving hug.

"I think," said Lord Ted as he sprung back into life, "I think that I cannot wait to see you next week either."

"That's a funny looking door," said Poppy nodding to the crooked door, "what's in there?"

"Well, it can be whatever you believe it to be," said Lord Ted.

"Poppy!" shouted Nanny from the hallway, "Daddy's here."

Poppy smiled and looked confused all at the same time. She gave Lord Ted a kiss on his head and returned him to his rightful place.

"Bye Lord Ted, see you next week," she said as she rolled off the bed straightening the covers.

"Cheerio Poppy – be good and work hard at school."

"I will!"

Poppy ran downstairs and packed all her belongings and kissed Nanny and Grandpa goodbye.

"Thank you for a lovely afternoon. I can't wait for next week."

"Thank you for being such a good girl Poppy. We're looking forward to next week too," replied Nanny as they finished their hug.

And with that Poppy turned and skipped down the path.

"Do you think she will say anything about Lord Ted?" asked Nanny.

"No, I don't think so," said Grandpa, "I never did."

"We are going to have some fun aren't we," said Nanny, "it's been a special day."

Poppy waved and Nanny and Grandpa waved back. As the car disappeared over the hill Grandpa put his arm around Nanny. "Yes, it's going to be fun," he said, "let her own adventures begin."

Nanny smiled.

2

As the late spring bank holiday approached, Poppy was getting excited at the prospect of her first camping holiday with Nanny and Grandpa, but most of all adventures with Lord Ted.

After meeting Lord Ted for the first time, Poppy had spent more time at Nanny and Grandpa's and got to understand just how special Lord Ted was.

"Why are you called Lord Ted and not just Ted, Lord Ted?" she asked one day.

"Well, that's a long story," Lord Ted replied.

"Grandpa says you know a lot of things and a lot of people too."

"I think I know a lot of people yes, but I will always be Grandpa's bear until he gives me to someone else."

Poppy smiled and hoped that one day Lord Ted would be her bear.

At last, the day of the camping trip arrived. It was a beautiful sunny day, with a clear blue sky yet slight chill in the air. Grandpa had just finished tidying the front garden when Poppy arrived. Just like the main cottage garden at the back of the house, it was full of colour at this time of year.

It had seemed to take forever to arrive, but Daddy finally dropped off Poppy with all the things she needed, from her clothes to her toothbrush but no toys.

"I don't need any toys; I'll be too busy. Plus, I have Lord Ted with me, so I'll be OK," she had told her mother, "I just need my backpack for Lord Ted and some books."

Poppy, Nanny and Grandpa stood by the front gate and waved as Daddy disappeared around the bend waving behind him as he went.

"Look Nanny, my two front teeth are wobbly at last!" said Poppy using her finger to wobble her teeth.

"Oh wow, I wondered when they would make an appearance, they've taken their time haven't they, but they look like they'll be out soon enough," said Nanny sweetly. "Run upstairs and fetch Lord Ted, I'm sure he'll be pleased to see you, and your wobbly teeth."

"Look Grandpa." again Poppy was wobbling her teeth this time in the direction of her grandpa.

"I see," said Grandpa, "exciting."

"That's good timing isn't it?" he said to Nanny.

"Absolutely," replied Nanny.

Poppy ran upstairs into the back bedroom. Lord Ted was in his usual place, propped up against the cushions on the big bed in the sunshine. Poppy's eye was drawn to the crooked door with the big brass doorknob to her right; in front was a rather old looking faded green backpack.

Poppy climbed onto the bed and picked up Lord Ted giving him a loving squeeze.

"Hello Poppy," said Lord Ted as if he had woken from a sleep, "I'm so happy you're here."

"Me too, and look Lord Ted, my front teeth are wobbly at last," again moving them with her finger.

"Well, the tooth fairies will be busy won't they?" said Lord Ted. "Are we all packed and ready to go?"

"No not yet I don't think. Grandpa said I could help him pack the car."

"I'm amazed how it all fits in, if you look down there you'll see my backpack to carry me in."

"I've brought my school backpack to carry you in Lord Ted," said Poppy happily.

"Oh OK, it's just I have all my things in there. All the things a bear needs," said Lord Ted.

"Like what?"

"Well bear things, plus its really comfy in there."

"Oh, OK," Poppy responded happily, *if that's Lord Ted's backpack then that is what we will use,* she thought.

In the hallway Nanny had started to pile up the bedding, clothes bags and food boxes ready to take to the car.

"Grandpa is in the garage ready to start putting all the stuff in the car Poppy," said Nanny, "he's waiting for you I think."

"OK Nanny, yes, he said I could help him."

Poppy skipped out of the front door with Lord Ted bouncing around on her back in his green backpack and down the path towards the garage, where Grandpa was moving things around ready to put in the car.

The back of the car was already open, and Poppy could see that half the back seat was folded down.

"Hi Popsicle. Pop Lord Ted on the back seat then we can start packing," said Grandpa.

Poppy opened the car door, took Lord Ted out of his backpack and placed him carefully in their seat. "I'll be back in a minute or two," she said turning to walk into the garage.

As she did so the first thing she noticed was how big the garage was with bikes, a workbench, shelves, boxes and hanging tools all neat and tidy and then there was the smell –the mixed smell of oil, wood and grass from the lawnmower; they all combined to make a smell only a grandpa's garage would have.

Poppy was amazed to see just how much 'stuff', as Nanny called it, was needed. Blow up beds, table and chairs, a flat-pack kitchen with a cooker, a box full of kitchen bits and bobs and then the bedding, clothes and food from the hallway – and last of all the tent.

"We put this in last as it'll be first out," said Grandpa as they both lifted the heavy tent into the back of the car, "that's it now, all done, thank you so much for your help Poppy. Time to fetch Nanny then we can be on our way."

"I'll let her know we're ready Grandpa," she said as she skipped back to the house, "I just need to wash my hands."

Grandpa locked up the garage just as Nanny and Poppy appeared after locking the house and checking all was ready to go.

"OK," said Nanny, "LG."

"LG?" enquired Poppy

"LG – Let's Go," said Nanny laughing.

"LG," repeated Grandpa.

They all got into the car and Nanny made sure that Poppy's seat belt was secure. Poppy placed Lord Ted on her knee so he could see out of the window.

Grandpa turned out of the drive. "Are we there yet?" asked Poppy giggling.

Nanny and Grandpa started to laugh.

After lots of laughing and chatting about what they need to do when they got there, Poppy fell asleep with Lord Ted snuggled into her arms. *This is going to be such fun*, thought Lord Ted.

About an hour later Grandpa turned the car into Meadow Island campsite. Grandpa had been coming to the same campsite since he was a boy and Katharine, the owner, saw them as they drove in – she waved and shouted, "Normal spot, I'll come and see you in a while."

Grandpa put his thumbs up and continued past the shop through to the orchard. This was to be home for the next few nights.

Poppy was still fast asleep so Nanny and Grandpa thought they would get as much done as they could before she woke up. The tent was up in no time at all. By the time Poppy opened her eyes Grandpa was taking the last box of food into the tent.

Poppy got out of the car with Lord Ted and could see that Nanny was talking to a lady with a dog.

"Poppy this is Katharine I was telling you about; Katharine owns the campsite."

"Hello Poppy," said Katharine kindly, "it's so nice to meet you. I've heard a lot about you, and this is Tripp, our dog, she's very friendly."

"It's so nice to meet you too, I've got wobbly front teeth at last, hello Tripp," replied Poppy wobbling her teeth again, "and this is Lord Ted, but I think you've probably already met."

"So, you have, and yes, a very long time ago," said Katharine as she reached out to give Lord Ted's ear a little loving squeeze, "well, it's so lovely to have you all to stay. How long are you staying for?" she continued, as Poppy stroked Tripp's head who wagged her tail in response. Tripp was a brown and white spaniel with long fluffy brown ears and a pink nose.

"Just three or four nights," replied Grandpa, "depends on the weather really; the forecast is not too bad but let's see. Nothing worse than taking a wet tent home."

"We should be OK, another warm bank holiday weekend in prospect," replied Katharine as she turned back towards the shop, "see you later!"

Poppy turned to look at the tent – it was enormous and green in colour. Poppy was sure Grandpa could have parked the car in it. The kitchen, now fully assembled, was down one side, food boxes on the other with the bedrooms at the back. A table in the middle with chairs around and a lamp hanging above.

Nanny was making a cup of tea while Grandpa was clearing away a few things back in the car.

"Oh fiddlesticks!" shouted Nanny.

"What's the matter Nanny?"

"I've gone and left the milk in the fridge at home," she said raising her eyebrows "Poppy, would you go to the shop and ask Katharine for a bottle of milk please and put it on our account?"

"Of course, can I take Lord Ted?"

"Yes, when you come back you can both go and explore the campsite."

"LG Lord Ted," said Poppy giving Lord Ted a squeeze

"LG," replied Lord Ted.

As they walked across the orchard towards the shop Poppy saw a duck waddling towards them. Grey and brown with a white flash underneath his yellow bill, he looked quite handsome for a duck.

"Here's Reg," said Lord Ted, "he thinks he's a chicken."

Poppy laughed out loud, "Why does he think he's a chicken?" she asked, still laughing.

"Because Mrs P, one of the chickens, sat on his egg and when he hatched Mrs P was the first thing he saw, so as far as he knows she's his mum," said Lord Ted, "he doesn't know any different so don't say anything to him about it."

Sure enough a few chickens appeared behind Reg, led by his mother. Mrs P was nothing like Poppy had seen before and she was not quite sure she was a chicken either; she was a lot smaller than Reg and the other chickens, mainly black in colour with a few brown feathers, she looked like she was wearing a black and white flowery hat for a wedding and had black baggy trousers on.

How wonderful, thought Poppy who had never seen a duck who thought he was a chicken before, or a chicken dressed for a wedding.

"Hi Lord Ted," said Reg.

Poppy stopped in her tracks with her eyes and mouth wide open just as when she'd heard Lord Ted talk for the first time.

"Hi Reg," said Lord Ted, "this is Poppy."

"Hello Poppy."

"You can t-t-talk," she stuttered.

"Well, yes. And this is my mum," said Reg nodding towards Mrs P, "and my brothers and sisters."

"Err, well err, hello everyone," said Poppy still in a state of shock.

"Hello Poppy," was the combined response from the chickens and Reg, who is also a chicken of sorts.

"We're off to the shop to get some milk," said Lord Ted.

"Has she forgotten the milk again?" asked Reg with a laugh that sounded like quack quack quack.

Poppy's state of shock had eased to more a state of surprise by the time she entered the shop. The shop was much bigger inside than Poppy had imagined. Groceries lined one wall and on the other side were cakes and breads that filled the air with a freshly baked bread smell. Just inside the door was a freezer full of ice lollies that made Poppy's eyes light up and next to that a few outdoor toys and camping essentials.

"I see you've met Reg then," said Katharine smiling from behind the counter.

"Yes," said Poppy still gazing at the freezer.

"He's quite the character is our Reggie. So, I'm guessing your nanny has sent you for some milk?"

"Yes, please," said Poppy now turning to the counter.

"Yep, here you go. I'll put it on their account. Anything else?"

"May I ask you a question err Mrs … "

"Please call me Katharine, and yes you may."

"Err, thank you. Do err, all the animals uhm, speak Katharine?"

Katharine smiled. "To Lord Ted, yes."

"Oh."

"But let's keep that to ourselves shall we?" Katharine replied with a wink, "better get that milk back to Nanny so she can make you a cup of tea."

"Yes, yes, of course thank you Mrs, err Katharine."

Poppy turned and left the shop and quickly walked back to the tent with the milk for Nanny.

"Here you go Nanny."

"Thank you my darling," said Nanny, "I see you've met Reg, bless him, so confused that one."

"Yes, yes, I have."

"Let's have a cup of tea then you can help Grandpa gather wood for the fire later."

Poppy sat next to Grandpa at the table, which had been moved outside into the sunshine, with Lord Ted on her knee as Nanny brought the tea and homemade biscuits over.

"You see something new every day Poppy," said Grandpa, "I think these next few days will be fun."

Poppy looked up at her grandpa, nodded and smiled.

3

As they were finishing their tea Poppy could see Katharine walking over towards them looking slightly flustered.

"Hello you lot," she said now smiling, "don't suppose you can help me out can you?"

"Of course," said Nanny, "what's up?"

"Dad's not well and he was going to mow the grass today before the masses arrive; don't suppose you could help me out?"

"I think we have just the team here," replied Nanny looking at Grandpa, Poppy and Lord Ted

"Yep, we're the team you need Katharine," said Grandpa standing up, "LG Poppy?"

"LG Grandpa," said Poppy also standing to attention and grinning.

"Excellent, excellent – you know where everything is," said Katharine sounding relieved.

"Yes, leave it with me, Poppy and Lord Ted."

"Thanks ever so," said Katharine now walking back towards the shop waving, "the sheds are open!" she shouted.

Grandpa gulped down the last of his tea and gathered up the cups and plates. "I'll just take these into the kitchen then we can get going Poppy."

"OK," said Poppy excitedly. "What will you be doing Nanny?"

"Well three things. Firstly, I'll watch you fly around on the mower, then when you're out of sight I'll read my book … "

"And thirdly she'll fall asleep Poppy," said Grandpa, laughing.

"I may do," said Nanny, smiling, "or I may just get the dinner ready."

"Come on Poppy, let's go and mow the grass and explore the campsite at the same time."

"OK. Bye Nanny."

"Bye Poppy, have fun and be careful."

Poppy put Lord Ted in his backpack with his head and arms popping out of the top and made sure he was secure, then ran to catch up with Grandpa as he was walking to the shed.

"This should be fun; I love driving these mowers, I'll hitch up the trailer and we can collect any firewood as we go," he continued.

As they got to the shed, which was bigger than any garden shed Poppy had ever seen before, Grandpa slid the door open.

Just as he did so a loud hissing and spitting noise made Poppy jump as three huge white geese came running out of the door. They were hissing and snapping as they ran past, which scared the life out of Poppy who instinctively hid behind Grandpa's legs. Their bright orange and yellow beaks were wide open showing their pink tongues as they hissed.

"Gerrout of it!" shouted Grandpa waving his arms.

Poppy was visibly shaken. The geese were so noisy and aggressive.

"Don't worry Popsicle. They're gone now."

"I didn't like that Grandpa, even Lord Ted disappeared into his backpack."

"No Lord Ted doesn't like them either. That's Roland, Ronan and Rebekah – they can be quite nasty so stay well clear of them!"

Grandpa picked Poppy up and gave her a hug.

Lord Ted got caught in the hug. "Have they gone?" came a muffled voice from the backpack.

"Yes, they're gone now," said Poppy, and as Grandpa put her down Lord Ted popped his head out of the backpack.

Grandpa checked the shed was clear and they walked in – the shed was vast, and the smell hit Poppy straight away – it was a bit like Grandpa's garage. In the centre of the shed was a bright red sit-on lawn mower with two black shiny seats.

"OK Poppy let's get you strapped in."

Poppy climbed up and Grandpa secured the safety belt. Lord Ted stayed in his backpack and was looking over Poppy's shoulder. Grandpa dragged a small trailer and hooked it up to the back of the mower ready to collect any firewood then climbed aboard.

"You ready Popsicle?"

"Ready Grandpa, LG," she said smiling already forgetting about the geese incident.

Grandpa fired up the mower and a puff of black smoke blew out of the back. He carefully reversed out of the shed and off they went. What fun they had driving around the camp site; Nanny was waving as they went in and out of the trees in the orchard cutting the grass as they went; Poppy could not stop laughing as they bumped around. She could now get to see how big the whole site was. There were more trees behind Nanny and Grandpa's tent and one of them had ladders to an enormous treehouse; beyond that the river bent around the back of the big sheds with a weir behind the trees.

As they swerved around Grandpa drove on to the track and off they went, past the shop and entrance to the caravan park. People waved and shouted, but Poppy could not hear over the noise of the mower but waved back anyway. She had no idea who they were, but they all seemed to know Grandpa.

Katharine waved as they entered the caravan park as she was chatting to some new arrivals. This area was much bigger, and Poppy saw the river properly for the first time with the island in the middle – Meadow Island. Children were playing in small boats.

In and out of the caravans they went making sure they cut all the grass. As they went by the riverbank Poppy could see more of the river and the island. A small wooden jetty made its way out into the water with a few small boats tied up.

Every so often Grandpa would stop and collect sticks and wood for the campfire. "You mustn't go too close to the river without Nanny or me Poppy."

"Of course, Grandpa."

Eventually Grandpa headed back past the shop towards the sheds. Katharine gave them a wave and Grandpa shouted, "all done!" Poppy saw Katharine put her thumbs up, so she did so too, then looked across and saw Nanny waving. Poppy waved back as they bumped along the track but then turned off towards the tent and stopped outside.

Grandpa unfastened Poppy's safety belt and she climbed down.

"That was great fun Grandpa."

"Yes, it was, great fun. Can you help me with some of these sticks please Poppy?"

Poppy took Lord Ted's backpack off and helped her grandpa. After all the sticks were unloaded Poppy picked up Lord Ted and the backpack and walked into the tent while Grandpa drove the lawnmower back to the shed.

"Perfect timing Poppy, dinner will be ready soon. Let's get your hands washed," said Nanny, "was that fun?"

"Apart from the geese Nanny, it was great fun."

"Ah, you've met those three have you, they're not very friendly are they?"

"No, I know, but I don't think I have ever laughed so much bouncing around on the lawnmower, I'm surprised my front teeth are still in, Grandpa went ever so fast."

Grandpa was soon back and washed his hands just as Nanny was serving dinner.

"I'll do the washing up," said Grandpa when they'd finished, "Poppy, you go with Nanny to have a shower and put your jammies on, then we can sit by the fire once I've made it up."

By the time they'd returned Grandpa had cleared all the pots and dishes away and was just about to light the campfire.

The campfire was roaring away soon enough, and Grandpa fetched the chairs so they could sit around it – close enough to keep warm but far enough away to be safe. Nanny had made tea along with a hot chocolate for Poppy and brought out some marshmallows and sticks.

"No camp is complete without S 'Mores Poppy," said Nanny.

"What are S 'Mores?" enquired Poppy.

"You'll see," replied Nanny as she began to toast the marshmallow on the end of one of the sticks over the fire embers. Poppy had never tasted anything so amazing and with her hot chocolate it was a perfect end to a busy day.

"There's a treehouse behind the tent Grandpa, is that where the fairies live?" asked Poppy after what seemed an age just staring into the fire.

"No Popsicle, the fairies live around us in the orchard. The tree house is for you to play in if you'd like," replied Grandpa as he got up to put some more wood on the fire.

"Thank you Grandpa, I'd love that," said Poppy trying to get back to the fairy topic. "So, the fairies live in these trees here," she said pointing at the surrounding apple and pear trees, "how do we see them?"

"Yes, all around us. Well, fairies like music and dancing and on a full moon they'll come out of their doors when it gets dark and dance. When the morning sun appears, they vanish back behind their doors. The next full moon is in a couple of weeks though, the Strawberry Moon in June, so we'll miss all the dancing, but you may see them in between times," explained Grandpa, "if you believe, you'll see them and their doors in the trees. If you take Lord Ted with you, he can show you where they are, but you will only see them if you believe. Many don't and that's OK too."

"Can I look now please?"

"Yes of course. Pop Lord Ted on your shoulders and he'll show you," said Nanny, "but put a cardigan on as you'll be colder away from the fire."

Poppy ran into the tent.

"Do you think she'll see them?" Nanny asked Grandpa.

"Yes, I think so, I think she believes enough."

Poppy found her cardigan in her bag, put it on and gave Lord Ted a squeeze.

"You OK to sit on my shoulders Lord Ted? And hang on to my head."

"Yes, no problem."

"And you know where the fairies live?"

"Yes, of course," said Lord Ted, "but you'll only see them if you believe."

"I do, I do," said Poppy now quite excited.

"LG then," said Lord Ted.

Poppy ran out of the tent and into the orchard with Nanny and Grandpa looking on. She stopped at the bottom of a tree with a jump.

"Here?" she asked eagerly.

"Slow down, you'll scare them," explained Lord Ted, "let's just walk around quietly. It's getting darker now so they will be difficult to see unless they have fairy lights."

"Fairy lights? I could get a torch," said Poppy.

"No, that will definitely mean you won't see them."

Poppy started to walk more slowly but was trembling with excitement.

"And you'll have to whisper too," whispered Lord Ted to make the point, "just keep walking around."

After what seemed forever Lord Ted suddenly whispered in Poppy's ear, "Stop!"

It made Poppy jump a little, but she stopped still. "Look up slowly," said Lord Ted, "can you see just above the second branch, a small purple door?"

Poppy looked up and tried to focus. She tried and tried but could not see anything. Minutes past and she was getting a little upset. Her bottom lip began to tremble, and her eyes began to fill with tears "I can't see them Lord Ted," she whispered with a whimper.

"There are a few appearing now," said Lord Ted, "close your eyes tightly."

Poppy closed her eyes tight and a tear ran down her face.

"Keep them closed as tight as you can."

"OK."

"Do you believe in fairies?"

"Yes!" whispered Poppy frustratingly and slightly louder than Lord Ted had anticipated.

"OK then slowly open your eyes and look up."

Poppy did as she was told, tilted her head back and slowly opened her eyes. To her amazement she could see the purple door and then small twinkling lights and a red door, yellow door, green door and more. They kept appearing. The tears had gone and the biggest grin that anyone could ever do appeared on her face.

"Whhhooooooooowwwwwwwhhhhh," whispered Poppy.

Poppy looked in amazement as she saw more and more doors appear in the orchard trees.

As she walked around with Lord Ted balanced on her shoulders, she saw most of the trees had different coloured small doors; some had twinkly lights, some had none.

"Why have some got lights on, Lord Ted?" she whispered.

"I think it's because some are at home and some are out. We may get lucky and see one or two of the fairies, but they prefer a full moon."

"It's so pretty Lord Ted."

From a distance Nanny and Grandpa could see Poppy looking around in amazement.

"I think she's found some," said Nanny holding Grandpa's hand as a small tear rolled down her face, "how wonderful."

Grandpa looked on with a smile on his face. He knew just how Poppy was feeling, Lord Ted had helped him see them for the first time when he was about Poppy's age.

Poppy continued to look around and point out new ones to Lord Ted as they appeared.

"Look at that bright red door," whispered Poppy pointing, "isn't that one pretty?"

"Yes," said Lord Ted, "Elvina and Oona live there, they're very nice fairies and in charge really."

"You know their names?" whispered Poppy very loudly, "how do you know their names?"

"Just do. Gullveig and Jareth live behind the blue door, they're tooth fairies and always arguing but they're very funny."

"Tooth fairies," whispered Poppy very loudly again, "real tooth fairies!"

"Not so loud, you'll scare them. Nixie and Alfred live at the yellow one, they're brother and sister."

"How many do you know?"

"A few. As well as Elvina, Oona, Nixie, Jareth, Alfred, Gullveig and friends there's Sophie, Belle, Zuzana, Deri, April, Emma and Maisy to name a few. There are a lot here."

"Wooooowwwaaahhhhh," whispered Poppy again looking around in wonder and amazement.

After a while Grandpa appeared by her side, "What do you think Poppy?"

"Oh Grandpa, they are real aren't they, it's so pretty. Do you think we'll see any fairies tonight?"

"I'm not so sure tonight. What do you think Lord Ted?"

"No, I don't think so, not tonight."

"Time for bed then I think Poppy, you've had a very eventful day."

"OK Grandpa," said Poppy reluctantly.

"They'll be here again tomorrow," said Lord Ted.

Poppy took Grandpa's hand and they walked back towards the tent.

"I knew you believed in fairies Popsicle, very few do and even then, very few get to see them. I'm sure they were looking out of their windows at you too. That makes you very special." said Grandpa softly.

"Thank you Grandpa," said Poppy.

Once back at the tent Poppy cleaned her teeth gently as tooth fairies only collect clean white teeth and finally snuggled into bed. Nanny and Grandpa hugged and kissed her goodnight and Poppy was asleep with a fixed smile with Lord Ted by her side before they could zip up her bedroom.

"What a day," said Nanny, as they returned to the fire to clear up for the night.

4

"Cock-a-doodle-doo!"

Poppy woke with a jolt, *what on earth is that noise*, she thought giving Lord Ted a squeeze. "Lord Ted, what's that noise?" she whispered as she could hear Grandpa snoring next door.

"That's Grandpa snoring."

"No not that noise," whispered Poppy.

"Cock-a-doodle-doo!" came the noise again.

"Oh, that's just the cockerel waking up all his hens, and Reg of course."

"Oh, right I see. What's a cockerel again?"

"Cock-a-doodle-doo!!"

"He's the daddy hen and his name's Jack," whispered Lord Ted. The early morning light was shining through the tent and Poppy thought it must be quite late, but it was only five thirty in the morning, "it's very early, so let's go back to sleep now."

Poppy turned over and stared up at the tent ceiling thinking about the night before.

"Did we really see all those fairy doors Lord Ted or was it a dream?" she asked after a few minutes.

"Cock-a-doodle-doo!"

"And how am I supposed to sleep with that noise too?" continued Poppy.

"Yes, we saw lots of fairy doors last night," said Lord Ted, "in fact I don't think I have ever seen so many."

"Really?"

"Cock-a-doodle-doo!"

"Oh, for goodness sake," said Poppy.

Poppy closed her eyes and thought of the fairies and the doors.

"Poppy… Poppy… Poppy," said Nanny gently. "It's 9 o'clock, time to get up," she said stroking Poppy's hair.

23

Poppy opened one eye. "Good morning Nanny."

"Good morning my lovely, you've slept well."

"Apart from the cockerel."

"Ahh, Jack. He's beautiful but noisy." Poppy could see Nanny was dressed. "Grandpa is making bacon sandwiches for breakfast. We're going to go for a walk by the river today."

Poppy could now smell the wonderful aroma of bacon frying from the kitchen.

"That sounds fun," said Poppy.

"Mornin' Popsicle!" shouted Grandpa from the kitchen.

"Morning Grandpa!"

Soon enough Poppy was sitting at the table tucking into bacon sandwiches with a lovely cup of tea. Just then the largest, most colourful hen walked into sight and Poppy stared. Jack, who was a cockerel and not a hen, was indeed very colourful. Chestnut brown and very dark green shiny feathers with flecks of red and white, he was much bigger than the hens, with what looked like a red hat and floppy red chin under his small beak. He stood very proudly like a sergeant major on parade.

"Hello Jack," said Nanny, "you come for some crumbs?" Nanny brushed the breadcrumbs from the breadboard onto the grass and Jack pecked away.

The day seemed to pass so quickly. Lord Ted joined Poppy, Nanny and Grandpa for a walk around the riverbank and even went to the island in a boat. The island was very small, but it was fun to run around, and the sun shone all day. Once back at the orchard Poppy played in the tree house and read her schoolbooks to Nanny and Lord Ted.

Before she knew it Poppy was getting ready for bed again as Grandpa was tending the campfire. Poppy and Lord Ted sat in her chair between Nanny and Grandpa sipping her hot chocolate as they chatted about the day but all she could think of were the fairy doors.

"Nanny, Grandpa, do think it would be OK for me and Lord Ted to see if we could see the fairy doors again please?"

"Yes, of course Poppy," said Nanny. "Pop your cardigan on again though, as there's a chill in the air."

Poppy was soon ready with Lord Ted on her shoulders walking carefully towards the trees in the orchard, learning from the night before that running was not the best idea. There were some more tents around, so she was careful to avoid those but walked to the tree where the bright red door was, the one where Elvina and Oona lived.

Again, nothing was appearing, but Poppy did not get upset.

"Close your eyes again Poppy," whispered Lord Ted, "and believe."

Poppy closed her eyes tight for a while and then looked up again; the doors, some with sparkly lights, began to appear.

"It's so pretty Lord Ted," she whispered.

"It is," whispered Lord Ted who also just stared at the beautiful sight of twinkly fairy doors.

After a while of looking up Poppy and Lord Ted made their way back to the campfire and sat down.

"It's so pretty and magical Nanny and Grandpa," she said, "did Daddy see the fairies when he was little?"

"No," said Grandpa, "he didn't believe enough to see them. Not everyone does and that's OK. If everyone saw them it wouldn't be as special."

"What about the tooth fairies though?"

"Well, they certainly left him money for his teeth because they were white and shiny like yours," said Grandpa.

"It's late now so time for bed I think Poppy," said Nanny.

"Thank you for a lovely day," said Poppy.

She cleaned her teeth ever so carefully as they were now quite wobbly, wobbly enough to move around with her tongue and was soon in bed cuddled up to Lord Ted.

"What do the fairies do with all the teeth they collect?" she whispered to Lord Ted, giving him a squeeze at the same time.

"Well, they only collect the white ones, which is another very good reason to clean your teeth properly, then they grind them down to make fairy dust."

"Fairy dust from teeth?"

"Yes, that's how they make it. They use it for all sorts of things but mainly to help them fly around and collect the good teeth. The children are rewarded for keeping their teeth clean."

"Oh, I see. Night night Lord Ted," thinking that sounded quite bonkers but now she'd seen fairy doors anything could be true.

"Night night Poppy," said Lord Ted.

5

The next day started in a very similar fashion. Jack did his best to wake the whole campsite very early, but this time Poppy slept right through the noise to be woken again by Nanny and the smell of bacon wafting through the tent.

Today the decision was to stay around the campsite, explore and play games with some of the other children and then eat out in the evening. How very grown up Poppy felt.

The sun was shining yet again but it was not too hot so being outside was just the right place to be. Birds were singing and Poppy could hear the weir from the river in the distance.

"Can Lord Ted and I go and see the weir please?" asked Poppy.

"Not without Grandpa or me Poppy, it can be quite dangerous there."

"Oh, OK, then perhaps along the riverbank?" said Poppy with the sound of disappointment in her voice.

"A little later. You should always have someone with you near the river, that's really important Poppy, either me or Grandpa will go with you."

"OK Nanny."

"I'll tell you what you could do though. Please could you go to the shop and get a few things, maybe a ball or two so we can play some games later. You can decide what you think we need?"

"Yes of course," replied Poppy, again feeling grown up as she was asked to go shopping. Poppy gave Lord Ted a squeeze.

"Come on Lord Ted, let's go shopping!"

"OK," said Lord Ted.

Poppy tucked Lord Ted under her arm and walked towards the shop. "It's very lovely here isn't it," said Poppy happily, "it's so quiet."

Before Lord Ted could answer the silence was broken with a commotion by the sheds. Roland, Ronan and Rebekah were being very loud, hissing and spitting and flapping their wings.

Poppy looked and then slowly started to walk towards the three geese who were snarling and hissing, she knew something was wrong.

"Where are you going Poppy?" said Lord Ted anxiously, "Nanny said go to the shop!"

But Poppy did not reply, she kept walking toward the sheds.

"Poppy!" shouted Lord Ted.

As they got closer to the sheds Poppy held Lord Ted more tightly to her side and at the same time they both noticed what was going on.

Somehow Reg had been separated from the rest of the chickens and Roland, Ronan and Rebekah had surrounded him. As well as hissing and spitting they were snapping and pecking at him. Poor Reg looked absolutely terrified.

As they got closer Poppy and Lord Ted could understand what they were saying …

"You're not a chicken you're a duck!" cackled one of the geese.

"And a stupid duck!"

"Mrs P is not your mum," they hissed nastily.

"I'm not a duck, I'm a chicken," said Reg in a shocked whimpering voice. The geese continued to cackle and laugh at poor Reg.

"You're a duck and an ugly duck – have you looked at your reflection, yuk!" they snapped trying to peck at him as Reg was pressed up against the shed wall trembling.

Poppy was a lot closer now. "STOP THIS RIGHT NOW!" shouted Poppy in a very commanding voice.

Suddenly the geese stopped, and slowly turned around together to face Poppy and Lord Ted looking very menacing. Reg looked up to see what had happened.

Poppy stared right back and quickly realised she could be in a spot of trouble as the geese were a lot bigger than she had realised as they raised themselves to their full height and spread their wings. They were taller than Poppy who was not little for her age by any means.

"Holy… Moly," said Lord Ted very slowly.

"Sssssssssssoooooooooooo you've come to protect the ugly duck have you?" hissed Roland who was by far the biggest goose.

"Yes, I have, and he's a chicken and a very handsome one too!" said Poppy who was now not feeling so brave.

Roland, Ronan and Rebekah hissed and cackled with their pink tongues sticking out at Poppy – then suddenly stopped.

28

"GET HER!" shouted Roland.

Poppy froze then realised she needed to turn and run very fast because these geese were quick. Just as she did so Reg saw an opportunity to escape but not before he pulled a big white feather out of Ronan's bottom who let out a loud hiss. With the white feather in his beak Reg made a break for it while the geese lunged forward towards Poppy and Lord Ted.

"RUN!" shouted Lord Ted.

Poppy screamed and turned to run without knowing where she was heading. She was a little disorientated but kept going jumping over clumps of grass, but the geese kept up with her.

She was not really sure what happened next as it was all so fast. She could see that she was heading straight for the river and had to stop but as she did so she dropped Lord Ted. As Poppy turned to face her fate and protect him, a glass wall materialised out of nowhere in front of her that sparkled and glittered with lights, just as two of the geese slammed straight into it and let out a squeal and hiss as the pain shot down their necks.

At the same time Lord Ted appeared to take off into the air just as Rebekah stopped and tried to grab him, all the while hissing and spitting with her long pink tongue sticking out. Rebekah then looked up to see Roland and Ronan screaming in pain and falling to the floor.

A few seconds later Roland and Ronan got to their feet, shook their heads and flapped their wings then turned and ran back towards the sheds with Rebekah not far behind them just as the sparkly glass wall faded away.

Poppy just stood still trying to take it all in, with a mixture of being scared and relieved all at the same time. Then panic set in as she realised Lord Ted was not there.

"Poppy!" shouted Lord Ted, "Poppy, I'm up here!"

Poppy looked up. Lord Ted was sitting on the branch of a tree.

"Oh Lord Ted I am so –" Poppy stopped mid-sentence, "– sorry." Poppy stared with her mouth open.

"This is Elvina and Oona," said Lord Ted, "from the red door, they rescued me."

Sitting either side of Lord Ted with their legs crossed and dangling down were two very pretty fairies. Slightly smaller than Lord Ted, they were dressed in red and green with sparkly wings behind them, little pointy ears and big smiles on their faces.

"Hi Poppy," they said together in rather high voices and a wave that was more like a salute, "are you OK?"

"Yes, yes I'm OK thank you."

"Above you in the other tree are Belle, Sophie, Zuzana and Deri," said Lord Ted.

"Hi Poppy," came a few voices from above her.

"They placed the fairy dust wall to protect you," said Lord Ted.

"Oh, th-thank you s-so much," said Poppy looking up.

"That's OK Poppy," said Sophie, "you were very brave to stand up to those bullies. I don't think they will bother you, or Reg again."

As Sophie was talking Elvina and Oona picked up Lord Ted and lowered him gently into Poppy's arms.

"Oh Lord Ted, I am so sorry, I will never let you go again," she said as she hugged him, "thank you all ever so much," she continued looking up at the fairies.

Just as she did so Tripp and Grandpa, closely followed by Nanny and Katharine, came running around the corner all breathing very heavily.

"Poppy, Poppy what's going on, we heard you scream," said Grandpa frantically.

"I'm OK Grandpa, the geese chased me and Lord Ted, but Elvina and the fairies saved us," she said pointing up into the tree, but the fairies had gone as quick as they appeared.

Tripp barked in the direction of the sheds.

"I told you not to go near the weir darling," said Nanny with a look that made Poppy turn her head and realise where she was.

"I panicked and ran the wrong way Nanny, I'm sorry."

"That's OK as long as you're safe. Let's get you cleaned up and have some lunch then maybe you can go to shop and buy the things you were supposed to be getting earlier."

"Sorry Nanny."

"I'll sort the geese out Poppy, I'm sorry they frightened you," said Katharine.

"It's OK, they were picking on poor Reg, but I don't think they'll bother him again," said Poppy with a reassurance that made Katharine understand what she meant.

Poppy went with Nanny and, once washed and freshened up, helped prepare the lunch.

Lord Ted sat on one of the chairs by the table and watched Poppy help her nanny. *What a wonderful girl Poppy is*, he thought.

Poppy walked over carrying a plate of sandwiches ready for lunch just as Reg, Mrs P and a few other chickens came walking around the tent quacking and clucking.

Poppy picked up Lord Ted and gave him a squeeze so she would be able to understand what was being said.

"Hi Reg," said Lord Ted.

"Hello," replied Reg, "I just wanted to say thank you to Poppy for saving me. I do know I'm a duck really, but in my heart I'm a chicken."

"That's OK Reg, I am glad we were there. You're a chicken to us and a very good looking one too," replied Poppy with a smile.

"Thank you," said Reg feeling himself blush a little.

"And thank you from me too Poppy," said Mrs P, "I think you were very brave."

Now it was Poppy's turn to blush.

"Just stay with your mummy from now on Reg but I don't think they will bother you again, the fairies have made sure of that."

"I will, thanks again both," said Reg as he waddled off towards the shop with the other chickens following on swiftly behind.

Poppy, Lord Ted, Nanny and Grandpa sat and had their lunch while other families arrived. Grandpa was pretending to read a book but was watching them over his glasses put their tents up with the odd tut and shake of his head. He did make Poppy smile.

"I'll help Nanny clear away and wash up Poppy, if you could go to the shop and get the things you were going to get earlier before you were distracted," said Grandpa with a knowing smile.

"OK Grandpa, thank you, I will," said Poppy, "come on Lord Ted, this time we are going straight to the shop."

"Yes, that's the best idea of the day so far."

As they entered the shop Katharine was behind the counter talking on the phone. She waved as if to say, 'I'll speak to you in a minute,' so Poppy went to look at the toys glancing at the ice lollies as she went past, almost straining her neck in the process.

Poppy picked up a basket and chose a cricket set, three tennis balls, a very colourful bouncy football and a game with two Velcro plates and a very hairy tennis ball. She knew to pick the three extra tennis balls for the cricket set because Grandpa was bound to hit some into the river. As she walked over to the counter Katharine was just finishing her telephone call.

As she put the phone down she looked up and smiled at Poppy, "So then, are you OK?"

"Yes, I'm fine thanks Katharine, really I am," said Poppy, "and how is your daddy today?"

"He's much better, just an off day I think at his age, thank you for asking."

"I hope the geese are OK too?"

"Yes, yes, they're just sulking behind the sheds, they'll be OK, just licking their wounds so to speak. I'm sorry they chased you. Perhaps they learned a valuable lesson today."

And the geese did learn a lesson never behaving like that again.

"Yes hopefully. Please may I get these?" replied Poppy lifting the basket on to the counter.

"Yes of course, I'll put them on the account. I'll bring them over with you as I want to chat with your grandpa and you have your hands full."

"I can manage," she said holding up her right hand with Lord Ted tucked under her left arm.

"Well you'll need that hand for your ice lolly, go and help yourself and I'll follow you across."

"Really?" said Poppy with a grin, "thank you!"

Poppy picked a colourful stripped lolly and skipped back towards the tent with Katharine following on behind with the basket.

"Where did you get that?" asked Nanny excitedly already knowing the answer as nannies always seem to.

"Kafferwin gawe itooo me," said Poppy with a mouthful of very cold ice lolly and trying to avoid her wobbly front teeth.

"You lucky girl, mind those teeth."

During the afternoon they all played games in the orchard. Other families joined in and, as expected, Grandpa hit two tennis balls into the river. Nanny played the Velcro hairy tennis ball catch game with Poppy while the 'boys' kicked the football around. At 5 o'clock they all went for showers and got ready to go to the pub for dinner.

Poppy was wearing her hair in bunches and a pretty little summer dress.

"Don't you look pretty?" said Katharine as they passed the shop

"Thank you," said Poppy, "we're off out."

"So I see."

Once they were all ready, Grandpa zipped up the tent and Poppy tucked Lord Ted under one arm and held Nanny's hand with the other, they made their way down the path by the side of the old church, into the village and into the pub.

Their table was waiting for them, Grandpa had asked for one by the window and Poppy sat Lord Ted at the table next to her.

When the waitress came to take their order, Poppy felt very grown up and, after checking it was not a chicken she had recently met, chose chicken and chips. Grandpa decided on the same and Nanny had a steak.

After chatting for a while, the dinners arrived – then it happened – first the left and then the right – Poppy's front teeth decided to come out there and then. It was not painful at all, in fact, if she had not nearly swallowed the first one she would not have noticed. Nanny kindly passed a tissue for Poppy to wrap them up. There was no fuss, no bleeding, and no pain but it took Poppy a little longer to eat her dinner having to chew on one side then the other to miss the new gap. There was no way Poppy was leaving any of this dinner as it was so delicious. However, after careful consideration and with help from Nanny, she decided on ice cream for her pudding.

"You were very brave and well behaved at the table Poppy, thank you," said Grandpa, "no one would have known that your teeth had come out."

"Thank you Grandpa, does that mean the tooth fairies will come tonight?

"I expect so, what do you think Nanny?"

"I'd like to think so as they are so close by and your teeth are very clean and white because you've looked after them so well." said Nanny

"And, I know what you did today, you were very brave there too. Standing up to bullies is not easy," said Grandpa.

"Thank you Grandpa, they said some very nasty things to Reg."

"You know if your feet slip you can recover your balance but if your tongue slips you can never recover your words. Once they're out, they're out so it's better to be kind," said Grandpa, "there is no place for bullies in this world. I am very proud of you Poppy."

"Thank you," said Poppy looking at her grandpa and grinning with a big gap in her teeth.

"I understand the fairies came to your rescue too, that makes you very special Popsicle so I am sure the tooth fairies will come tonight."

"Thank you Grandpa, I hope so," said Poppy, with her new smile.

They sat and chatted for a while longer, but Nanny could see that Poppy was getting tired and it was getting late.

"Come on," she said, "let's be getting back."

Poppy was so tired that Grandpa ended up carrying her all the way back to Meadow Island and she fell fast asleep in his arms. Nanny carried Lord Ted back and on their return she put both to bed, carefully placing the tissue with Poppy's front teeth in under her pillow. There would be no more adventures today, Poppy was exhausted.

6

Poppy opened one eye, it was still dark. She wasn't sure what the rustling noise was, but it was in her right ear as she lay on her pillow. Then some whispering voices…

"Put your back into it," came the loud whisper.

"I am, you're not pulling hard enough."

"I am, it's you."

"It's not me it's you."

"We'll have to wait until she turns over, she's right on top of them."

"Come on, one last try – ready ... one … two …"

Before they could get to three, Poppy lifted her head off the pillow and out flew Gullveig and Jareth bouncing against the tent wall and on to the groundsheet next to Poppy's clothes bag.

"Thrrreeeeeeeee … ooommmppffff," said Gullveig as he and Jareth hit the ground.

"Ow," said Jareth.

Poppy rolled on to her left side to see a dazed Gullveig and Jareth on the floor shaking their heads.

"Hello," she said, "you must be Gullveig and Jareth the tooth fairies, you live behind the blue door don't you?"

"Oh, hi Miss Poppy, miss," said Gullveig and Jareth together both elbowing each other at the same time.

"Yes we do Miss Poppy," continued Gullveig, "and this has never happened before. We've been doing this for about 436 years 4 months 1 week and a day and this is the first time anyone has woken up."

"I'm not surprised the racket you were making," said Jareth.

"It was you, not me," snapped Gullveig.

"It was not, you started it."

"I didn't, you did."

They were both holding each end of the folded tissue that contained Poppy's front teeth.

"Give that here," said Gullveig as they each pulled an end of the tissue.

"No, it's mine."

"I got it first."

"No, you didn't, I did."

"You did not, I ... "

"Boys, Boys!" whispered Poppy, "ssshhhh," she continued putting her finger to her lips, "you'll wake Nanny and Grandpa, or even worse Jack, then the whole world will be awake."

"Sorry Miss Poppy miss," they both said together just as the tissue ripped straight down the middle and out flew two shiny front teeth.

"That's torn it," said Jareth and Gullveig started laughing. Then Jareth started laughing followed by Poppy.

"Zzzzzhhhhh," said Poppy trying not to laugh really loudly but was finding it hard watching these two little fairies rolling around in front of her with torn tissue all over them.

"Stop it."

Poppy gave Lord Ted a squeeze.

"Hello you two," whispered Lord Ted.

"Oh, hi Lord Ted," they both said together, still giggling but whispering at the same time. "Sorry about this, we should get the teeth and go, we have a lot to do tonight," said Gullveig.

"Where are they?" said Jareth.

"I dunno, you had them."

"I did not, you did."

"No, I didn't, you did, they were in your half of the tissue."

"They were not, they were in …"

"Boys!" whispered Poppy loudly.

"Ssssshhhhhh," whispered Gullveig and Jareth together putting their fingers to their lips mocking Poppy, and they all started laughing again.

After a few minutes they calmed down.

"Right." said Gullveig finally, "we really do have to find the teeth, they're a couple of good ones."

Poppy got out of her camp bed. "I think one went behind my bag, I'll get that one and one went under the bed, Jareth you get that one."

"I'll get that one," said Gullveig.

"No you won't, Miss Poppy asked me first."

"But I am closest."

"But Miss Poppy asked me."

"Boys!" snapped Poppy, "Gullveig, I'll move my bag and you can get that one, OK?"

"Yes Miss Poppy miss, sorry."

"Found it," said Jareth eventually.

"Found mine too," said Gullveig.

Both now moved back to where they'd landed putting the teeth into their little bags, Poppy sat on the edge of the bed with Lord Ted in her arms. She looked at them properly now. Dressed in green and gold with red hats, their wings glowed when they hovered and went dark when they stood or sat down. Their faces were quite old looking and Poppy could see that Gullveig had grey hair like Grandpa's, sticking out from underneath his red hat. They both sat cross legged as if Poppy was the teacher and it was story time in the classroom.

"How long did you say you've been tooth fairies?" she whispered.

"For 436 years, 4 months, 1 week and a day," said Gullveig.

"That's a very long time," said Poppy.

"Not really," said Jareth, "we're quite new at it really."

"Yes, we can see that." said Lord Ted.

Both the fairies wrinkled their noses and folded their arms in Lord Teds direction.

"So, how old are you Gullveig?" asked Poppy.

"I'm 474."

"And I'm 475," said Jareth.

"No you're not," snapped Gullveig.

"I am so."

"You're not older than me."

"Boys, please!" whispered Poppy now wrinkling her nose and folding her arms too.

"Sorry Miss Poppy, miss," they both said together.

"And how long have you been arguing like this?" continued Poppy.

"About 436 years, 4 months, 1 week, a day and about 15 minutes," said Lord Ted, laughing.

Again, they all had the giggles.

After what seemed like a long time Poppy finally said, "Well it is lovely to meet you both."

"And you too Miss Poppy, miss," they both replied.

"Please just call me Poppy, not Miss Poppy. I'm only seven."

"Soon to be eight I hear too," said Jareth, "Oona told me."

"Yes," smiled Poppy, "I met Oona with Elvina, Belle, Sophie, Zuzana and Deri earlier."

"Yes, she told me what happened," said Jareth, "you were very brave."

"She told me too," said Gullveig.

"No she didn't."

"Yes she did, she told me first."

"Good grief," said Poppy, "do you two ever stop?"

"Yes, we do," said Gullveig.

"No, we don't," said Jareth and they all started laughing again.

Poppy fell back on the bed laughing and it seems she fell asleep just like that for that's how Nanny found her in the morning with Lord Ted in her arms, her new gappy smile etched across her face.

"Poppy … Poppy … " whispered Nanny.

"Oh, you two do make me laugh," said Poppy wearily and her eyes still closed.

"Well, I'm glad we do," replied Nanny.

Poppy sat bolt upright, "Oh, not you Nanny," she said quickly.

"Oh."

"Oh, I mean you do of course and Grandpa, oh dear." Poppy fell back on the bed as she and Nanny started to laugh.

"What are you two laughing at?" came Grandpa's voice from the kitchen followed swiftly by the smell of bacon cooking.

"Nothing Grandpa," said Nanny and Poppy both at the same time laughing.

Poppy loved her nanny. Nanny was a little bit parent, a little bit teacher, a little bit best friend and a little bit partner in crime.

"Now then, did the tooth fairies come last night?" asked Nanny kindly.

"Yes. They were very noisy though," said Poppy.

"Oh really?"

"Yes, but very funny Nanny."

"Oh OK. And did they leave you anything?"

"I'm not sure."

Poppy moved her pillow and underneath were two new shimmering pound coins, one for each tooth.

"Oh wow," said Poppy. "Grandpa!" she shouted, "Jareth and Gullveig left me some money!"

"Oh, that's great Popsicle."

Poppy gave Nanny a big hug then ran across the tent and hugged her grandpa.

"Good morning Popsicle."

"Good morning Grandpa."

After delicious bacon sandwiches, which tasted just as good chewing side to side as chewed normally, showers and careful teeth cleaning it was time to start packing up.

Poppy looked around at all the things, all the stuff that Nanny had talked about and she had helped Grandpa pack in the car a few days before but now had no idea how all of this was going to fit back into the car.

"We're going to need a bigger car Grandpa."

"Nonsense, it will be fine," said Grandpa smiling.

Everything seemed to just fold into itself – beds, tables, kitchen and chairs seemed to be flattened within no time at all. Finally, all that was left was the tent.

"Let's let the tent air for a bit in the sunshine and go and see Katharine. I need to settle the bill," said Grandpa.

Poppy ran to get Lord Ted, tucked him under her arm and they walked to the shop.

"Hello you lot," said Katharine with her normal cheery smile, "did you have a nice meal last night?"

"Certainly did thanks," said Grandpa.

"And I see your teeth have finally gone Poppy, you didn't swallow them did you?"

Poppy laughed, "No but the tooth fairies left me two shiny pound coins under my pillow last night." she said. "That's all my old teeth gone now I think."

"Oh wowser," said Katharine, "what a lucky young lady."

Poppy smiled to herself, *young lady* she thought, *and the fairies called me Miss Poppy last night too.*

Grandpa paid the bill and they talked for a little while longer.

"Well, I hope you enjoyed your first stay here," said Katharine to Poppy, "it's certainly been very eventful for you."

"Yes, thank you, it's sort of, well, sort of erm, magical. Thank you for letting us stay."

"It's my pleasure and sorry about the geese again. They seem very pleasant this morning though."

"It's OK, I'm sure they'll be kind to everyone from now on."

"Thanks again Katharine," said Grandpa and after hugs all round they went back to the tent to fold it away and put it in the car.

In no time at all they were waving to Katharine through the car window as they left Meadow Island. Poppy sat back in her seat and gave Lord Ted a squeeze.

"Well that was brilliant Lord Ted."

"Yes, it was, I love Meadow Island."

"Me too," said Poppy.

Poppy gazed out of the window watching the countryside go by, thinking about her next adventures – what would they do, where would they go?

Soon enough they were turning into the drive at Nanny and Grandpa's house with Grandpa carefully reversing the car up to the garage.

"Let's get unpacked then we can have a cup of tea," said Grandpa.

Some things like bedding, clothes and remaining food went to the house and the camping stuff returned to the garage.

"It's all cleaned down at the campsite, so it's ready to go next time," explained Grandpa who was taking care to tell Poppy all the ins and outs, so she understood things. "When we're done here fancy helping me water the garden with the hosepipe?"

"Yes, OK Grandpa."

"It'll be a while before Daddy is here to pick you up, you can go and unravel the hose for me if you'd like, that will be a big help."

"Please may I do the watering too?"

"Yes, of course, you like doing that don't you?"

"Yes, I do, it's funny."

"OK, you can do it," said Grandpa, laughing.

"Thanks Grandpa."

Poppy took care to make sure she watered each plant. There was something special about helping Grandpa in the garden. After a while the vegetable plot was well watered.

"That's it, let's have a cup of tea now," said Grandpa, as he could see Nanny had bought out tea and biscuits at the top of the garden, "then we can do the flowers and all the pots."

They sat and had their tea and chatted about their little holiday and then Grandpa stared at the tree house.

"I reckon I'll get that all fixed up this summer so you can play in it and even sleep in it too if you'd like Poppy," he said. "Needs the roof doing, the window replacing, few bits in the floor and a general spruce up. Maybe a new ladder and a new bed too."

"And I could make a few things for it too Poppy," said Nanny.

"That would be brilliant, thank you," said Poppy excitedly.

"If we run some power to it you can have a light too for night-time," continued Grandpa as if he was thinking out loud.

"Maybe some fairy lights too," said Nanny looking at Poppy who was already there in her head and ginning her new gappy smile.

"Well, that's a project to get stuck into over the summer isn't it." said Grandpa, "come on let's get the watering finished before Daddy gets here."

Once done Poppy returned Lord Ted to the back bedroom and sat on the window sill, staring out to the garden and the fields and barn roofs beyond. She could see her grandpa sweeping the path making sure the garden was always tidy.

"I'll miss you Lord Ted."

"You too Poppy but you'll be here next week, and it'll be your birthday soon."

"I know but I will still miss you. Could you come home with me?"

"Maybe one day, but I am Grandpa's bear, and this is where I live for now," said Lord Ted kindly.

"I know, but still… "

Poppy heard the front doorbell and Nanny shout that her daddy was here, she got off the windowsill and put Lord Ted on the bed.

"Where does your backpack go Lord Ted?"

"In the door over there," he replied looking towards the crooked door.

"OK, I'll put it back for you."

Poppy picked up the bag and walked towards the door. As her hand was about to touch the big brass doorknob she froze.

"What's in here again?" she asked with some hesitation.

"Whatever you want it to be," replied Lord Ted.

"It's just a big cupboard isn't it?"

"If that's what you want it to be then, yes."

41

Poppy stayed still for a few seconds not really sure what to expect. She took a gulp, closed her eyes and opened the door which creaked. She opened one eye, then the other.

Inside was just a cupboard with a few empty wooden shelves. It was quite big inside with white painted walls and a small box in the corner.

"You see, just want you wanted it to be," said Lord Ted.

Poppy placed Lord Ted's backpack on the bottom shelf and closed the door.

"OK, I see. I love you Lord Ted," she said giving Lord Ted another hug.

"I love you too Poppy."

She kissed his head, placed him up against the cushions in his spot on the bed looking out of the window.

"Bye, Lord Ted."

"Bye Poppy, see you next week."

7

As time went by it was getting ever closer to Poppy's eighth birthday. She was going to have a party at home with her friends on her actual birthday but the week before was her end of year school trip and she was very excited.

"We're off to the Tower of London next week Nanny," she explained one night after tea.

"Oh, that sounds exciting," replied Nanny.

"Yes, kings and queens have lived there and some bad people and some have even lost their heads too, including a queen," continued Poppy without taking a breath. "And now ravens live there, Beefeaters and the queen keeps her jewels and her crown in the Tower."

"Will you see those too?" asked Grandpa.

"Yes, I think so, but I don't think I'll see the queen even though I'd love too, she looks a lovely lady. I am ever so excited. We get to go on a big coach, and I'm sitting next to my friend Sarah."

"Oh lovely," said Nanny.

As it happened both Nanny and Grandpa already knew all about Poppy's school trip as she was to stay the night before. Grandpa and Nanny were going to take her to school that day as they would have to leave really early as her daddy was working away.

This was going to be the first time Poppy was staying overnight so Nanny and Grandpa had decided to decorate the back bedroom so it was more fitting for a young lady.

Next week came quite quickly and Poppy arrived with her daddy and an overnight bag with all the things she needed for the school trip.

She took her bag upstairs and opened the door to the back bedroom, her bedroom. The first thing she noticed were the curtains, long fresh white curtains with bright red poppies all over them. On the bed sat Lord Ted surrounded by new cushions that matched the curtains. The walls were now a light pink and everything looked so pretty. On the wall above the bed was a large picture of herself holding Lord Ted – a photograph that Katharine had taken of them at Meadow Island a few weeks before.

Poppy dropped her bag on the floor and jumped up on the bed, picked up Lord Ted and gave him a squeeze. "Hello, Lord Ted."

"Hi Poppy."

"I'm staying here tonight."

"I know, do you like your new bedroom?"

"It's very pretty, I love it."

"Grandpa has been working on the treehouse too. There has been lots of sawing, drilling and banging going on today."

"Really?" said Poppy excitedly now scrambling off the bed to look out of the window.

At the bottom of the garden she could see three sets of ladders propped up against the oak tree, Grandpa's legs were on one set and another pair of legs were on another.

"Who's that with Grandpa?"

"Oh, that's Dave Johnson, the farmer, they call him Jonny, he's been helping your grandpa today," said Lord Ted.

"That's nice of him, shall we go and see what they're doing?"

"Yes please, I'd like to see it."

Poppy put Lord Ted under her arm and went downstairs. Nanny was in the kitchen.

"Thank you for my new bedroom Nanny, I love the curtains," she said giving her nanny a big hug.

"I'm glad you like it Poppy, I couldn't resist the poppy-pattern material, I thought it was just right. I'm going to use it in your treehouse too. Shall we go and see?"

Poppy held Nanny's hand and with Lord Ted under the other arm they walked down the garden. Just as they did so both Grandpa and Jonny were coming down the ladders.

"Thanks for all your help Jonny and the loan of the ladders, I know you're really busy at the moment."

"No problem my friend," said Jonny turning to look at Nanny and the little girl next to her with a grin and a teddy under her arm, "and you must be Poppy?"

"Hello Mr Johnson."

"Well hello there, nice to meet you at last. I've heard so much about you."

"Thank you, very nice to meet you too. And thank you for helping my grandpa."

Poppy looked up at Jonny Johnson. He was enormous, quite possibly the tallest man she had ever seen with lots of grey hair, hands the size of Grandpa's garden spades and two funny shaped ears. She was not quite sure he needed the ladders at all.

Jonny could see she was looking at his ears and smiled.

"Got these playing rugby with your grandpa," he said pointing at his ears, "quite a player in his day he was."

Grandpa raised his eyebrows, "hardly," he said.

"It's been a pleasure spending the day here and helping your grandpa, always a good laugh and your nanny has fed me until I'm about to burst too," he said, smiling. "Time I was getting back."

"Thanks again Jonny," said Grandpa, "I owe you."

"No problem."

"I'll help you with the ladders."

"It's OK, I'll just carry them over the field and pop them back in the barn."

Poppy watched the enormous farmer pick up the enormous ladders as if they were matchsticks, hang them over his shoulder and walk off down the garden with her grandpa, who held the gate open for him, shook his hand and exchanged a few words.

In no time at all Grandpa was walking back up the garden.

"What a nice guy," said Grandpa.

"Thank you so much for my new bedroom," said Poppy, "it's beautiful."

"That's OK Popsicle, I'm glad you like it."

"It's lovely."

"The treehouse is almost done too, well its watertight thanks to Jonny today, he helped with the roof, so just a bit of paint and we are done."

"And the curtains and cushions excuse me," said Nanny, "this is a girl's hangout now, not a boy's," she said, laughing.

"Ha ha, yes that's true, want to pop up and have a look Poppy?"

"Oh yes please."

Poppy, with Lord Ted under her arm, started to climb the new ladders which were wide with flat treads and rubber grips – so easy to climb. She got to the top, which was quite high up in the branches and looked on in amazement.

Nanny and Grandpa stayed at the bottom for a while to help her explore.

In front of Poppy was a small terrace area with two steps to a door. To the side of the door was a small window. Poppy opened the door and went inside. It was really big, big enough even for Jonny Johnson to stand up in. Another window to the side let in lots of light. She looked out and could see the fields with the path through the green barley and could just make out Jonny propping his ladders up against the side of the barn. Under the window was a small built-in desk with a lid and a bench seat and along the back wall a much larger bench with a hinged lid. Poppy opened the lid, it was empty. She had not noticed Nanny and Grandpa climb the ladder, but a little bell sounded at the door

"Can we come in?" asked Nanny.

"Oh yes please," replied Poppy still holding the lid open.

"I've made a built-in bed for you there," said Grandpa proudly. "I'll put a mattress on it and you can store things underneath it too if you'd like. Nanny is going to make some nice things to brighten it up and it needs painting obviously. There's a light switch here," he continued.

As he was talking Poppy carefully lowered the lid, which had rubber stoppers on it so it didn't bang, she sat Lord Ted on it and slowly walked over to her grandpa. Her eyes were full of happy tears as she just looked up at him and hugged him.

"And this one switches on the light. The big window opens too so you can get some air in while you are sitting at your desk. I thought you could … "

Nanny prodded Grandpa and he looked down at Poppy. At last he finally noticed Poppy hugging him, he picked her up and hugged her back.

"Oh, Grandpa it's amazing," she said with tears streaming down her face, "thank you so much."

"It's our pleasure Popsicle. Still a bit to do but should be ready when you come and stay after your birthday."

"And we are looking forward to that week too," said Nanny.

"I'm coming for a week?"

"Yes, to give your daddy time to get some work done on the house you can come and stay with us and Lord Ted," said Nanny.

"Oh brilliant, thank you," said Poppy now standing back on the floor.

"Right, I'll get tidied up and showered," said Grandpa, "then its teatime!"

Poppy helped Nanny get the dinner ready while Grandpa finished putting things away in the garage, wiping down tools and ensuring everything was where it needed to be. After a quick shower he joined them at the table.

"Sorry about that, took a bit longer than I thought," he said and they tucked into their dinner.

"Early night tonight Poppy," said Nanny, "we have a very early start in the morning. Exciting day tomorrow."

"I think the Tower of London is going to have to be something quite special now looking at our treehouse," Poppy said smiling, her new teeth growing nice and straight now where her gap had been only a few short weeks before.

Before long Poppy was in bed with Lord Ted by her side, in her cosy new bedroom with Nanny reading a story about four children and a dog going on an adventure. Nanny continued to read for a while after Poppy's eyes were tight shut, then put the book on her bedside table and kissed her forehead.

"Night night, you beautiful girl," she said as she switched out the light and left Poppy to sleep soundly until the morning.

It was still dark when Nanny came in to wake Poppy up. It took some time but eventually Poppy opened her eyes.

"And there you are," said Nanny kindly, "I thought you were never going to open your eyes."

Poppy smiled and stretched her arms, "Good morning Nanny."

"Cock-a-doodle-doo!" came Grandpa's voice from the landing.

Poppy laughed. "Mornin' Grandparrrr."

"Good morning Popsicle, chop chop now."

After her shower Nanny put Poppy's hair in a nice plait for the day's school trip, Poppy said goodbye to Lord Ted and went downstairs. Grandpa had made boiled eggs and toast so that she didn't go hungry through the day and a nice packed lunch to take with her in her school backpack.

"Got to start a busy day with a good breakfast," he said.

The sun was now making an appearance as they all got in the car and drove to the school ready for her trip.

"I wish Lord Ted could come with me Grandpa," she said as they were approaching the school, "I think he would love the Tower of London."

"Yes, I know he would, but he wouldn't like all the people I think," said Grandpa, "here we are then."

Poppy got out of the car and hugged Nanny and Grandpa.

"You have a lovely day Poppy and most of all a lovely birthday next week and we will see you after your party," said Nanny.

"Thank you." And with that Poppy skipped off to see her friends and teachers. Moments later she came running back with another girl.

"This is my nanny and grandpa. Nanny, Grandpa, this is Sarah. She's my best friend."

"Hello Sarah," said Nanny and Grandpa together.

"We've heard a lot about you," continued Nanny.

"Hello," said Sarah very shyly.

"Run along then Poppy, they're getting on the coach look, you don't want a rubbish seat, try and get to the back, it's more fun there," laughed Grandpa as Nanny elbowed him in the ribs.

Poppy and Sarah ran back waving as they went.

"Have a great day!" Nanny shouted.

8

With a school trip and a birthday party all happening so close together, Poppy had a lot to tell Nanny, Grandpa and Lord Ted when she came to stay. This was the second week of the summer holidays and the sun was shining brightly as Poppy's daddy dropped her off with all her things.

"Blimey Charlie," said Grandpa, "how long are you staying for?"

"Only a week," smiled Poppy.

"Looks like you're moving in," laughed Grandpa.

After waving her daddy goodbye both Poppy and Grandpa took her bags upstairs into her bedroom, now known as Poppy's room as there was a new sign on the door with her name on it with a bright red Poppy by the side.

"So, it's your room officially now," said Grandpa looking at her nameplate, "it's not the back bedroom anymore."

"Thanks Grandpa," said Poppy dropping her bags on the floor and picking up Lord Ted all at the same time. She gave him a squeeze.

"Hi Poppy!" said Lord Ted.

"Hello Lord Ted, I've so much to tell you all."

"Right then. The wardrobe is full at the moment with Nanny's dresses and my old suits, still got to sort that out sorry, but that can be a wardrobe if you like," said Grandpa pointing at the crooked door, "hang your things in there and use the chest of drawers, and I'll go and help Nanny with tea."

"OK Grandpa thank you."

"Then we can hear all about your trip and party over dinner," he said as he left the room.

"So, you had a good time then?" asked Lord Ted, "did you meet the queen?"

"Yes. We had a great time, but I didn't meet the queen, I don't think she lives there, she lives in the palace."

"She does, I'm sure she would love to meet you though."

"Wouldn't that be exciting," she laughed, "I'll unpack my things now."

Poppy placed Lord Ted back on the bed and picked up her bags to put next to him, chatting away as she went back and forth to the dresser. She stopped to look out of the window and stared down the garden. In the distance she could see how the fields had changed colour in such a short time, turning from green to light brown as the barley fields prepared themselves for harvesting. But what caught her eye the most was a bright red door in the oak tree.

"Oh wow, look at the door of the treehouse!"

"Yes, it's great isn't it. Grandpa decided to paint it bright red like Elvina and Oona's door."

Poppy was excited to go and see her finished treehouse so hurried with unpacking.

"Did Grandpa say this was a wardrobe now?" she asked Lord Ted as she pointed towards the crooked door, "I thought it was a cupboard."

"Well remember it can be whatever you want it to be," replied Lord Ted.

Poppy picked up some dresses and walked towards the door and hesitated again with her hand hovering over the big brass doorknob. She moved her hand down and carefully opened the door. Inside was different now, not as deep as before with a rail full of hangers ready for clothes and a shelf at the bottom for shoes.

"Oh," she said, "that's different."

"It's what you wanted it to be though?" asked Lord Ted.

"Err, well yes, it is," said Poppy still quite surprised.

Poppy couldn't quite reach the hanging rail so moved a small chair to stand on. Once all her dresses were on their hangers, she closed the door and looked back at it staring for a while.

"So, behind that door is whatever you want it to be?"

"Yes, correct," said Lord Ted.

"OK," she said looking a little confused.

After clearing away her bags and taking her toiletries to the bathroom, Poppy and Lord Ted went downstairs and saw Nanny in the kitchen.

"I love my name on the door Nanny, thank you, and I've put all my clothes away. I think I'll go and look at the treehouse if I can please?"

"Yes, of course you can, Grandpa is pulling up lettuce in the veg garden."

"OK," she said, "LG Lord Ted."

Poppy skipped down the path glancing at the treehouse but going straight past and on to the vegetable plot. Sure enough, Grandpa was there just knocking the soil off the bottom of a lettuce and placing it into a basket next to a cucumber and some tomatoes.

"Hi Grandpa, Nanny said you were down here. I'm going to look at the treehouse if I may?"

"Of course Popsicle, it's all finished now. Finished it yesterday, well your nanny did, she's done a great job I think. See you back at the house."

"OK, thank you," she said as she turned and ran back to the bottom of the ladders. She noticed a cord hanging down the side of the ladders and decided to pull it. Nothing seemed to happen, so she pulled it again and heard the ring of a bell coming from the treehouse. She also noticed a light switch, she pressed it and a row of small fairy lights that ran up either side of the ladder into the tree above, sprung into life.

With Lord Ted under her arm, she climbed the ladder and followed the lights to the top. Here she found another light switch which this time turned the fairy lights off, she put them back on again and looked at the door. It was bright red, just like Elvina and Oona's and so shiny it could have been made of glass with fairy lights around the frame.

Poppy opened the door and walked in. It looked a lot cosier than before. The walls were now painted the same pink as her bedroom with the same cushions and curtains. There was now a bed and a cushion on the bench seat in front of the now varnished desk. Poppy opened the desk lid and inside were some colouring books, crayons, pens and pencils, paper and a pair of binoculars to see as far as she could out of the window. There was a little table next to the bed with a lamp and a bookshelf on the other wall with some of the books Nanny had been reading to her. Above the bookshelf was a clock. Hanging from the ceiling was a pink light shade and on the floor was now a carpet to make the whole treehouse as cosy as possible.

"Oh my," said Poppy sitting on the edge of the bed, "it's amazing, what a great den."

"It's fantastic Poppy. How lucky are you!"

"I think I may well be spending the next few days in our treehouse Lord Ted."

"Me too," he said.

The bell rang by the door. Poppy opened the door and walked to the top of the ladders and looked down at her grandpa.

"What do you think Popsicle?" he said looking up at his smiling granddaughter.

"Oh Grandpa, it's amazing, thank you ever so much!" she said excitedly, "it's just brilliant."

"Good oh," he said now walking up the garden with his basket of vegetables, "dinner won't be long!"

A little later Poppy, with Lord Ted by her side, was sitting at the table which Nanny had set up outside in the sunshine, eating their dinner. Poppy told them all about her birthday party, the games and the bouncy castle and then all about her school trip. The big white tower, the big metal suit that King Henry used, who she thought must have been the same size as Jonny Johnson, and finally the crown jewels.

"They were amazing Nanny, and the queen's crown was stunning,", she continued between mouthfuls of pizza, "with a big red ruby and her robes were beautiful too. We have to draw a picture for my art folder, so I might do that in my own tower in the oak tree," she laughed.

"We are both glad you like it Poppy; would you like to sleep in there?"

"I'm not sure," said Poppy, "do you think it will be OK?"

"Sure," said Grandpa, "it will be just like camping all over again."

After helping clear the table Poppy and Lord Ted went back to the treehouse to play. After running up and down the ladders a few times, seeing what books were on the shelves and looking at everything she could see through the binoculars it was starting to get a little dark so Poppy put the lights on. Just then there was a ring at the door. Poppy got up and opened the door, no one was there so she looked down the ladders.

"Ten more minutes then it's bath and bedtime Poppy," said Nanny kindly.

"OK Nanny, 10 more minutes."

"Thank you," said Nanny disappearing back up the garden.

Poppy went back into the treehouse and sat at her desk to clear a few things away when the bell rang again.

"That's not 10 minutes Lord Ted," she said as she got up and answered the door. Again with no one there she looked down the ladders, but no one was there either. Slightly confused she turned to go back inside when she was startled by what she saw. There, sitting on the handrail around the balcony, with their legs swinging, were Elvina and Oona looking just as pretty as she remembered.

"Hello Poppy," they both said together.

"Didn't mean to scare you," said Oona.

"Oh, err, hello," said Poppy, "what are you doing here?"

"Come to see your new treehouse," said Elvina.

"Right, I see, good, well err, come in. It's lovely to see you."

Poppy went inside and Elvina and Oona flew in behind her.

"Hi Lord Ted."

"Hi guys, what are you doing here," said Lord Ted just as surprised as Poppy.

"Come to see the treehouse and ask for your help," said Elvina as they both settled on the edge of the bookshelf.

"Nanny and Grandpa finished it today, its great isn't it?" said Poppy.

"Yes, it's amazing," said Oona smiling, "I like bright red doors."

"So, what can we do for you?" said Lord Ted.

"Well we need somewhere to live," said Elvina, who went on the explain that the orchard is getting a bit crowded at Meadow Island and, unfortunately, one of the apple trees needed to be chopped down as it was too old and struggling to stand up. So some of the fairies needed to find a new home.

"…and well, we heard about your tree house and wondered if you'd like some new neighbours?" she finished.

Poppy was staring with her mouth open.

"That would just be amazing wouldn't it Poppy," said Lord Ted.

"Yes amazing," repeated Poppy.

"Yes amazing," said Lord Ted again, "err, when are you thinking?"

Elvina began "Well it's a full moon tomorrow, the Sturgeon Moon, so there will be lots of music and dancing and we were hoping..."

Before she could finish here sentence Poppy interrupted.

"YES!" she said very happily, "Yes of course you can. Nanny and Grandpa won't mind will they Lord Ted?"

"Not at all, in fact I think they would be absolutely thrilled."

"So, when you say *we*, how many are coming?" asked Poppy.

"Well, a few actually if that's OK. There's us then Nixie and Alfred, Sophie, Belle, Zuzana, Deri, April, Emma and Maisy to start with."

"Yes of course," said Poppy.

"And Jareth and Gullveig," said Elvina very, very, quickly trying to brush over the subject.

"Excuse me?" said Poppy.

"Jareth and Gullveig," she repeated very quickly.

"Those two make me laugh, that's great," said Poppy.

"Oh good, good. It's just I know they made a bit of a mess of your tooth collection that's all," said Oona, "they're very good at it really."

"I know, it's not a problem," said Poppy, "when are you thinking of moving in exactly?"

"Well, err, they're all outside,"

Poppy went to the door and there they all were, lined up like birds on a wire.

"Hi Poppy," they all said together with the familiar wave that was more like a salute.

"Oh, hi guys."

Poppy returned inside followed by a herd of fairies glowing behind her, some lining up on the bookshelf to join Elvina and Oona and others on Poppy's desk.

"What if we had said no?" Poppy smirked.

"Like that was ever going to happen," said Lord Ted, and they all laughed.

"See, I said it would be OK," barked Gullveig.

"No, you didn't," said Jareth.

"Yes, I did!"

"No, you didn't."

"I did so!"

"Boys!" snapped Poppy.

"Sorry Miss Poppy, miss," replied Jareth and Gullveig together and again they all burst out laughing.

"Well I have to get ready for bed now, how long does it take to, you know, build your houses?" said Poppy.

"Well we've already built them around the treehouse," said Elvina.

"Really?"

Poppy and Lord Ted went outside followed by all the fairies and looked up and could see a few doors up in the tree.

"Oh wow," said Poppy.

"I hope its OK Poppy," asked Belle.

"Yes, yes, its brilliant," said Poppy still looking up, "so Grandpa already knew?"

"Yes," said Zuzana.

Poppy smiled. "OK I have to go now but I'm so pleased you're all here," she said, "see you tomorrow?"

"Yes, we'll be here," said Elvina, "and thank you Poppy."

Poppy smiled at her new, now local friends, shut the door and returned down the ladders finally switching off the ladder lights when reaching the bottom. As she walked back to the house, she glanced back to see the little doors shining in the treetop. *How brilliant,* she thought.

"Look at that Lord Ted, isn't it just the best."

"It's wonderful," said Lord Ted, "so that's why Grandpa thinks it's OK for you to sleep there sometimes, you'll be very safe with the fairies looking after you."

"But I have a new bedroom too."

"Yes, aren't you a lucky one, you'll have to alternate between the two."

"Yes, I am, I really am, and I'll have to."

As she went back inside she could see Grandpa in his chair watching the news on the television and ran up to give him the biggest hug ever.

"Ah, that's nice. I was going to tell you but thought they would want to tell you themselves," he winked and gave Lord Teds ear a little squeeze too.

"Thank you Grandpa."

"You off to bed now?"

"Yes, Nanny's going to read me a story."

"OK Popsicle, nighty nighty," he said giving her a kiss, "sleep well."

"Goodnight Grandpa."

9

Poppy woke quite early the next morning with Lord Ted snuggled in by her side. She gave him a little squeeze.

"Good morning," she said sleepily.

"Good morning Poppy, it looks like another sunny day."

Poppy could hear Nanny and Grandpa downstairs so decided to go down to join them with Lord Ted.

"Morning sleepy, thought I'd do a camping breakfast this morning – bacon sandwiches OK?" asked Grandpa

"Good morning Grandpa, yes please, morning Nanny."

"Good morning my lovely," said Nanny who was half watching the breakfast news on the television, "just waiting for the local news and the weather to come on, then I'll make a pot of tea."

Nanny watched the television carefully as if she was waiting for something, finally she looked up and called Grandpa over…

"Here it is," she said turning the volume up. Poppy and Grandpa watched too…

"… *local sources say that the robberies are becoming more frequent and that local farmers should be vigilant, keeping an eye on barns and outbuildings that contain valuable farm machinery. So far there have been 18 such incidents and the police are no nearer to catching the offenders…*"

"We need to let Jonny know," said Nanny.

"He knows already," said Grandpa, "he was telling me about this, his barns are well hidden in the dip, so he's moved some of his tractors down there ready for the harvest. He thinks he'll be OK, but he's going to put cameras up at the weekend."

"… *and now the weather for the weekend with Robert …*"

"Oh good, I like a bit of Robert in the morning," said Nanny, laughing.

"*Hello, good morning everyone. Plenty of sunshine today with temperatures around 25 to 26 which is just above average for this time of year. Tonight, warm with clear skies means a bright night with a full moon, the Sturgeon Moon, which is named after North America's largest fish, the lake sturgeon apparently. Answers on a postcard on that one please – tomorrow morning remains clear which means a chilly start with temperatures rising to a high of 26 but getting…"*

The weather reporter suddenly stopped and put his fingers to his ear

"…err, and, err now quickly back to our London studio for some breaking news …"

Nanny, Grandpa, Poppy and Lord Ted all focussed on the television as the picture went back to the national news studio

"…early reports are coming in from the Tower of London of a daring and what seems to be, on the face of it, a successful robbery. These first reports say that the crown jewels and many other artefacts along with the queen's gold reserves have been stolen from the Jewel House and Martin Tower, several guards have been injured and one taken hostage but we do not have any further information at this time, as soon as we do, we will come straight back to you … so, let's go to Carol for the weather…"

Carol was obviously not expecting to be on camera so quickly and stood there with her mouth open at the news. Poppy watched Carol, the national weather reporter, stumble over her words then she turned to listen to Nanny and Grandpa.

"Oh my," said Nanny.

"Oh dear," said Grandpa.

"I was there a couple of weeks ago," said Poppy, "it wasn't me!"

They laughed but then realised the seriousness of the situation.

"That's not good is it Nanny," said Poppy.

"No poppet it's not good, not good at all."

"They can't get far surely," said Grandpa who looked quite shaken by the news.

Nanny made the pot of tea and eventually cleared things away while keeping an eye on the television. News reporters were outside the Tower now, behind them a sea of flashing blue lights but no further news from the incident. All programmes were moved as the news stayed on air to bring the latest but no one seemed to know what was going on – what had exactly happened? How did they get in? How are the guards? Where is the hostage? Have they heard anything? What's been taken exactly? How did they get away? Any news from the queen? All these questions were being asked. It seemed no one knew anything or saw anything. Lots of diagrams, lots of discussion about the vault, doors and guards but no updated news.

Poppy got washed and dressed and decided to go to the treehouse. It was a lot quieter in her den, away from the goings on of the world. She lay on the bed with Lord Ted and started to read her book but her mind kept drifting back to the morning's news on the television.

"Poor queen," she said eventually.

"Yes," said Ted, "she'll be very upset. There are over 20,000 jewels you know."

"That's a lot of sparkly stuff," said Poppy. "I'm not sure how they'll get away with it, what are they going to do with it all?"

They both sat there in silence for a while then Lord Ted said something that made Poppy sit up with a jolt.

"Grandpa knows the queen you know."

"Does he?" asked Poppy, the words taking her by surprise as the book fell to the floor.

"Yes, he's known her since he was your age, he and I went to meet her."

"Did you?" asked Poppy now turning to look Lord Ted in the face.

"Yes, we took her some banana bread."

"Oh, I see," said Poppy not expecting banana bread to be brought into any conversation about the queen's jewels being taken, "banana bread, right."

"Yes, he wanted to go and see her, so we did, and his grandma made us some banana bread to take with us," said Lord Ted, as if this was a very normal thing to do.

"His Grandma and Grandpa were wonderful," continued Lord Ted

Nothing really surprised Poppy anymore when it came to Lord Ted, she had learned that being with him was magical, that magical things happened, but this was another level in the world of Lord Ted.

"And what did you do when you met her?"

"We had tea and banana bread in Buckingham Palace."

"Grandpa said you know a lot of people, but I didn't know you knew the queen as well," said Poppy, excited at this revelation.

"Yes, and she is a very lovely lady, I really hope she's OK."

"Me too," said Poppy, "can I meet her do you think?"

"Yes, I think so, but maybe not today, I think she might have quite a lot on her mind."

"Yes, yes, I expect she will, poor queen."

Poppy's thoughts now turned to happier things and the fact it was a full moon.

"So, tonight is a full moon, does that mean the fairies will be out with lots of music and dancing?"

"It does and that will be fun."

"I need to ask Nanny and Grandpa if we can sleep in the treehouse tonight, then don't I?"

"Yes, we should really but it will be fine, they made it for you to sleep in after all."

"OK I'll ask over lunch."

Poppy picked up her book and lay back down. She really enjoyed reading and getting lost in the adventures. Today she was reading about Julian, Anne, Dick and George, who was a girl, and her dog Timmy, in a story about smugglers. Although Poppy was only eight she had been reading much more grown up books for a long time now and only needed help with a few words or the meaning of some words. Her teachers were also encouraging her to read more and more and Poppy loved it. She rarely watched television or bothered with computer games, her passion was books and the treehouse was her new reading den. Nanny and Grandpa had bought her the complete set of Famous Five books for her birthday, all 22 of them, and she proudly lined them up on the bookshelf in the treehouse alongside the books she had brought from home. After a few chapters, and what seemed like hours, the bell rang.

Poppy got up, opened the door and looked down the ladders. Nanny was at the bottom and she looked up

"Excuse me miss," she said, laughing pretending to be a maid, "please may we have the pleasure of your company for lunch."

"Why of course m'lady," Poppy said, joking.

"Be ready in 10!" replied Nanny on her way back to the house.

Poppy went back in and picked up Lord Ted and gave him a squeeze.

"Lunch Lord Ted?"

"LG, maybe there will be some more news on the robbery?"

"Maybe, let's go and see."

Poppy ran back up to the house, washed her hands and sat back at the kitchen table with Lord Ted by her side, where Nanny had laid out some sandwiches, crisps and drinks. Grandpa switched on the television for the 1 o'clock news. There was no introduction music or headlines, the presenter just said, *"Now it's time for the 1 o'clock news."* And it went straight to a lady, hosting the news directly outside the Tower of London. They all sat and watched the screen. Poppy could see that there were still lots of blue flashing lights behind the host, who was called Fiona, as she ran through an overview of what happened before she got into any detail…

"…many of the objects within the crown jewels have been taken, including, we understand, sovereign crowns and consort crowns along with the priceless St Edward crown, robes, rings, sceptres, swords and parts of the secular and alter plates used during coronations. Much of the gold reserves, which are hidden from public view, have also been taken.

"The hostage is one of the long-standing Yeomen Warders or Beefeaters, named as George Featherbottom, 63 years old and a grandfather of four, from Fotheringham in North Yorkshire. George, a former paratrooper, has been a warder for 11 years and was due to retire at the end of this year. Seven other warders have been injured but none seriously. It is reported that they fought bravely to protect the crown jewels.

"The queen is said to be heartbroken at the news of George, and we understand his family have joined her at Buckingham Palace.

"I'm joined now by Chief Inspector Pickles-Cunningham. Chief Inspector if I may start with the whereabouts of the gang and more importantly the whereabouts of Mr Featherbottom?

"Yes, good afternoon, thank you. At this moment in time, we have no further information on the condition or the whereabouts of Mr Featherbottom, the gang or indeed the crown jewels. Our first priority is to find Mr Featherbottom and return him safely to his family and our thoughts are with them at this time."

"Absolutely," said Grandpa not moving his eyes from the television.

"Indeed, and may I ask do you have any more details on the robbery itself?" continued Fiona.

"Yes, we have more information coming through all the time as you would expect. There have been several extensive building works along the bank of the River Thames, behind us here, in relation to the London Underground. It seems the audacious group of men began their own works alongside these several weeks ago. No one seemed to notice, and all assumed that they were there as part of the actual works, even wearing the same clothing. In reality, they have been tunnelling towards the Tower

and entered the vaults and strong rooms at several points just after 3 o'clock this morning. It seems they made their exit back through the tunnels, split up and left in both directions along the river. We estimate, from the statements we have received, that there were around nine men in total in..."

The reporter interrupted the police chief inspector, *"And do you believe Mr Featherbottom to be one of the gang, an inside job as it were?"*

"Absolutely not!"

"... so, you say they split up and went in both directions on the river, presumably boats, do you know how many, is there CCTV footage?"

"Yes, we do have CCTV footage but let me make this very clear. This is a very professional and ruthless gang, who have obviously been extremely well financed and have been planning this for many, many months. Interestingly no firearms were reported being used during the robbery but there was use of force. This does not mean they do not have firearms now, so we urge the public to be very cautious and not to approach them. They knew exactly where all the CCTV cameras were and minutes before any boat landed up or down river, cameras nearby were disabled, so we know there are more people than just the nine or so within the Tower and this enabled them to move out of the city undetected. At this time, we do not know the vehicles used but they must be vans and lorries knowing the number of items taken. We are undertaking many house-to-house enquiries in these areas, interviewing workers close by and looking at CCTV going back months to see if we can identify anyone as part of the works but this will take time as you can imagine, and time, for Mr Featherbottom, is not on our side..."

"And if I may, one further question?"

"Yes, one more, then, as you will gather, I have to return to the job in hand."

"Yes of course, thank you. Do you have an estimate of the value of the items taken?"

"It runs into the hundreds of millions I'm sure, but much of the collection is priceless as you know and because of this, of course, they are not insured. But at this stage I have no more information on this, I think that question is for others and not the police."

"Thank you, chief inspector. Chief Inspector James Pickles-Cunningham there who is leading the investigation into the robbery here

today and the whereabouts of Mr Featherbottom. So, let's review again where we are ... "

"Well, that sounds like a very well-planned operation," said Grandpa, turning down the volume on the television.

"Isn't it shocking that no one questioned a load of workmen digging for all those weeks, how did they get rid of all the soil?" said Nanny.

"I bet they just used the system they're using for the new underground line, just fitted in, best form of camouflage is in plain sight," continued Grandpa, "very clever, but they do sound a nasty bunch. I wouldn't like to come across them on a dark night."

The television was on in the background and Poppy could not take her eyes off it as Nanny and Grandpa discussed the day's events

"Come now Poppy, let's eat our lunch," said Nanny. "I thought you could come to the shops with me this afternoon. I've only got to walk to the post office, then we can play that hairy tennis ball catch game later if you like, I got it out of the garage earlier."

"Yes please Nanny, that would be fun. And I was wondering, as it's a full moon, could I sleep out in the treehouse tonight?"

"What do you think Grandpa?" asked Nanny.

"I think that's a great idea. We can leave the back door open so if you need a, err get cold, you can just come in and get into your cosy bed," said Grandpa, "how does that sound?"

"Lovely Grandpa thank you. And thank you Nanny."

"That's OK Poppy, right let's finish lunch, get cleared up and go to the post office and I'll pick up a few bits from the shop too. What are you up to this afternoon?" she asked looking at Grandpa.

"I think I'll just watch this a little longer," he said looking at the television, "then nip out to see Jonny."

The afternoon went quite quickly. Poppy and Nanny went to the shops for a few groceries and a little walk around the village. Nanny and Grandpa lived in a large house, on its own, on Honeypot Lane, in Diddlesdale village in Derbyshire. Diddlesdale village had a small river that ran through the village green, with a pond with lots of ducks and a few geese. Around the green was a post office, a small village store selling groceries, a hairdresser, a pub with black and white walls and a thatched roof. The pub, called The Mallard had an award-winning restaurant with an enviable reputation called The Greedy Duckling to the side. To the left of these was a fish and chip shop and the Honeypot Tea

Rooms. The river then ran on through to Diddlesdale itself, then onto the farm which backed onto Nanny and Grandpa's house on Honeypot Lane. While Nanny was in the post office, Poppy sat on one of the benches by the green with Lord Ted by her side.

One of the ducks walked towards them so Poppy gave Lord Ted a quick squeeze.

"Hi Lord Ted," said the duck as he got closer and Poppy was not surprised at all.

"Hello Gerald," said Lord Ted, "how are you?"

"I'm OK thanks."

"This is Poppy," said Lord Ted.

"Hello Poppy. It is nice to meet you at last."

"Likewise, Gerald," said Poppy.

With that Gerald turned around and waddled back towards the pond.

"Well, that was short and sweet," said Poppy, "do you know all the ducks around here too?"

"Most of them," said Lord Ted and giggled.

Poppy smiled and sat there with Lord Ted for a while longer, looking around the pretty little village houses with their colourful front gardens. Some of the houses had cars parked outside but one had a large dark blue van that caught her eye with two men sitting in it. They were just staring across the green. It made Poppy feel a little uncomfortable so, with Lord Ted under her arm, she got up and joined Nanny in the post office just as she was finishing a conversation with Mrs Jones who was behind the counter.

"Hello Poppy," said Mrs Jones kindly.

"Hello Mrs Jones," said Poppy trying not to stare at the big hairy pimple that Mrs Jones had on the end of her nose.

As they left the shop Poppy glanced across towards where the blue van was parked but it was gone so Poppy thought no more of it and they continued their walk.

After they'd returned Poppy helped Nanny unpack the shopping then they both played catch in the garden with the very hairy tennis ball. Poppy was going to mention Mrs Jones's hairy pimple when catching the ball but decided that it was not a kind thing to say so didn't bother. She then sat in the sunshine and read a little more of her book with Lord Ted. Later, Nanny fetched a quilt, pillow and blankets for the treehouse and helped Poppy set up her bed.

"Well, that does look cosy, I'm quite jealous Poppy. I might join you," said Nanny, laughing, as they both stood back and admired their handywork in the treehouse "and remember, if you don't like it later, just come back to the house, we'll listen out for you."

"Thank you, Nanny. The fairies will be dancing tonight as it's a full moon, so it'll be fun."

"It will. You are a very lucky girl to know so many fairies, and have them move in too."

"I know, it's all thanks to Lord Ted."

"It is. He is quite a bear isn't he."

"Yes, Grandpa's bear."

Just then the bell rang, and Poppy opened the door, again knowing just to look down.

"Helloooo Grandparrrr."

"Why Princess Rapunzel I assume."

Poppy laughed.

"May I come up and join you?" asked Grandpa.

"Yes please, Nanny is here too."

"Oh great, we can have a party."

Grandpa climbed the ladders and joined Nanny, Poppy and Lord Ted.

"Well, this is looking good now isn't it, I'm quite jealous."

"That's what Nanny said."

"I did, and I think we might move in here when Poppy goes home," said Nanny.

They all laughed.

"Jonny OK?" asked Nanny.

"Yes, he's fine, I was just helping him with a few things. Said I'd go around on Saturday and help put the cameras up. You can come too Poppy if you'd like?"

"Yes, please Grandpa."

"Good oh, right what's for dinner, I'm starving."

"Steak and kidney pie and chips or fish and chips."

"From the chip shop?" asked Grandpa.

"Yes, me and Poppy have been far too busy and, in all honesty, didn't realise the time so chip shop it is."

"Fab, love pie and chips. Want to come with me Poppy?"

"LG Grandpa!"

10

Poppy tucked into fish and chips with Nanny but Grandpa, as always, had steak and kidney pie and chips. They chatted more about the news, about the poor man who was missing, the queen and how she must be feeling. After washing up and putting everything away Poppy sat on Grandpa's lap with Lord Ted as he announced he was going to switch on the television to see the latest on the day's events.

"Let's see what's going on," he said, "hopefully some good news."

They listened and watched a different host, a man called Huw. He spoke to lots of reporters all stationed around London, places where boats had landed, cars were changed, this person saw this and heard that but there was nothing about Mr Featherbottom, the gang or the whereabouts of the crown jewels.

"The police must know something by now," said Nanny, "they're just not making things public at the moment, surely," she continued trying to reassure herself, but the reality was that the police were no closer to knowing where anyone or anything was. It was as if the stolen items had disappeared into thin air along with poor George Featherbottom.

"They might be a rough bunch, but I tell you what, they knew what they were doing," said Grandpa, "this is stuff of Hollywood isn't it. How on earth have they got away so cleanly, amazing."

"Lord Ted told me you've met the queen, Grandpa" said Poppy quietly and changing the subject slightly.

"Did he indeed?" he smiled, "yes a few times actually, and your nanny has."

"Oh wow."

"Yes, she'll be very upset," said Nanny.

They continued to watch the television and listen to Huw explain everything over and over again, but nothing new was reported.

"Come on then Poppy," said Nanny, "bath time, jammies on, then a big night tonight."

Once Poppy had finished her bath Nanny selected her warmer pink pyjamas just in case she got cold in the night, although it was the middle of summer and Robert the weatherman had said it would be warm, Nanny was doubtful.

They returned downstairs to find Grandpa in the garden making up the firepit. He'd put the chairs around in a semi-circle looking down towards the treehouse and was about to light the fire.

"With Poppy camping out in the treehouse tonight, I thought it would be nice to have a campfire, just like our little holiday."

"Oh, fab idea, hot chocolate and s'more S 'Mores then?" Nanny said, jokingly.

"I'd love s'more S 'Mores please Nanny."

They sat around the fire, Lord Ted tucked in beside Poppy, just like Meadow Island, drinking their hot drinks and feeling the warmth from the fire on their legs.

"So, you just need to let the music start tonight Poppy, they'll come to you when they're ready," said Grandpa eventually, "you'll hear it."

"OK Grandpa."

The conversation then turned to the events of the day again.

"With all the events happening in London not much has been said about the farm robberies, has there been any more about them on the evening news?" asked Nanny.

"No," replied Grandpa, "seems the whole country is out looking for the crown jewels and poor Mr Featherthingy. No other news at all. They need to catch those guys soon, with it coming up to harvest time the farmers will need all their equipment. Jonny was saying it's a bumper crop this year too."

"Well, the cameras will help," said Nanny.

"Yes, we'll get them up at the weekend then he'll feel safer I'm sure."

"What do they do with the equipment they steal Grandpa?" asked Poppy.

"Well, I presume they either sell it or break it up for parts or even take it overseas somehow," he replied, "I don't really know."

"Oh. I see, and meanwhile the farmers can't collect their barley can they?"

"No, that's his livelihood all wrapped up in the fields, so it's important they find these people quickly," said Grandpa.

"And what is barley used for exactly?" asked Poppy.

"Well, it's used for a lot of things but mainly, and I have to say most importantly, it's used in the making of beer, and that Popsicle, is the drink of the gods," said Grandpa smiling.

"Oh OK," said Poppy, "not for me then," she laughed.

"No," said Nanny, "but it can be used in breads, soups and stews and I think animal feed too."

"What a waste of good barley," said Grandpa, laughing.

They continued to chat away and it made Poppy realise how important being kind and honest really was. There seemed to be far too many bad people in the world and Poppy was determined not to be one of them.

"Right then, one s'more, S'More then it's time to scrub those teeth after all those marshmallows and get yourself tucked up in bed in the treehouse," said Nanny.

Poppy nodded and smiled. She was very excited about staying in the treehouse, she felt a little apprehensive at first but now she couldn't wait.

"And remember we're just inside Poppy and will leave the back door unlocked in case you need the loo too, OK?"

"Yes Grandpa, thank you."

After Poppy had finished scrubbing her teeth, she washed her hands and face, picked up a few bits and of course Lord Ted, she went to say goodnight to her grandpa.

"Night night then Grandpa," she said giving him the biggest hug she could manage.

"Night night Popsicle, remember what I said and sleep well my lovely."

"I will."

Poppy walked to the treehouse with Nanny.

"Do you want me to come on up and tuck you in and read for a while?"

"Yes, please Nanny."

Poppy switched on the fairy lights and they walked up the ladders. Poppy went in first. It was darker than she expected inside even though the moon was already beginning to shine brightly in the darkening night sky, so she switched on the small lamp on the table and snuggled down in bed with Lord Ted by her side.

"So how far have you got with *Smugglers Top* then?"

"There should be a marker in it Nanny."

"Oh yes, my you have read a lot today, we'll finish this one tonight I'm sure."

And with that Nanny continued the story. Poppy felt her eyelids starting to droop but was determined to stay awake so she would not miss the music and the dancing in the full moon. She could see the bright moon in the slight gap at the top of the curtains. Try as she might, she could not stay awake and eventually succumbed to the power of sleep.

Nanny continued to read for a page or two then put the marker back in the book where she knew Poppy had fallen asleep. Grandpa had fitted a dimmer switch to the lamp so Nanny turned it down low, so when Poppy woke, she would know where she was.

She gave Lord Ted's ear a squeeze, "Look after her please Lord Ted," she whispered. She placed the book on the side table, gave Poppy a kiss on her head then quietly closed the door behind her as she left.

She joined Grandpa back by the firepit which was now just glowing embers and looked down to the treehouse with the pretty fairy lights leading up the ladders.

"It's great in there you know, you did a good job, old man."

"Well, you made it look better didn't you, young lady."

They laughed.

"She'll be OK, won't she?" asked Nanny.

"With Ted and the fairies around her, she is very safe."

"Just checking," said Nanny.

11

Poppy had been asleep for a few hours when she woke up. She was disturbed by a beautiful sound like a symphony of glass bells in the air, the gold strands of a harp sound coiled like a snake around her head. Poppy sat up, the moonlight shone through the gap in the curtains and lit up the hands of the clock showing it was just past 1 o'clock in the morning.

The sound was so intoxicating.

She gave Lord Ted a squeeze "Listen to that Lord Ted," she said in astonishment. "It's beautiful isn't it. Is that the fairies?"

"Yes, they start with this then later they'll play different music so they can dance and celebrate the new moon," he said knowledgably.

"How long have they been playing?"

"A while."

Poppy sat on the edge of the bed with her head tilted slightly back and her eyes closed listening to the harmonies floating around her. She stayed there for a while longer then got up and with Lord Ted under her arm, went outside.

It was still very warm, and the sky was lit by a very bright and very big moon. She could see some of the fairies in the tree playing their music. Once they saw Poppy they stopped.

"Oh, please don't stop, it's so beautiful."

"We've been waiting for you Poppy," said Sophie who appeared on the balcony railing, "we wanted to start the dancing when you were here."

"Oh lovely," said Poppy.

"Come on!" Sophie shouted to the others. All the fairies started to appear on the balcony. Some had small harps, some had little fiddles, and some had small tambourines ready to make their music, others were just ready to dance.

"Hi Poppy," said Zuzana, "I hope you like it."

Suddenly the music started, it was wonderful, and Poppy couldn't help but tap her feet. Then, without knowing, she was dancing with Lord

Ted, round and round they went as the fairies played and danced around her. It was so enchanting.

She could see Gullveig and Jareth with Belle, Zuzana and April playing their fiddles and harps with Oona and Elvina tapping the tambourines in time with the music. They were so happy, dancing while all the others were spinning around, just like Poppy and Lord Ted.

Poppy continued to dance with Lord Ted laughing while the fairies, who were enjoying entertaining their guests for the night, continued to play.

Eventually Poppy had to stop to get her breath. She went back into the treehouse to take a sip of water, the music still playing and fairies still dancing behind her. She pulled open the curtains to look at the moon, but her eyes were drawn to something else. In the distance, by farmer Johnson's barns were car headlights, some moving around as if they were just arriving. She put her drink down and opened the lid of the desk to find Grandpa's binoculars.

"What are you looking at Poppy," said Lord Ted as Poppy focussed the binoculars in the distance

"Oh no, I think Mr Johnson's barns are being robbed!"

"Let's get Grandpa," said Lord Ted firmly.

"Well let's just check it is first, it might be Mr Johnson himself."

"Not at this time in the morning," pointed out Lord Ted.

"Maybe."

Poppy picked up Lord Ted and went outside to find Oona and Elvina, already formulating a plan in her head as she did so. She got their attention and they came over, the music still playing on the balcony.

"Elvina, Oona, I think Mr Johnsons barns are being robbed. We need to go and check it's not him then phone the police."

"I don't think that's a good idea Poppy," Lord Ted interrupted, "I think we should call the police now plus Nanny said I was to look after you."

"Let's go and have a look first, they might be gone by the time the police get there," said Poppy taking command. "Lord Ted will come with me. Elvina, Oona, I know it's a full moon and you're all dancing, but can you get everyone together and follow me up."

"Of course, no problem."

Poppy went back to put her trainers on so she could run if needed.

"Are you sure this is a good idea Poppy?" asked Lord Ted.

"Yes, let's just go and have a look, see what's there then we can let the police know so they know what to do and what to expect," she said quite impressively now making her way out and down the ladders.

"We'll be right behind you Poppy," said Elvina as Poppy passed her. The music had now stopped, and Elvina was readying her troops.

"Thank you," said Poppy.

Lord Ted understood what Poppy was doing, and also knew that with him and the fairies by her side she would be safe, nevertheless he still thought just ringing the police might be a better idea.

When Poppy got to the bottom of the ladders she turned and ran down the garden path, easily seeing where she was going with the moonlight illuminating the way. Once she reached the gate, she opened it and was halfway down the narrow path and through the barley field in no time at all, then she stopped to catch her breath.

"We need to be quiet now," she whispered hidden by the tall barley either side of her as she crouched down.

She could see movement ahead and could hear voices too, so held back. Then all the individuals seem to go inside so she carefully walked through the rest of the field and an open area before reaching the barn. She was quite shocked to see how big the barns actually were, from the treehouse they looked fairly normal barn-sized buildings, but these were supersize for Mr Johnson to store his combine harvesters, tractors and then the dried grain. She crouched down beside the side of the barn where she could hear the voices clearly.

"This is ridiculous," said one man's voice.

"I had no idea, honest Charlie," said another.

"Well, we can't stay here can we."

"B-b-but there were no vehicles in here on Thursday, honest."

"Well, there is now ain't there. And what we gonna do with him?" snarled Charlie "it was your idea to bring him weren't it?" he continued.

"I'll take care of him," said another deeper voice in a nasty manner.

"So, what's the plan now then Charlie?" asked someone else. "Can't even get a phone signal, we're in the middle of nowhere here."

"Well, that's why we found this place, thought it would still be deserted, and switch off your phone, that's how they will track us," came a reply.

"Well, it's not deserted now is it," growled Charlie again sounding quite anxious. "It's harvest time ain't it so all the stuff is in here. We need to get rid of him and get out of here. Let me just think a minute. We're OK here for a couple of hours I reckon. No one knows we're here, but we'll need to move before folk around here start waking up."

"We will need to split the gold boxes Charlie, they're way too heavy for a couple of the cars. We should put the jewels an' stuff in the cars and the gold in the vans before we leave," said a new voice.

"OK, OK, let me think," snapped Charlie.

"This is stupid, I thought you had everything planned," said the very menacing deep voice, "we were supposed to be splitting the loot up here then going our separate ways. And where's Ron and Ray? What's going on?"

"They ain't got here yet have they?" snapped Charlie again.

As an argument started in the barn, Poppy realised that they were not robbing Mr Johnson at all, they had just robbed the queen! Inside were quite a few men and she assumed George Featherbottom.

"This is worse than we thought Lord Ted," she whispered just as Elvina and Oona arrived with everyone lined up behind them.

"You're not kidding," he whispered back, "we need to get the police here quick."

"Agreed but we need to try and stop them getting away," she said. "Elvina can you take Deri and Emma and see if you can get in to see how many people there are and see if George is OK then come and let me know?"

"Yes, will do," she said standing to attention.

"Oona, can you, Belle and Sophie take the rest and let all the air out of the tyres of the cars and vans?"

"Roger that, on our way."

"Who's Roger?"

"No idea," said Oona and with that they were gone.

"That was a good idea Poppy," said Lord Ted.

"Well, it will slow them down if they start to get away before the police get here."

Poppy continued to listen to the robbers with Lord Ted. The arguing was still going on and getting quite heated. There were some angry conversations but Charlie, who seemed to be the leader, was taking charge.

"Keep your voices down, we need to think," he snapped.

Then there was a discussion about how they needed to split up and where they would go, just as Elvina, Emma and Deri returned.

"OK," said Elvina, "there are a lot of them, all getting quite twitchy, I counted 18, Deri 19 and Emma 20 because they keep moving around so let's say 20."

"What about George?" asked Lord Ted while still trying to listen to the robbers through the wall.

"He's OK," whispered Deri, "well I think he is. He's sitting on the floor in the far corner with his hands tied up but looking very scared."

Just as Deri finished explaining the barn door opened and a man came out to light a cigarette, kicking the door shut behind him. He was still dressed in his bright orange train tunnel overalls. They all froze, including the fairies who were busy letting the air out of tyres.

Poppy needed to think because she needed to get back to call the police while the moon was still quite bright.

She whispered as softly as she could to the others.

"OK we have no choice," she said, "I'm going to make a run for it. He'll probably see me and follow. Lord Ted will trip him, can you pin him down?"

"Yes, no problem," said Elvina.

"And can you secure all the doors?"

"Again, no problem, Emma and Deri will sort him out and I'll grab the others to secure the barn."

"We need to move fast," said Poppy, "Lord Ted, are you ready?"

"Yes," said Lord Ted who understood the plan, "ready when you are but don't let me go too soon."

"Emma, Deri – ready?"

"Yes, whenever you are," they replied.

"OK. Ready one … two … three … go!"

Poppy shot up and out from her hiding place like a bullet from a gun and ran as fast as she could into the barley field holding Lord Ted, followed by Emma and Deri.

"Oi!" came a voice behind her, "get back 'ere'!"

Elvina also had to move quickly as she knew the rest of the robbers would have heard the commotion outside. She shouted, "Secure the barn!" as loudly as she could to all the other fairies.

They all immediately stopped what they were doing and flew towards the barn. Instantaneously Elvina and Zuzana covered the doors in fairy dust that spun gold thread through and around the iron handles, the others secured windows and another bigger door for the vehicles in the same way. This was just in time as one of the robbers ran to the door to get out and see what the shouting was all about outside. He smashed into the door falling back on the floor. Mayhem broke out in the barn as the robbers were trying to get out, but the fairy locks were holding firm.

Meanwhile Poppy was halfway through the barley field with the robber catching up fast.

"OK, ready when you are!" shouted Deri.

"You ready Lord Ted?" she asked breathlessly as she was running towards Grandpa's gate forgetting that it was uphill and a lot harder than she had anticipated.

"Yes!" Lord Ted shouted.

Poppy dropped Lord Ted gently on the path and carried on as fast as she could with no idea if the plan would work. Lord Ted only had to wait seconds, as the robber continued his pursuit of Poppy, Ted stuck out his leg and tripped the man mid-stride. The robber stood no chance and went sprawling forward, planting his face firmly on the path with a grunt. Deri and Emma did not hesitate, covering him in fairy dust that instantly turned into heavy netting, the robber was pinned to the ground and could not move.

Emma stayed to make sure the robber remained secured while Deri scooped up Lord Ted and caught up with Poppy who was now past the vegetable patch and partway up the garden. She dropped Lord Ted into Poppy's arms just as she reached the house.

"Thanks Deri," said Poppy now totally out of breath, "all OK?"

"Yes, all OK, I'll get back to help them now," she said turning to fly back to the barn.

"You OK Lord Ted?" asked Poppy still panting while brushing the dust and bits of barley out of his fur.

"Yes, that was fun, now let's get the police."

Back at the barn all hell had broken loose. The robbers were kicking at the doors and walls and trying to start the farm vehicles engines so they could ram the main door. All the fairies were maintaining their hold over the exits, apart from Gullveig and Jareth who continued to let all the air out of the tyres. For once they were not arguing.

All the shouting and noise had woken Grandpa and Nanny who were coming down the stairs just as Poppy was entering the kitchen with Lord Ted.

"Grandpa!"

12

Poppy ran and hugged her grandpa has hard as she could, then moved quickly to hug Nanny.

"What on earth is going on?" asked Grandpa with a feeling of unease, "are you both OK, it's past 3 o'clock in the morning?"

"Yes, Yes Grandpa, we're fine, honestly, but we must phone the police straightaway."

"Is Jonny being robbed?" asked Nanny

"No, well sort of, well no, actually, err, it's worse."

"Worse?"

"Yes Grandpa, the people who stole the crown jewels and gold are trapped inside Mr Johnson's barn!"

"What! how do you know that?"

"We saw headlights at the barn so went to see and saw it was the queen's robbers. The fairies have trapped them inside and Lord Ted tripped one of them who was chasing us, so Emma and Deri pinned him to the ground but I'm not sure how long they can hold out. We need to get the police there before they escape," she said without taking a breath.

"Chased you?" gasped Nanny.

"It's OK Nanny, honest, we planned it," said Poppy very authoritatively, "we're fine, everything went to plan."

"You planned it! Oh my giddy aunt," said Nanny sitting down.

"OK let's call 999 but we'd better not mention the fairies otherwise they'll think we are drunk or something at this time of the morning, not everyone believes remember," said Grandpa, "then we can discuss what on earth you were doing there."

"Yes Grandpa, sorry."

Grandpa dialled and the call was quickly answered.

"How may I direct your call – what's the emergency?"

"Police please," said Grandpa.

"Police, what's the emergency?" came a lady's voice almost immediately.

"Yes, err good evening, sorry morning, err can we have the police please. I suggest you send as many as possible. The crown jewel thieves are trapped in a barn on the farm that backs onto our house in Diddlesdale village."

"Oh really, oh my word, right, err yes, OK, err hold on."

The line went quiet and Grandpa thought they had cut him off.

"I think they've cut me off," he said. "Hello... hello."

"Hello sir, sorry about that," came another voice, a man's this time, "can you repeat that please?"

"Yes, I know it's hard to believe but there are around, hold on," said Grandpa now looking at Poppy, "how many Poppy?"

"About 20 Grandpa."

"20! Oh my giddy aunt!" gasped Nanny again.

"Sorry, err yes," continued Grandpa, "around 20 of the robbers who stole the crown jewels are trapped in a barn on Diddlesdale farm," he paused again to look at Poppy, "and Mr Featherwhatsit?"

"He's not in a good way and tied up in the corner," said Poppy confidently.

"On my!" gasped Nanny a third time.

"Yes, sorry, and the hostage is not in a good way," Grandpa continued.

"And how are they trapped in the barn?" asked the man on the phone.

Grandpa had feared that would be asked and knew that telling him the fairies were holding 20 desperate robbers at bay might not seem a good call at 3 o'clock in the morning.

"My granddaughter has seen to that."

"Oh, I see. Can I speak to her please?"

"Err, yes of course," he said handing the phone to Poppy, hoping she would not talk about fairies and talking teddy bears, but he also knew that Poppy was an extremely smart young lady.

"Here you go Poppy, they want to speak to you," he said with his eyes widening and nodding at her with a confident, 'you can do this' way.

"Hello," said Poppy.

"Yes, hello miss err?"

"Poppy, my name is Poppy."

"Yes, Poppy, can you tell me what has happened?"

"Yes, but before I do can we get the police here as quickly as you can please, I am not sure how long they will be here for. I overheard Charlie, who I think is the leader, say two hours but that's before they knew they were trapped."

"Charlie you say?"

"Yes Charlie."

"OK, OK hold on," came the voice.

Poppy waited for a minute then a new voice came on the line.

"Hello Poppy, my name is Chief Inspector James Pickles-Cunningham," said a kind voice.

"Hello sir," she said.

"Please call me Jimmy. Can I ask how old you are Poppy?"

"I was told you should never ask a lady her age, chief inspector," said Poppy as if she was a school headmistress

Grandpa and Nanny stared at her with their mouths open and Grandpa let out a snort of laughter.

"Yes, indeed but..."

"Chief inspector, honestly, the longer we talk the more time they have to get away. There are around 20 men held up in Mr Johnsons barn. Inside they also have Mr Featherbottom... "

"Featherbottom, yes that's it," said Grandpa rolling his eyes.

"... who's tied up in the far corner on the east side of the barn," continued Poppy with Lord Ted, Nanny and Grandpa staring at her impressive performance. "There seems to be a leader called Charlie. They were obviously not expecting the barns to be in use, but Mr Johnson recently moved his farm machinery there ready for the harvest, trying to avoid the other robbers who are stealing the tractors. They checked, according to one of them, on Thursday that the barns were still empty which would have been true because Grandpa said Mr Johnson had only just moved the combine harvester and tractors. They have six cars and four vans and are using the barn as a meeting point. We've let all the air out of the tyres so they will find it hard to get away because some of the cars were struggling with the weight of the gold anyway. The doors to the barns are secured but I am not sure how long for."

"Yes, I see. When you say we...?"

"Inspector please!"

"Response teams are being mobilised now. I estimate in around 25 minutes they'll be there."

"OK."

"Do you know if they are armed?"

"Do you mean guns?"

Nanny gasped again.

"Yes guns."

"No, I don't think so. We didn't see any and none were mentioned."

"Good, yes that fits. Well Poppy, thank you. We knew they were heading north but that's about as much as we could figure out, so we have teams in all areas on standby so hopefully we'll be there quite quickly. I will come and see you after this is over."

"Yes, that would be lovely, we can have a cup of tea and some of Nanny's cake."

"Well, err yes, thank you. Can I ask again how old you are?"

"Chief Inspector!"

Grandpa beckoned for Poppy to hand him the phone

"…my grandpa would like to speak to you."

"Yes of course, thank you Poppy,"

"Hello chief inspector, I'm Poppy's grandfather."

"She's an impressive young lady, isn't she?"

"Yes, very impressive. I just wanted to give you more details on where to find us and how to get to the barn, as its not visible from the road at all… "

As Grandpa continued with the details, Nanny put the kettle on for a cup of tea and got all the cakes out ready as nannies do. Poppy sat back down and gave Lord Ted a squeeze.

"That was well done Poppy," he said.

"I skipped the bit about you and the fairies as I thought they may think I am a bit of a weird kid," she said, "but we need to go and warn the others that the police are coming."

"Yes, one of your better ideas," he smiled.

"… yes, yes, thank you chief inspector, I see yes, thank you, bye," finished Grandpa on the phone, "right then, they're on their way and will be here soon, I expect that there will be hundreds of police officers crawling around the barns soon enough."

"Great," said Poppy, "right I need to go and let Deri and Emma know so they can warn the others."

"No Poppy," said Nanny.

"I have to Nanny, I'm only going just past the gate, Grandpa will come with me won't you."

"Of course, I will, just give me two minutes to get changed," he said now running upstairs, actually quite excited at the thought of catching robbers.

"I don't like it," said Nanny.

"It's OK honestly Nanny, I will let them know, they can tell the others so they're safe, and then we can watch from the top of the field. Honestly Nanny I promise, then we can have a cup of tea with the chief inspector."

Grandpa came thundering down the stairs, "Right come on then," he said.

Poppy, with Lord Ted under her arm, led the way down the garden with Grandpa following. The first thing that hit them was the noise coming from the barn. Poppy broke into a run towards the gate and Grandpa did the same. Poppy ran through the gate to near where one of the robbers was still pinned to the ground.

"Deri! Emma!" shouted Poppy.

Emma appeared, "Oh, Poppy at last," she said, "we can't hold on much longer. They've managed to start one of the tractors and are ramming the doors."

The noise was deafening with banging and shouting.

"Is everyone OK though?" asked Poppy, nervously.

"Yes, but we're getting very tired. It's not really a fairy's job this is it?"

"No not at all, I'm so sorry I had no idea this would happen."

"I'm joking!" Emma laughed. "We've not had this much fun for hundreds of years!"

Poppy laughed. "OK, well the police will be here shortly," she said, just as the loud banging stopped in the barn. It seemed the robbers had given up ramming the doors but there was still plenty of shouting.

"Is George OK?" asked Lord Ted.

"Oh, hi Lord Ted, yes, Elvina managed to get in and put a shield around him, she is such a brave fairy. It's really freaked them all out though, which was why they were trying to get out using the tractor."

As they were talking a helicopter flew right over their heads down to the barn, then another followed by a third, nearly flattening the barley with the wind from their propellers as they went. They all hovered over the barn with lights shining directly downwards.

"Emma, you'd better let everyone know that the police are here, as if they hadn't guessed, I do not want them to get caught up in anything," said Poppy.

"OK will do.." And Emma flew off. The robber on the floor was knocked out cold and not going anywhere.

"What happened to him?" asked Grandpa looking down at the unconscious man, almost as big as Jonny Johnson.

"Lord Ted got to him." Poppy laughed.

"Hi Poppy," said Deri as she flew back to stand watch over the robber, "Wooo hooo this is great fun," she flew around in circles, "such fun."

"Hi Deri, all OK."

"You bet!"

Poppy watched as they saw police arrive, with blue lights and sirens – all lined up in the distance. If no one was awake in the village, due to the helicopters, they soon would be.

"Good grief," said Grandpa, "look at that lot."

"Holy moly," said Lord Ted.

Within what seemed only a couple of minutes they could see officers surrounding the buildings. There was still a lot of shouting and arguing going on in the barn, they were obviously very distressed in there and Poppy was really worried about George.

Suddenly a voice came from a loudhailer, "Charlie Wilson!"

There was a pause for a minute or so as everyone just stood still and stared waiting to see what would happen next.

"Charlie Wilson!" came the loudhailer again.

The arguing stopped in the barn. It fell silent.

At that very moment the fairies, unseen by all, dropped the hold they had on the doors and windows. Just like the glass wall that had protected Poppy a few weeks before with the geese, everything just melted away into thin air. They flew and joined Poppy, Lord Ted and Grandpa. Elvina stayed to keep a shield around George, but no one could see her and they would not have believed it even if they could.

"Charlie Wilson we know you are in there – come out peacefully. You are totally surrounded!"

"We're trapped in here; you'll have to come and get us!" came a frustrated voice from inside.

There was a tense pause, "Come out peacefully!" came the voice on the loudhailer again.

"I've just told you we're trapped ain't we, we've been trying for ages."

Just as the sun was starting to come up Poppy could see one of the officers lead a team, dressed head to toe in black, to the front door of the barn. They stood with their backs against the barn wall either side of the door.

"This is your last warning!" said the loudhailer.

Inside the barn was more shouting, they knew the game was up. All that planning, all the financing, all that work blown, in less than 24 hours they would have nothing.

Grandpa, Lord Ted and Poppy and most of the fairies looked on with Deri keeping an eye on the robber on the floor.

"Is Elvina OK Oona?" asked Poppy. Oona had decided to sit on Poppy's shoulder to watch, she was exhausted but smiling.

"Yes, as soon as they come out Elvina will join us, she is well hidden but let's face it I doubt anyone in there will believe in fairies anyway so it's all good," she laughed.

Just then, as the first sunlight of the morning hit the front of the barn, one of the officers lent across the door and flicked the handle. The door just swung open. Inside the robbers looked on in astonishment and fell silent.

The helicopters continued to hover high above the barns.

The police waited…

Poppy, Grandpa and Lord Ted waited…

Elvina waited…

Then, with his hands above his head, they saw one man walk out of the barn, followed by another and another. They were all shouted at and instructed to lie on the floor. A total of 19 men walked out of the barn.

"See 19, I win," said Deri laughing.

"I said 19 too," said Gullveig.

"No, you didn't," said Jareth.

"I did so!"

"You did not."

"Boys," shouted Poppy.

"Sorry Miss Poppy, miss."

Everyone laughed.

"Good job," said Elvina just arriving, "how much fun was that?" she could see everyone was laughing.

"Oh Elvina, you're safe," said Poppy.

"Of course."

"And George?" asked Lord Ted.

"He'll be fine," said Elvina. "Right come on you lot let's get back, see you all later." she said and all the fairies flew off back to their new homes in the old oak tree where Poppy had her new reading den.

"I'll hold on here," said Deri nodding towards the chap on the floor.

"OK," said Elvina, "good idea, don't be long."

"Well, that was a welcome and a half to Honeypot Lane for the fairies," said Lord Ted, "they won't forget that full moon in a hurry will they?"

Deri laughed, she was having a ball, "Best night of my life so far!"

Poppy, Lord Ted and Grandpa continued to watch for a while. They saw George being brought out. He was walking but went straight into an ambulance and will probably never be able to explain how on earth he was so well protected in the barn.

"OK Poppy," said Grandpa, "enough excitement for one morning, it's nearly 6 o'clock already and you must be absolutely exhausted. Go in and have a shower then we can chat later, OK?"

"OK Grandpa," she said sheepishly.

"You're not in any trouble Popsicle, but you must take care, promise?"

"I promise."

"I'll just nip down and tell them there's another chap here so they can come and get him, I'll be up in a bit."

As Poppy went back through the gate to join Nanny, Grandpa went to speak to the police to let them know about the other robber. As the police arrived Deri released the netting as if it had never been there and went to join the rest of the fairies. The robber, with the aid of a much smaller policeman, stumbled to his feet completely unaware of what had happened. He was led back down the field in handcuffs to the waiting vans.

Grandpa stared across the barley fields at the chaos in front of him, thinking of his brave, beautiful granddaughter and wondering how the police would ever believe an eight-year-old, a talking teddy bear and a bunch of fairies brought down a very experienced and ruthless gang of thieves.

He turned and walked back to the house, closing the gate behind him. As he walked past the treehouse, he switched off the fairy lights on the ladder, knowing that all the fairies would now be fast asleep, he joined Poppy and Nanny in the kitchen.

13

"Well, well, well," said Grandpa as he entered the kitchen, "not sure I've ever had a morning like that before or ever will again."

"Was that man OK Grandpa?"

"Yes Poppy, I don't think he knew what had hit him really."

Poppy was drinking a hot mug of tea with Lord Ted by her side and Nanny was just finishing buttering some toast for her, as she was very hungry.

"Fancy some toast too old man?" Nanny asked Grandpa.

"Oh yes please. It's chaos down there. I'll call Jonny in a bit."

Poppy sat and ate her toast and was waiting for the inevitable question.

"So, Popsicle," said Grandpa eventually, "what exactly happened?"

Poppy took a big gulp of tea and proceeded to tell Nanny and Grandpa every little detail she could remember until the point she ran in to call the police. It took a while, but Poppy made sure she did not leave anything out.

"Amazing Poppy," said Nanny, "but Lord Ted was right, you should have called the police first."

"But then they might have got away Nanny, plus I didn't know it was those robbers, I thought it was the tractor robbers or maybe Mr Johnson himself."

"Not at that time in the morning," pointed out Grandpa.

"That's just what Lord Ted said."

"Well, you were amazing Popsicle, we're very proud of you."

"Yes, we are, very proud indeed," confirmed Grandpa, "but I think we need to slightly bend the truth here, otherwise people will think we're a bit bonkers, and more importantly I do not want Poppy being in the news for her own safety."

"Agreed," said Nanny, "right Poppy, you go and have a shower and we'll sort it out."

"OK Nanny."

Poppy finished off her tea and went upstairs with Lord Ted. She walked into her bedroom and looked out of the window. The sun was shining brightly. Looking down the hill towards the barns she could see some movement, but as the view from her bedroom was nowhere near as good as the view from her treehouse, she couldn't make out what was happening. The helicopters were gone so it had fallen silent, although when Poppy opened the window, she could hear that there was still plenty of activity.

She hopped up on the bed and lay down for a few minutes with every intention of going for a shower. As the adrenalin of the morning's activities started to wear off, she realised she was absolutely exhausted and within minutes, with Lord Ted snuggled into her side, she was fast asleep.

Poppy woke some hours later. Nanny had been up to see where she was and saw her on the bed so decided to put her under the covers so she could sleep properly. For a few seconds Poppy could not remember where she was or the events earlier in the day. She could hear voices coming from downstairs and gave Lord Ted a squeeze.

"My you've been asleep for a while," he said kindly.

"What time is it?" she asked stretching and yawning all in one movement.

"Lunchtime I think, certainly by the sounds of it downstairs anyway."

Poppy could hear the clinking of cups and saucers and different voices, she got out of bed, and after freshening up, made her way downstairs with Lord Ted.

Before she went into the kitchen she stopped and listened to try and work out who was there. Nanny and Grandpa obviously, what sounded like Jonny Johnson and a man and lady that sounded familiar, but she was not quite sure who they were.

"Well, I think that's the best solution all round," she heard Grandpa say. "Thanks Jonny, really appreciate it."

"No problem," said Jonny.

"Yes, I do not want this to leave this room please, the last thing I want is for Poppy to be part of the media circus," said Grandpa quite firmly.

"Agreed said all the voices together."

"Have you seen all the television crews in the village?" said the lady's voice. "The whole world's media is outside."

"Yes, and I do not want them outside my house either, please make that a priority," said Nanny also in a very firm voice.

"Yes, you can rely on that," said the male voice.

Poppy decided to enter the kitchen. The talking stopped as everyone turned around to look at her. Poppy could see that along with Nanny, Grandpa and Jonny Johnson there were two senior police officers. She knew they were senior by the silver pips on their shoulders.

The man looked quite shocked at how young Poppy was, a little girl, in her pink pyjamas with a teddy bear under her arm did not seem like the girl that he spoke to earlier in the morning.

"Hello sweetie," said Nanny kindly, "you've slept well, would you like a cup of tea?"

"Yes, I have and yes please Nanny."

"Poppy," said Grandpa. "This is Assistant Chief Constable Mary Underberry and Chief Inspector James Pickles-Cunningham."

Poppy could see that the chief inspector was looking at her with a surprised look so knew she had to be confident

"Chief inspector, nice to meet you, and I'm eight before you ask me again. And assistant chief constable, hello too. And hello Mr Johnson."

"Hello Poppy," they both said together shocked at how this little girl had brought down a gang of experienced thieves. Jonny Johnson smiled, winked and sort of waved.

"We were just telling them exactly what happened Poppy," said Grandpa.

"Oh good, right."

"Yes," continued Grandpa, "that Jonny here, thought ahead and laid some tyre spikes on the tracks leading to the barn to try and stop the tractor robbers."

There was silence as they all awaited Poppy's response.

"Yes, what a good idea Mr Johnson," said Poppy eventually, widening her eyes.

"And somehow they got trapped inside the barn," finished Grandpa.

"Yes, I've been meaning to get those locks fixed for some time now," said Jonny.

There was a pause as Poppy took that all in. She looked around the room as everyone was staring at her. She sat down at the table as Nanny put her cup of tea in front of her. She held Lord Ted close to her then looked Chief Inspector Pickles-Cunningham straight in the eye.

"Yes, chief inspector, yes that's exactly how it happened," she said as firmly as Grandpa said earlier, "and Mr Johnson you do need to get those locks mended sooner rather than later."

There was a silence.

"Yes, I do, I really do," smiled Jonny Johnson.

There were lots of smiles in the room and Poppy then let out a laugh.

"Thank you Poppy," said the chief inspector, "that's what is going in our report."

"And what about the other robber found in the field?" asked Poppy.

"Oh, he just tripped apparently, he has no idea how he got there," said the assistant chief constable, "I'm Mary, Poppy. Thank you for all you have done," she winked at Poppy and held out her hand to shake it.

Poppy shook her hand.

"So, I think that's everything is it?" asked Grandpa.

"Well apart from my barn is a bit of a mess and I have lost a tractor or two," said Jonny with his arms folded.

"Yes, we will ensure that gets sorted for you Mr Johnson," said assistant chief constable, "no problem at all."

"I would like to ask Poppy a question if that's OK," asked the chief inspector.

Grandpa looked at Poppy as if to say up to you.

"Yes of course," said Poppy

"Thank you. Well firstly I want to thank you, I am not quite sure I have met an eight-year-old quite like you before, you are quite a young lady."

"Why thank you chief inspector," she said in as lady like a way as she could muster.

"Yes, uhm, anyway one question. Did you see or hear anything else that may help us, I know we have them bang to rights as we say, but anything else that you think could help at all?"

"Yes, one of the men in the barn did ask where Ray and Ron were," said Poppy.

"Really, that's very useful thank you, anything else?"

Poppy thought for a while. "No, I don't think so, err… yes hold on. Yesterday, when Nanny and I went for a walk in the village, and Nanny was talking to Mrs Jones in the post office, I saw two men in a dark blue van just staring across the green down Beehive Lane, towards the farm."

"Did you get a look at the men?"

"No not really, they made me feel a little uneasy."

"Yes, I should think so," said the chief inspector.

"You never told me that Poppy," said Nanny.

"I didn't think anything of it really."

"Did you get a look at the number plate by any chance?" continued the chief inspector.

"No but I bet I could find out, Gerald would know."

"Who's Gerald?"

"Err, could I get back to you on that one, it's a bit complicated," said Poppy.

"Yes, uhm OK," responded the chief inspector not pushing anything or doubting this quite remarkable girl in front of him. "No problem at all, your grandpa has my phone number, just ring me when you remember."

"Yes of course chief inspector," said Poppy smiling.

"Great," said Grandpa, "time to get back to normal in here if we can."

"Yes, yes of course," said the assistant chief constable, "thanks again and thank you for the tea."

"Our pleasure," said Nanny.

The assistant chief constable turned and looked at Poppy, "You know," she said, "you are a very extraordinary and lucky young lady." She rested her hand on Poppy's shoulder and smiled, "I believe too."

Poppy looked up and smiled, "Thank you," she said.

The assistant chief constable and chief inspector left through the back garden, past the treehouse and through the gate so they would not be seen by the media that had now descended upon the small Diddlesdale village.

"I'd better be off too then," said Jonny, "I'm going to be interviewed within an inch of my life I guess."

"Sorry Jonny," said Grandpa.

"It's OK, my friend, the last thing we would want is for Poppy to be involved."

"No, her mummy and daddy would not be happy either. Same story to everyone outside this room Poppy OK?"

"Yes Grandpa."

"OK, I'll be off then, see you on the tele," said Jonny, laughing.

"Mr Johnson?" asked Poppy just as he was leaving.

"Yes my lovely?"

"Thank you, thank you very much and I am really sorry about your barn and tractors."

"No problem, they can all be replaced. Between you and me I wanted a couple of new ones anyway, so you've done me a favour," he said laughing.

Poppy smiled as Jonny Johnson made his way down the garden to avoid being seen out of the front of the house.

"I called your mummy and daddy, Poppy, to say all was OK, they were worried of course. Perhaps you should call them, now you are up, then we can have some lunch," said Nanny.

"OK Nanny thank you, then we need to go and see Gerald please."

"OK, we'll see."

After Poppy had had her shower, called her daddy and had something to eat she was ready to go into the village.

"OK Nanny, I'm ready, can we go into the village now?"

"Oh, I don't know Poppy, it will be very busy down there and … "

"Please Nanny, it's important."

Poppy looked at her nanny. How could Nanny avoid that look?

"OK then, give me a minute or two."

"Thank you, where's Grandpa?"

"Being nosy at the bottom of the garden pretending to work on his vegetable patch," said Nanny, smiling.

"He is funny, OK I'll go and tell him we're going into the village. Also, please can we make some fairy cakes later as I think I owe a group of very brave fairies something."

"Yes of course poppet, we can pick up a few bits from the shop."

"Thank you, Nanny."

Poppy walked down the garden and glanced up at the treehouse wondering how all the fairies were, then on to see her grandpa.

Grandpa was standing at the gate gazing down the field.

"Ahem," Poppy coughed.

"Ah hello there, Popsicle, I was just taking a breather," said Grandpa, laughing.

"That's OK Grandpa, you must be very tired."

"I am a little bit yes."

"Nanny and I are going into the village then going to make some fairy cakes to share with the fairies tonight if that's OK?"

"Yes of course, you need to say thank you to them too and let them know what the story is, not that they are going to tell anyone of course."

"No of course but they were amazing, do you want anything from the shops?"

"Just you and Nanny back safely please, there're robbers about you know!"

"OK Grandpa."

Poppy gave her grandpa a big hug, "See you later."

Poppy skipped back towards the house where Nanny was waiting for her ready to walk to the village.

14

Nanny and Poppy, with Lord Ted in his now usual place under her arm, left through the front door and walked up Honeypot Lane towards the village. There were a lot more cars parked on the side of the road making it hard for other cars to pass and making it a little unsafe to walk.

"This does not bode well Poppy, it's going to be mayhem on the green I am sure."

"Nanny, do you think I can stay here for the rest of the summer holidays please?" asked Poppy staring up at her nanny as another car squeezed by.

"Well of course you can if you like, you'll have to ask your mummy and daddy though."

"I asked them when I called earlier."

"Oh, did you?" asked Nanny in surprise, "and what did they say?"

"They said if you're OK with it, then that would be OK."

"Well, that's just wonderful, yes of course you can," said Nanny smiling, "I couldn't think of anything better. We're off to the Lake District for a little holiday in a few days, there's plenty of room for you so you can come on holiday with us. We're staying at a friend's house on the side of the lake."

"I would love that, thank you Nanny."

"I'll call your daddy tonight. Do you need anything else from home?"

"I have everything I need right here," said Poppy and gave her nanny's hand a tight squeeze.

They walked a little further on, having to wait a few times for passing cars looking for somewhere to park.

"They better not park on our drive," said Nanny sternly, followed by, "Oh my word!" as they followed the bend in the road and on into the village.

In front of them was the vision the assistant chief constable had described, a media circus. The village green and pond could hardly be seen, and the shops had disappeared behind a collection of white vans with satellite dishes on their roofs. In front were dozens of people, reporters with microphones talking into cameras, others holding the cameras and long furry microphones. Some bright lights were shining on the reporters as they fed their accounts to their relevant television stations in various languages.

Poppy, Lord Ted and Nanny walked around the back of the vans. There was the longest queue ever seen at the tea shop as they passed to get into the post office to see Mrs Jones. The noise of hundreds of people talking was shut out as they closed the door behind them for the tranquillity of Mrs Jones's post office.

"Hello Agatha," said Nanny.

"Oh, a friendly face at last," replied Mrs Jones, "Hello both, what a circus. I never thought I'd see the day. Unbelievable isn't it? The drama of it all here in Diddlesdale. Did you see all the mayhem this morning and the noise, quite extraordinary wasn't it?"

"Yes indeed."

"Could you see much from where you are?"

"No, nothing really, it's all in the dip so hidden away."

"Yes, yes of course. Poppy did it keep you awake?"

"No not really Mrs Jones, it's very exciting though," said Poppy thinking that Mrs Jones had turned into a television reporter herself, asking all these questions.

"Yes, I suppose it is in a funny way but still terrible that people like that think they can get away with such things. Anyway, I'm sure we'll be talking about this for years to come, what can I get you?"

"Just need to post these birthday cards then we'll battle our way to the store to get a few bits."

"I'm going to make some cakes," said Poppy, who was now wondering where Gerald might be with all the people outside.

"Oh nice," said Mrs Jones and then for no reason it seemed, said, "I have some bread here to feed the ducks and geese, would you like to do it today, as I do not want to go out there with that lot, not until I've put my face on anyway."

"Yes of course," said Poppy thankful for a reason to go looking for the ducks.

As Nanny continued with the birthday cards and Mrs Jones persisted with the gossip and questions, Poppy and Lord Ted looked out of the window. She could see the assistant chief constable being interviewed with about 20 microphones in her face. To the left she could see Mr Johnson's head above the crowds as he was also being bombarded by microphones and flashing lights from the cameras. Poppy gave Lord Ted a squeeze.

"Poor Mr Johnson."

"Yes, poor man, he's going to be there for a while I'm sure."

"Can you see Gerald, Lord Ted?"

"No. But I'm sure they will all be around the other side of the pond."

"How did all these people get here so quickly?"

"I've absolutely no idea," said Lord Ted, "it takes ages to get anywhere around here."

"Right then," came Nanny's voice, "LG Poppy."

Mrs Jones gave Poppy the small bag of bread for the ducks as they opened the door. A cacophony of noise hit them as Poppy said thank you for the bag, but it was probably lost in the noise. The once quiet village had been transformed into Piccadilly Circus overnight. Nanny headed for the village store to get all they needed for the cakes and something nice for tea.

"I'll go and feed the ducks!" said Poppy loudly trying to be heard.

"OK!" replied Nanny, "stay where I can easily see you please."

"I will, I'll just be at the pond and will wait there for you Nanny."

Poppy and Lord Ted continued past the shop as Nanny entered. Then Poppy moved around the back of all the vans. She could hear the assistant chief constable being inundated with questions then heard her say something about the robbers being trapped but Poppy continued on to the pond where she could see some of the ducks huddled together looking quite pensive wondering what on earth had happened to their peaceful oasis. Further behind the ducks were the geese grouped on the bank behind the reeds with their beaks tucked under their wings.

As she approached the ducks they looked up, pleased to see a friendly face that they knew. Poppy gave Lord Ted a squeeze again.

"Hi guys," said Lord Ted to the assembled team of ducks.

"Hi Lord Ted," they all said together, "what's going on?" asked Rafferty.

Lord Ted gave a quick explanation of why all these vans and people were there as Poppy broke up some bread and threw it on the grass.

"And how long will they be here?" asked Rafferty with a mouthful of bread spraying crumbs in all directions as the others impatiently pecked at the bread all around him.

"Steady on, there's plenty for all," said Poppy.

"I'm not sure how long they'll be here for, a couple of days I guess," said Lord Ted, "do you know where Gerald is?"

"Here I am!" shouted Gerald, waddling as fast as he could out from behind the bushes at the sight of the bread. "hello Poppy and Lord Ted," he continued making a dive for the last few crumbs. Poppy threw some more pieces of bread down for him and he gobbled it up.

"Hi Gerald," said Poppy, "can I ask you a question?"

"Of course," he said spitting breadcrumbs.

"Well, you remember the other day when we met?"

"You mean yesterday…" interrupted Gerald.

"Gosh, was it, it seems like ages ago, anyway. Yes, yesterday, there was a dark blue van…"

"Yes, it nearly ran me over!" interrupted Gerald again.

"Oh my, I'm sorry about that."

"I think they deliberately headed for us all too," said Rafferty.

"Well, that's awful but can you remember anything about the van or the men in it?" asked Poppy. "It's important if you can."

"The two men did not look very nice," said Rafferty, "and it was all red behind where they were sitting."

"Yes, it was, I remember that now," said Poppy, "anything else like a number plate or anything."

"I hate to disappoint you Poppy, but we're ducks," said Gerald, "we can't read."

"Oh yes, right, sorry, I thought, well, never mind, sorry."

"But the geese can," said Rafferty happily.

"Oh, can they?" said Poppy now confused, surprised and pleased all in one go.

"I didn't know that either Poppy," said Lord Ted.

"Yes Sally, the mother goose, said the number plate had my name and age on it," said Gerald, "Gerald aged three, as it nearly hit me," he continued.

"Gerald aged three?" said Poppy, "that's not a normal number plate."

"No, it's not," said Lord Ted.

"We can go and ask Sally."

"I wouldn't go near them at the moment Poppy," said Rafferty, "they are sleeping, or trying too. They've not had much sleep and are very grumpy with all this going on. I would steer well clear of them for now."

"Oh OK, yes I've had a run in with geese before," said Poppy, just as Nanny appeared.

"Hi Poppy, you all done? got what you needed?"

"Err, yes Nanny, for now," she said hesitantly. "Bye guys," she said to the ducks as she turned away. They all quacked in response.

"Come on then," said Nanny, "let's get back and make the cakes, away from all this nonsense going on."

They made their way around the vans, through the crowds and queues almost unnoticed by the reporters, who had no idea that the little girl with the teddy under her arm was the one they really needed to speak to. Poppy could still see poor Mr Johnson being interviewed, although he did look rather like he was enjoying himself, and the assistant chief constable was now with another group of reporters.

"Poor Jonny," said Nanny, "I think we owe him for this one."

After they had squeezed past all the parked cars, they eventually made it home and unpacked the shopping. Grandpa was making a cup of tea and got out two extra cups.

"It's chaos out there," said Nanny, "but the best news is that Poppy is staying for the rest of the holidays and coming to The Lakes with us," she said, very happily.

"Really? that's amazing news," said Grandpa with an enormous smile across his face, "we have our own boat on the lake too Poppy, so it will be great fun."

"Oh that's exciting Grandpa."

"And even more exiting is that Jonny called me just after you left … "

"We saw him being interviewed," said Poppy.

"Poor guy, anyway he said he has to fly down to Porthcastle in Cornwall in the morning to do a deal with a brewer for his barley and said we could go with him. We can go to the beach as the airfield is only a short walk away and it will be a glorious day tomorrow. What do you think Poppy?"

"Oh, Grandpa that's amazing," then after a short pause, "Mr Johnson has a plane?" she asked, astonished.

"Yes, a small one, seats four, he travels all over the place in it. The airfield is only a few minutes away from here. Be good to get away from all this don't you think?"

"Fantastic," said Poppy, "that's really amazing."

"Only trouble is it's an early start so its sleep in your bedroom tonight then treehouse tomorrow with the fairy cakes if you are not too tired, I know they won't mind, OK?"

"Oh, OK Grandpa, yes I am sure they will be fine," said Poppy, "can we make the cakes soon though Nanny please?"

"Of course, Poppy, what an exciting few days ahead, it's a bit late now anyway," said Nanny sweetly.

"I've never been in a plane before," said Poppy.

"Well, that's doubly exciting then," replied Grandpa as he smiled. "What fun. You coming too Nanny?"

"You try and stop me," she laughed. "Right then dinner time, then we can watch Jonny on the news."

After Poppy had helped Nanny and Grandpa clear away all the dinner plates, she went to get ready for bed so that straight after the news she would be ready to snuggle down and be prepared for an early start in the morning.

"Hurry up Poppy!" came Grandpa's voice from downstairs. "The news is about to start."

Poppy, with Lord Ted under her arm, came thundering down the stairs just as Grandpa was turning the television on.

"Blimey Charlie, I thought it was a herd of elephants coming down the stairs," said Grandpa just as Poppy flew past him, taking a running jump and landing on the sofa.

"Ta Daaaa," she said, now rising to an upright position, hands in the air, just as the gymnasts do when finishing a routine. Lord Ted was still bouncing on the cushions.

"It's a 10 from me," said Nanny, laughing.

"I've been working on that," said Poppy laughing, picking up Lord Ted and sitting on her grandpa's lap ready for the news to start.

"Here we go," he said turning up the volume.

Fiona was the host outside the Tower of London and Huw was live from Diddlesdale.

"...and the headlines this evening. George Featherbottom is found safe and well, 19 have been arrested with two more still at large and the majority of the crown jewels and gold reserves have been recovered. We will join Huw at the scene where the arrests took place earlier today but let me give you some more details, more coming in all the time, of course.

"Charlie Wilson 43, from East London, Mark Jameson 34, from ... "

Fiona went on to list all the names of the robbers who had been caught earlier, showing their pictures as she went.

"Oh, not everything recovered then, interesting," said Grandpa.

"Good grief they look a rough lot, you were very brave Poppy," said Nanny.

"I never saw any of them really, I think I would have run the other way if I'd known."

"Me too," said Grandpa.

"...and John Klondike, 41 from Gravesend were all arrested in a barn at Diddlesdale in Derbyshire this morning.

"Earlier today we had an update from Assistant Chief Constable Mary Underberry who is at the scene in Diddlesdale ... "

The report now cut to an interview with the assistant chief constable, recorded earlier at the village green.

"Oooo here we are look, on the world map at last," said Nanny. "She is a nice lady, isn't she?"

"Yes, she is," said Poppy watching intently in case she was on the television at any point, then at the same time hoping she was not filmed talking to the ducks.

"...I can now give you more information, continued the assistant chief constable. There were 19 men arrested earlier today at a barn here in Diddlesdale, in the heart of rural Derbyshire. Much of the stolen items have been recovered and Mr Featherbottom was found well, although rather shaken by his ordeal. It seems the gang were using this as a rendezvous point before splitting up across the country, at this stage we have no idea why. They all took various routes to get here, thinking the barn was not in use. The barn is well hidden from view but only two days ago the local farmer moved machinery in readiness for the harvest, and to avoid another gang who are stealing farm machinery at this time. The farmer placed some tyre spikes, similar to the ones used in police operations, to stop the gang stealing farm machinery or to impede their getaway. It seems he caught a different gang. Somehow the locks dropped on the barn door and trapped them inside and with the noise they made trying to escape it alerted the local community. We were called at 3.14 a.m. this morning and were on the scene by 4 o'clock then eventually the arrests were made. I can also confirm that we are looking for two further suspects who are associated with many of the arrested men. These are bothers Ray and Ron Pearson from Clapham, North London. These are dangerous men and should not be approached…

"And why would, what would seem to be a sophisticated gang make such a fundamental error as to all meet up in a barn – why didn't they just continue to their separate hideouts?" interrupted one reporter.

"That's the question I'd like an answer too," replied the assistant chief constable.

"Wouldn't we all," said Grandpa.

The screen then showed pictures of the Pearson brothers. "Hmmm they look like a couple of tough guys too," said Grandpa

"…and there is also a selection of the crown jewels still not accounted for, these being the current sovereign crown and prince consort crown along with the St Edward crown, current sceptre and coronation rings…"

The television screen now showed pictures of the missing crown jewels.

"…these are priceless artefacts and we must assume that the Pearson brothers have these in their possession. The Crown Jeweller, the keeper of the jewels, is still collating the find and cross checking to ascertain if anything else is still missing…"

The picture now went back to Fiona as she interviewed other people, all lined up at the side of her in front of the Tower, about various topics.

Nanny, Grandpa, Poppy and Lord Ted all watched intently still not believing that less than 24 hours ago all this happened at the bottom of their garden in the quiet village of Diddlesdale.

The screen then changed to a reporter outside a hospital.

"Thank you, Fiona, yes, George Featherbottom was brought here earlier today. George is said to be well, sitting up although a little confused as to exactly what happened in the barn. His family are on their way to be at his bedside after spending the night at the palace with the queen and have asked for privacy at this time…"

Pictures of the ambulance arriving at the hospital were shown as the reporter went on to give more information about George, as a warder at the Tower and his life as a soldier.

"I love that, they have asked for privacy, so they go and show more information about him, his life and what he did," said Grandpa rolling his eyes.

Fiona now came back on the screen and suggested they now go to join Huw live from Diddlesdale.

"At last," said Nanny

"Yes, thank you Fiona, said Huw, you join me here in the heart of Derbyshire in the quiet village of Diddlesdale where earlier today 19 men were arrested ... "

In true news style Huw then went on to repeat everything that Fiona had said and that the assistant chief constable had announced earlier.

"...and I'm joined now by Agatha Jones, the local postmistress..."

"Oh, I knew Agatha was itching to get out on the village green at some point," said Nanny laughing.

Poppy and Grandpa laughed.

Huw placed the microphone to her face after he asked her what she had seen or heard earlier in the morning. He was understandably looking at the hairy pimple on her nose but continued like the professional newscaster he was.

"Well... " started Mrs Jones, who had clearly been to the hairdressers since Nanny and Poppy had been to the post office, had her make-up done and put on her best Sunday outfit for the occasion.

"...I could not believe the noise at about 4 o'clock this morning," she continued with a much posher voice than normal.

"Helicopters and then sirens with blue flashing lights all speeding through the village. They need to be careful around that bend, very dangerous the roads are around here."

"But did you see anything of the robbers?"

"Err, well no, but I saw them being taken away in police vans."

Grandpa, Nanny and Poppy all laughed at poor Mrs Jones, her five minutes of fame reduced to about 15 seconds.

"Thank you, Mrs Jones." The camera moved away from Mrs Jones and now focussed on Huw.

"Agatha Jones there, the local postmistress here in Diddlesdale. Right let's go now to an interview with Dave Jonny Johnson, who is the local farmer where all the action took place this morning and former England international rugby player of course ..."

"Here we go," said Grandpa, "let's hope he gets his story right."

"He played Rugby for England Grandpa?"

"He did quite a few times yes. Nanny and I went to watch him."

"Oh wow, I didn't know that. He was very good then?"

"One of the best, he's got a world cup medal to prove it too. His career was cut short through injury, very sad."

The screen had a smiling Jonny Johnson who towered above everyone else around him. He looked pleased to be there and was used to being interviewed after his time in the limelight as a professional sportsman.

"Yes, I laid out three lines of spikes to stop the thieves taking my tractors and combine harvesters, not a good time of year for that to happen with a decent harvest about to start," said Jonny Johnson in reply to the reporters first question. He also had around 20 microphones thrust under his chin too, with many of the arms holding them stretched up to catch his words. Poppy remembered the scene well as she was in the village when this had been recorded.

"And how did you find out they were in your barn?" asked one of the reporters.

"First I knew about it was the police knocking on my door after 5 o'clock this morning."

'And how were they trapped in'? asked another.

"I've been meaning to get those locks looked at, I got trapped in there the other day too."

"He's adding to it, like it," said Grandpa, "very convincing, good job Jonny."

"And can you tell us anything else?"

"Not really. I've got two bust tractors and a wrecked barn wall but apart from that all good. The queen has her stuff back, the chap is OK, and I've still got my harvest to get in." he said smiling away.

"Did you see any of the robbers?"

"Nope, nothing. As I say the first I knew was when the police knocked on the door, my farmhouse is quite a way from these barns, so I did not see or hear anything. By the time I'd got here the police had carted them all away."

The screen now moved back to Huw. Jonny's task was over. Just then the phone rang. Grandpa put the television sound on mute and picked up his phone.

"It's Jonny," he said to all, "Jonny!" he said down the phone.

Nanny and Poppy clapped.

"Yes, you did do a good job, the girls are applauding for you now," there was a pause.

"Yes, the story was perfect, I liked the 'I got trapped too' addition," again another pause. "No, it came across well, thank you," continued Grandpa, "really appreciate it mate, thanks."

Nanny beckoned Poppy over.

"Right go up and clean your teeth then, it's bedtime, then come and say goodnight to Grandpa. Too late for a story tonight I think, we have to be up early."

"OK Nanny."

Poppy went upstairs with Lord Ted as Grandpa continued on the phone with Jonny. She placed Lord Ted on the bed and looked out of her bedroom window towards the barns. There was still some activity with bright lights shining. She closed the curtains then went to have a wash and clean her teeth. After saying goodnight, she was soon snuggled in her big bed. Lord Ted was snuggled in beside her. Poppy gave him a squeeze.

"Well, what a day Lord Ted."

"It's been very eventful hasn't it."

"What do you make of the number plate, Gerald aged three?"

"No idea, we'll have to ask Sally when they're a little more friendly."

"Yes, be good to let the police know as soon as we could though."

"Let's sleep on it."

"Good idea Lord Ted, night night," said Poppy giving him a cuddle. "Thank you for everything."

"Night night Poppy."

15

Nanny woke Poppy who had been asleep for nearly 10 hours. The previous two days had clearly been exhausting.

"Good morning poppet," said Nanny, "you've slept well."

"Good morning Nanny," said Poppy who was wide awake very quickly.

"Exciting day today, Grandpa is just finishing a packed lunch then we'll have some breakfast after you've got ready and meet Jonny at the airfield. What did you do with your swimmers?"

"OK, great – they're in the bottom drawer."

"You go and get washed and dressed and I'll meet you downstairs, I've got everything else,"

"Will do Nanny."

Nanny disappeared downstairs as Poppy gave Lord Ted a squeeze.

"Hello you," she said, "you want to come on the plane I guess, right?"

"Err, I think so yes please," said Lord Ted.

"Good oh," replied Poppy.

After getting ready, Nanny, Grandpa and Poppy finished their breakfast.

"It's going to be a long day so best make sure we start it on full tummies," said Grandpa as he was clearing the table. "Jonny said to be at the airfield at 9 o'clock, so we'd best get going soon."

Poppy gathered up her things for the day, which was quite simple – Lord Ted and a book – Nanny had everything else all packed up including the lunch, swimsuits and towels.

"I called Daddy last night Poppy, just to make sure everything was OK for you to stay and come on holiday with us. He's going to bring round a few more clothes and things before we go."

"OK Nanny, thank you. I'm very excited to be going on holiday, and the boat and the plane today – every day is an adventure."

"Adventures fill your soul Poppy," said Grandpa, "and we certainly seem to be having our fair share of those at the moment, don't we?"

"I know," said Poppy with a big grin.

Poppy helped carry the bags to the car and within a short time they were on their way to the airfield. They drove past the village green. It was still a lot busier than normal, but over half the vans had now gone. Poppy, with Lord Ted on her lap, could see the ducks and geese on the pond looking slightly more relaxed. She wanted to stop and speak to Sally, the mother goose, but thought she would leave it for now. Her mind turned back to the number plate and how 'Gerald aged three' could even be a number plate at all.

"Gerald aged three," she whispered to Lord Ted giving him a squeeze, "any ideas?"

"I'm thinking but no nothing, I think we'll need to speak to Sally when we get back don't you?"

"Yes, I think so."

Nanny turned the car into the airfield and followed a road around the back of a long runway to some hangars where all the planes, and some helicopters, lived. This was the home of the local air ambulance too, which Poppy could often hear flying over Nanny and Grandpa's house; the bright red helicopter lying still, waiting for an emergency call.

Jonny Johnson was already there, preparing the plane ready for the journey. The white plane was not as big as Poppy had imagined. The doors were over the wings that swept underneath the body with wheels seemingly propping them up. A long red stripe along the body with letters and numbers on each side were towards the rear of the tail. Two small windows sat above the doors with the wider windscreen and a propeller at the front. It was very shiny and very smart.

Poppy skipped ahead to see Mr Johnson with Lord Ted bouncing around in his green backpack.

"Hello Mr Johnson," she said.

"Hi Poppy, you excited?"

"Yes, I'm so excited, I've never been in an aeroplane before."

"Well, there's a first time for everything, did you see me on the tele last night?"

"We did, and thank you again," said Poppy.

"No problem."

"Morning Jonny," said Nanny and Grandpa.

"Morning both," he replied smiling, "phone has been red hot this morning, be glad to get away for a few hours, I've told Sue not to answer the home phone and mine will be off."

"Sorry mate," said Grandpa.

"No worries, right then let's get those bags in and we'll be off, I've fuelled her up and ready to go, I reckon it will take us 90 minutes to get there."

Jonny opened a small, almost hidden door under the red lettering and Grandpa passed him the bags. He then asked Nanny and Grandpa to get in first.

"Thought you'd like to sit in the front Poppy, your nanny and grandpa said it would be OK."

"Oh, thank you, wow, yes that would be amazing."

Poppy watched carefully as Nanny and Grandpa squeezed themselves into the plane.

"Please can you pass Lord Ted to Grandpa. I think he might be safer in the back?"

"Of course."

Poppy passed Lord Ted to Jonny who reached round and passed him to Grandpa.

"You got plenty of room in there old boy?" he asked Grandpa smiling.

"Yep, all good ta."

"OK then Poppy," he continued, "reach above and hold that handle and put one foot into the foothold there under the wing and step up. Just walk across the black area on the wing and sit yourself down. I've put a couple of cushions so you can see out easily. I'll shut your door then I'll get in to explain what we need to do. Safety is the most important thing now."

Poppy nodded and did as she was asked. It looked like it might not be an easy thing to do but once she was on the wing it was just like getting into a car and about the same size. She sat on the seat and felt a little nervous as Jonny slammed the door shut. It made her jump.

"You OK Poppy?" asked Grandpa.

"Yes, I think so."

"Jonny will help you with your straps so no need to worry about that."

"OK."

In front of Poppy was a dashboard full of small screens, dials and buttons and a small, almost squashed, steering wheel that matched the other seat to her left. She had obviously no idea what they all did or meant but as long as Jonny knew that was OK. She could see the top of the propeller and the windows and windscreen gave her a good all-round view. Not what she had expected when she first saw the plane. Above her head were some more buttons and an air vent already blowing air on to her face, this was more than welcome. It was already a warm day.

Eventually Jonny sat beside her in the other front seat which was in front of Nanny. How he managed to squeeze his enormous frame into such a small space was beyond thinking but Poppy was glad he was there, he had an air of confidence about him that made Poppy relax.

"OK then Poppy, today you're my co-pilot, a very important role, are you up for it?" he asked kindly.

"Yes sir captain," said Poppy now feeling very important indeed.

Nanny, Grandpa and Lord Ted, who was sitting on Nanny's knee so he could not only see out of the window but also see Poppy, watched her every move. Nanny took Grandpa by the hand and smiled at him giving him a wink as she did so. They were both so proud of their granddaughter.

"OK so what I need you to do first is to flick that switch on the door to make sure it's closed properly then cross check mine, so we're both happy the doors are closed," said Jonny.

"OK done and I can see you've done yours."

"Great, now we need to make sure we all have our seatbelts on across our waist and over our shoulders."

Nanny and Grandpa helped by checking each other's, and Jonny helped Poppy with hers.

"Good, now I am just going to run down a checklist then we can be on our way. I need all of you to put on the headphones so we can talk to each other once we're in the air and you'll be able to listen in to me talking to air traffic control."

They all put their headsets on. Poppy's was quite big, so Jonny helped with the strap to make it more comfortable then put his thumbs up. Poppy responded with a thumbs up too and then the headphones sprang into life.

"CLEAR PROP!" Jonny shouted. It made everyone jump, "can you all hear me OK?" he asked.

Jonny's voice came in loud and clear and they all said they could hear. After a few minutes Jonny pressed a few buttons and pulled back the steering wheel.

"Mind your knees Poppy," he said as her steering wheel came out towards her.

A few seconds later the propeller started up. It was quite noisy, so Poppy was now very pleased that she was wearing the headphones. The plane then moved forward, and Jonny steered it along the tarmac road towards the open area and headed for the runway.

"Golf Delta Zero Three Niner requesting take off position on runway Two Two Bravo," said Jonny.

Poppy looked at him having no idea what he had just said and wondering if he was talking to her as another voice came over the headphones.

"Roger, Golf Delta Zero Three Niner take off on runway Two Two Bravo, wind north-easterly."

"Golf Delta Zero Three Niner runway Two Two Bravo, thank you," said Jonny as he now turned the plane towards the runway, "OK everyone, all set?"

"Yes," came the combined response of Nanny, Grandpa and Poppy as the plane turned and was now facing the long runway in front of her. Poppy turned and looked at Nanny who put her thumbs up. Poppy put her thumbs up too then looked back at the runway. She could not quite see the end of the runway but lots of white markings on the long black road that stretched out in front of her with a very large 22B painted in the middle was her current view.

"Golf Delta Zero Three Niner runway Two Two Bravo requesting take off," said Jonny.

"Golf Delta Zero Three Niner runway Two Two Bravo permission to take off, traffic light, have a safe flight."

"Golf Delta Zero Three Niner runway Two Two Bravo," said Jonny, "OK Poppy, your job is to look out of the windows and let me know if you can see any other planes."

"OK Mr Johnson."

The noise then suddenly increased and with a roar the little plane moved forward. Faster and faster it went picking up speed. Within seconds Poppy could see that they had left the ground and all around her the fields opened up. She looked on in amazement as the airfield disappeared.

"Golf Delta Zero Three Niner heading Two One 3,000 feet," said Jonny.

"Roger Golf Delta Zero Three Niner heading Two One," came the reply.

"OK, I'm going to be a little naughty and just fly over your house so you can take a picture. It will be on Poppy's side, camera at the ready," said Jonny.

Grandpa got his phone out and switched on the camera as Poppy looked out of her right-hand side window. She could not believe how high up they were and so quickly, as Jonny turned the plane around.

"There Poppy, can you see it?" said Grandpa taking lots of pictures.

"Yes, I can, wow!"

Nanny was straining over Grandpa to see her house but all she could see was the village green, with the white vans and wondering if Agatha Jones was still down there waiting for another chance with another television station.

"Right better get on track," said Jonny, "there's a bottle of water each by your sides if you get thirsty. Should be less than 90 minutes as the wind is with us on the way down."

"Thanks Jonny," said Grandpa.

"OK Poppy we'll go through three or four different airspaces, so over the radio we need to say goodbye to one and hello as we enter the other. You'll hear me talking to different people as we go then when we get closer to Porthcastle, I'll ask them for permission to land and they'll tell me which way to come into their airfield. It depends on other traffic and which way the wind is blowing. I need you to look out for other planes too, but the air traffic control can see me and anything else if needed."

"OK Mr Johnson," said Poppy now looking out eagerly across the sky but wondering why, as there was so much space surely there was room for a few more.

"Please call me Jonny, everyone else does."

"Thank you and where are all the really big planes Jonny," asked Poppy.

"Well, we need to avoid those, so we'll go around the main airports, it's not just a straight run. When they're up they fly at about 33,000 feet. We on the other hand are at 3,000, we just need to avoid their take-off and landing routes, that's why we have air traffic control," said Jonny now showing Poppy a map that was on his lap. "We'll fly across then down the Bristol Channel and around the Devon coast and down to Porthcastle in Cornwall."

Poppy had been looking at a map with Grandpa the day before so knew where Jonny was pointing.

"And what does the Golf Delta stuff mean?" asked Poppy.

"That's my plane number – GD039 – Golf Delta Zero Three Nine," said Jonny, "every plane has a number, a call sign. We use what we call the phonetic alphabet so there are no misunderstandings because 'C' could sound like 'D' or even 'E' over the radio. So, we say Alpha for 'A', Bravo for 'B', Charlie for 'C' and so on. So, if I was to spell out 'Poppy' using that alphabet I'd say Papa, Oscar, Papa, Papa, Yankee."

Poppy burst out laughing.

"That is quite a funny one actually," laughed Jonny.

"And who's Roger?" asked Poppy.

"No idea."

Poppy sat and wondered why people spoke to Roger, but no one knew who he was. The next hour or so seemed to flash by. She listened to Jonny talking his strange phonetic language to Roger and various people over the radio and watched what he was doing as well as keeping an eye out. She also looked down to see a view of the earth she had obviously never experienced before. She could make out the towns and villages and all the farmlands. Everywhere looked so green and as they flew over the coast the sea looked so blue. There was so much to see, and she was quite enchanted by it all. Jonny had taken the time to explain things to Poppy as they went he pointed out key things like bridges and towns.

"That coast is South Wales," said Jonny pointing to the right, "and that one England," he continued, as they flew down the Bristol Channel and pointed to the map.

"Right then I need a drink. Could you pass me that bottle please?" he asked Grandpa. Grandpa knew what was coming because Jonny did the same trick every time he had a new co-pilot.

Grandpa passed him his water bottle.

"OK Poppy can you hold the steering wheel for me while I take a drink?"

Poppy instinctively held the steering wheel thinking that Jonny needed help and also thinking he was joking at the same time.

"OK, you are now flying the plane Poppy."

"What?"

"Keep it steady, look ahead and keep the sea level just about the level of the dashboard, see?" he said calmly then taking a drink.

Poppy saw her knuckles turn white as she held on so tightly and gulped with nerves.

"That's it, relax, just hold the steering wheel lightly."

Poppy tried to relax a little.

"That's better," said Jonny taking another drink.

Not only was this the first time Poppy had ever been in a plane, but she was now flying it. Most of her friends had been on holiday in a plane but none of them had actually flown one. This was definitely a story for the class when she got back to school because she could not tell them about catching a gang of robbers with a talking teddy bear and a bunch of fairies. She continued to fly the plane for a few minutes before Jonny talked to the air traffic control at Porthcastle Airfield.

"Golf Delta Zero Three Niner requesting permission to land."

"Golf Delta Zero Three Niner Porthcastle tower here, welcome, approach east on runway Alpha Three," came the reply through Poppy's headphones.

"Golf Delta Zero Three Niner east on Alpha Three."

"Roger Golf Delta Zero Three Niner."

"OK I'll take her back now Poppy. You've done a great job thank you."

"Roger," she said wondering if that was right.

Poppy let go of the steering wheel almost having to peel her fingers off one by one and sat back and relaxed. She didn't realise just how stiff she had been and instantly relaxed back in her chair.

"Don't get too relaxed, we still need to keep an eye out."

"Roger Captain," said Poppy, loving the responsibility of being an actual co-pilot.

"Well done Poppy," came Nanny's voice over the headphones. "Great job, I felt very safe thank you." She was secretly very relieved that Jonny was now flying the plane again.

Jonny now reduced the height a little, but they seemed to be flying further out to sea, then, suddenly he turned left back towards the land.

"There's the runway in front of us Poppy, can you see it?"

"Yes, yes I can."

The runway was a long way away, but Poppy could make out what seemed to be a very short stretch of black tarmac. As they got closer, they started to drop. Poppy felt a little uneasy but, as the now appointed official co-pilot, felt she needed not to show just how scared she actually felt. This was worse than being chased by one of the crown jewel robbers.

Down and down they went. Poppy could now see the runway was getting bigger and see a big A3 painted at the beginning of the tarmac. She could see the beach and the fear now started to turn to excitement. Eventually the trees were at the same height and the aircraft kissed the tarmac and ran along towards the end.

"Golf Delta Zero Three Niner now on Alpha Three."

"Golf Delta Zero Three Niner head towards the end to exit Tango Four and park up in front of the left buildings please, welcome to Porthcastle."

"Golf Delta Zero Three Niner thank you."

Jonny steered the plane off the runway by a yellow sign with black T4 painted on it eventually stopping outside the airfield buildings next to another plane and cut the engine. The noise went and everyone took off their headphones.

"OK that's it," said Jonny.

"Thank you so much Mr Johnson, sorry Jonny, that was amazing," said Poppy.

"Yes, thanks Jonny, great flight by the flight crew," said Grandpa.

"No worries. OK I need to sign us in and pay the landing fees then I'll be off. I'll join you on the beach later for lunch about 1 o'clock. That OK?"

"Perfect," said Nanny, "plenty to go around."

"Excellent thanks, I knew there would be," said Jonny, laughing.

16

Getting out of the plane was a little harder than getting in, but eventually Grandpa was getting the bags out and they were making their way through a small gate towards the beach as Jonny disappeared into the air-field hut.

"Remember this number Poppy – one, seven, four, three – so we can get back in through this gate, otherwise we'll have to walk all the way round."

"OK Grandpa."

Poppy had taken Lord Ted out of his backpack and had him under her arm so she could carry another backpack that had her swimsuit and towel in. She gave him a squeeze.

"How was that then?" she asked.

"Pretty impressive co-pilot Poppy, pretty impressive indeed."

"I was scared stiff if I'm honest, but it was amazing too, everything looked so small from up there."

"I was fine," lied Lord Ted, "but more importantly I think I've worked out the number plate, I know the phonetic alphabet Jonny was on about and I think that might be the key."

"What do you mean?"

"What was Jonny's plane number, can you remember?" he said as they walked along towards the beach.

"Yes, we heard it a thousand times or more – Golf Delta Zero Three Nine."

"Exactly, GD, Golf Delta could be Gerald Duck, zero three, aged three – GD03 – start of the number plate – what do you think?" asked Lord Ted now thinking that it sounded quite silly.

"I think that might be it, it's worth a shot."

"I've got nothing else."

"OK I'll ask Grandpa if we can ring Mary, he kept her number in his phone."

Eventually they reached the beach. It was such a warm day with clear blue skies that the beach was the place to be. Poppy was surprised that there were not that many people on the beach itself, so they soon found a spot to sit in. Nanny laid out some rugs and they sat down.

"Last one in's a sissy," said Grandpa suddenly.

"Hold on, I've not got my swimsuit on yet," moaned Poppy.

"Come on then, quick," said Nanny, "we can beat Grandpa."

There then followed a frantic race of getting into their swimwear under towels that must have looked comical to onlookers. Poppy, who had Nanny to help pass clothes was first out of the blocks running towards the sea, but Grandpa was hot on her heels. Poppy had always loved the sea after holidays with her mummy and daddy and the cold water never bothered her, so she ran straight in with her hands in the air, the winner. Grandpa on the other hand stopped a little short and was now walking in.

"Blimey, its f-f-f-freezing."

"Come on you sissy," laughed Poppy.

After returning to Nanny for some sun cream, which was forgotten in the race to the sea, they had another race back to the water. For the next hour they played in the sea, running in and out, jumping over the small waves, building sandcastles laughing and giggling and totally forgetting the trials and tribulations of the previous 48 hours. Nanny was waving and taking pictures and enjoying sunbathing, she loved watching Poppy play with her grandpa. Lord Ted was sitting up on the blanket watching Poppy too. Poppy had not had so much fun for ages and was having a great time, but poor Grandpa was exhausted.

"I'm pooped," he said, "let's go and grab something to eat, Jonny will be here soon I'm sure."

"OK Grandpa" she replied and taking Grandpa by the hand they walked back to Nanny and dried themselves ready for lunch.

"Well you've both had a great time haven't you," said Nanny.

"We have and I'm starving now, I bet you are too Poppy."

"Please may I have a drink Nanny."

"Homemade raspberry lemonade?" asked Nanny.

"Yes please, thank you."

Nanny opened some of the food boxes that she and Grandpa had prepared earlier. There were all sorts of sandwiches, crisps, pork pies, fruit, cakes and drinks.

"Should we wait for Jonny?" asked Poppy.

"No, it's OK, he called to say they've made him lunch there, he was surprised but thought he should stay to do the right thing, so it's all ours," said Nanny, "he'll join us later."

With Poppy wrapped in a towel and Lord Ted on her lap, Nanny passed her a plate and the feast began. Nanny put a sun hat on Poppy to keep her head out of the sunshine as she tucked into the sandwiches and crisps on her plate. After lunch, leaving some for Jonny because he was bound to still be hungry on his return, they all lay back on the towels to enjoy the sun.

"Right who's for a game of catch?" asked Nanny eventually.

"Me!" shouted Poppy.

"And me!" followed Grandpa almost reluctantly but trying to make it sound as though he could not believe his luck.

After putting on some more sun cream they all played catch, Grandpa making an excuse fairly quickly so he could sit and watch instead. Poppy had Nanny running in and out of the sea after a short while, eventually coming back and getting wrapped in towels.

"Oh, I've not done that in years," said Nanny slightly out of breath.

"I know you haven't," said Grandpa, laughing.

They sat in silence for a while just watching and listening to the waves roll in. The golden beach, which stretched a lot further than the plane runway, was still quite empty for such a warm day in the school holidays. Behind the beach were a few cafes and an amusement arcade but not much else. It was about a five-minute walk into the pretty seaside town of Porthcastle where there were more shops and holiday homes.

"Fancy a go in the amusement arcade for half an hour Poppy?" asked Nanny all of a sudden.

"Oh yes please," said Poppy.

"Grandpa can look after Lord Ted for a while, can't you," Nanny said winking at him.

"I think he might be looking after me, I might have to close my peepers for a while," replied Grandpa.

"Come on then Poppy, pop your shorts on and let's go and lose some money."

"I'm sure we might win some Nanny. See you later Grandpa." And giving Lord Ted a kiss on his forehead she sat him down next to her grandpa.

"Have fun," said Grandpa already lying back with his eyes closed.

Hand in hand, Nanny and Poppy walked up the beach to the arcade. It was full of flashing lights and funny whooping and buzzing noises with bells going off every few seconds. Nanny changed some money into 10-pence pieces and twopence pieces.

"Right what do you fancy first?"

"Can we do the tipping one with the twopence pieces please?"

"Of course."

They walked over and tried to work out which one had the most chance of tipping over the edge. There were three tipping point machines, just like the ones on television. Eventually they decided on one where a lady said she had put so many twopences in, but nothing was coming out.

"That lot has got to fall eventually," said Nanny, "look at it all piled up. Right come on Poppy, I'm feeling lucky."

There was a small stool for Poppy to stand on, so Nanny passed her the coins and she dropped them in waiting specifically for the right time, just as the top row was coming towards her. After quite a few coins Poppy stopped, nothing was moving.

"I think they might all be glued together, but if I put one in the left slot instead it might work. What do you think Nanny?"

"I was just going to say the same thing, there's so much piled up there, it just needs a nudge, go for it."

Poppy waited and dropped the coin, but it rolled slightly to the right before it rested and missed the pile. She tried again but this time it kept wobbling so much it rested on the one she needed to push.

"Oh bum," she said, followed quickly by, "oops, sorry Nanny."

Nanny laughed, "I was just going to say the same thing too. Right two coins left, come on, we can do this."

Poppy took a deep breath and waited. She missed the first opportunity, almost too scared to drop the coin, so waited for the right time again. She dropped the coin.

It came to rest in the perfect place. This had to be it. It all seemed to go into slow motion. Then, with an enormous crash, hundreds of twopences fell into the trough by Poppy's feet. There were so many that they spilled out on to the floor.

"Wooo hooo, you've done it Poppy," shouted Nanny, "we're as rich as can be!"

"Nanny!" shouted Poppy at the same time.

The commotion attracted a small crowd who watched in disbelief at the avalanche of coins that fell from the machine.

"Right," said Nanny, "lets gather all this up and go and cash it all in. I think we may change our holiday from the Lake District to the Maldives."

Poppy helped Nanny pick up the coins and a young lady dressed in a very fetching purple Porthcastle Arcade uniform came over with a bucket to put all the coins in. They walked over to the cash desk area and waited for the massive total to be revealed.

"OK, I can tell you that this is the biggest win we have ever had on the twopence tipping machine 326 coins dropped, that's a record!" said the kind lady behind the counter, "so that's £6.52 we owe you."

"Nanny we're rich!"

"We certainly are, enough for an ice cream each," said Nanny, smiling.

Nanny thanked the lady and they both went to get an ice cream. After both choosing a 99 with a double flake and raspberry sauce they started to walk back to the beach.

"Double flake Nanny."

"Well, we can afford it now Poppy," said Nanny, laughing, "but not enough for poor Grandpa."

"He'll understand, you win some, you lose some," said Poppy.

"Come on cheeky," she said.

Arriving at the towels, Grandpa still had his eyes closed.

"Ahem," coughed Nanny.

"Yes, yes, I'm not asleep, just resting my eyes" smiled Grandpa with his eyes still shut.

"Grandpa, you'll never believe it, but we now hold the record for the biggest win on the tipping machine!"

"Oh wow, do you?" he said now sitting up looking much more interested.

"Yes, over 300 coins dropped."

"Pound coins?"

"Err no, twopences," said Poppy.

"We're rich!" shouted Grandpa.

"Well, we were but me and Poppy just had two 99s with double flakes," laughed Nanny.

"Oh, oh well it was nice while it lasted, so how much did you win exactly?"

"Six whole pounds and fifty-two pence," said Poppy proudly.

"Wowser, I hope you had raspberry sauce then."

"Of course," said Nanny quite smugly but with a smile Grandpa loved.

"There's some wipes in that box Poppy," said Nanny pointing, "wipe the sticky sauce off your fingers. Please could you pass me one?"

Poppy did as she was asked and then gave Lord Ted a squeeze.

"Oh Lord Ted, we were rich for about eight minutes," she laughed.

"I heard, good job."

"I'll ask Grandpa about calling Mary now."

Poppy turned to face her grandpa.

"Grandpa, I need to talk to you," she said.

"OKayyyyy," replied her grandpa inquisitively.

"Yes, well I think, with Lord Ted's help, well Lord Ted worked it out actually, we know the number plate of the blue van I saw in the village. I promised the chief inspector that I would call him when I remembered but I think I'd rather call the assistant chief constable if that's OK?"

"Yes of course that's OK, do you want to do that now?"

"Is that OK?"

"Yes, I have her number, I'll call her now."

Grandpa found the number and made the call. It seemed to take a while then her voice came on the phone. Poppy watched her grandpa explain who he was again and go on to say that Poppy had found out more detail regarding the van she saw.

"Yes of course, she's right here with me, we're at the beach today at Porthcastle, hold on," said Grandpa passing the phone to Poppy, "she'd like to speak to you Poppy."

Poppy took the phone, "Hello," she said.

"Hello Poppy, are you having a nice day?"

"Yes, thank you, great fun thanks."

"Good, that's nice. We're making progress here thanks to you. Your grandpa said you can remember the number plate?"

"Well yes, the beginning part anyway, I thought that would still help. Hopefully it's right anyway."

"Yes, that's great, we can try and track its movements. It may help, it may be nothing, but you never know."

"Yes hopefully, it's G for Golf, D for, erm, Duck, Zero Three – GD03"

"Golf Delta Zero Three."

"Yes Delta, not Duck, sorry."

"That's OK."

"And behind the driver and passenger, the wall behind them, was all red."

"That helps a lot actually, thank you. Anything else, anything unusual or any writing on the van?"

"No, it was all the same dark blue colour."

"OK Poppy thanks, you've been very helpful. If you think of anything else then call me OK?"

"Yes, I will, thank you."

"Goodbye then."

"Bye," and Poppy handed the phone back to her grandpa.

"All OK Popsicle?"

"Yes Grandpa, thank you."

"And are you sure that's right – it does sound rather like the plane's number?"

"No, I'm not sure but it's all we have. Hopefully it will help in some way," said Poppy now slightly regretting her phone call.

"I'm sure it will be fine," said Grandpa. "Oh, look here's Jonny."

Poppy turned around and saw Jonny marching down from the arcade.

"How'd it go Jonny?" asked Nanny.

"All good, done a great deal, just need to get the harvest in now. Very happy actually although they spent most of the time either talking about rugby or the crown jewels," said Jonny raising his eyebrows. "I was going to tell them a fighter pilot with a teddy and a bunch of fairies solved it all but they wouldn't have believed me so I stuck to the story," he laughed.

They all laughed and then Poppy went on to tell him about their day and the enormous win on the tipping machine.

"There's a bit of food left if you want it Jonny?"

"Yes please, sounds like you've had a fab day and nearly millionaires too."

"It's been brilliant," said Poppy, "thanks for bringing us down."

"My pleasure," replied Jonny, eating the remaining sandwiches, crisps and cakes.

After he'd polished off the food Grandpa and Nanny started to pack everything away. Poppy got changed back into her clothes and then helped fold the blankets and picked up Lord Ted ready for the walk back to the plane.

"Reckon we should be back by about 4 o'clock," said Jonny.

"Please may we make the fairy cakes for the fairies when we get back Nanny?"

"Yes of course my lovely," said Nanny kindly.

As they walked slowly back towards the airfield Poppy, with Lord Ted under her arm, glanced back at the beach. What a brilliant day it had been and now for the flight home.

"I think I'll sit in the back with you Lord Ted," she said giving Lord Ted a squeeze.

"I'd like that," he said.

"I think I'm a little tired to fly a plane again today."

Poppy caught up with the others just as they got to the gate.

"Oh dear, I've forgotten the number," said Grandpa.

"One, seven, four, three," said Poppy.

Grandpa pressed the buttons and the gate sprung open.

"Well done Popsicle."

"I think I'll sit in the back with Nanny for the journey home if that's OK?"

"Of course," said Jonny smiling.

Poppy and Nanny boarded the plane and got themselves settled in as Jonny loaded the bags, followed by Grandpa who got into the co-pilot's seat. Lord Ted sat on Poppy's lap so he could see out of the window. They put their headphones on and waited for Jonny to get in after he had done some checks. Before long they were hurtling down the runway and waving goodbye to Porthcastle beach.

"What a great day," said Grandpa over the headphones.

The conversation flowed but the voices seemed to drift away as Poppy closed her eyes and fell fast asleep.

17

Poppy woke with a jump as the plane landed back at Diddlesdale Airfield, she had slept all the way home. Nanny had been asleep too for a while and she also woke as they landed.

"Golf Delta Zero Three Niner now on Two Two Bravo," came Jonny's voice over the headphones.

"Golf Delta Zero Three Niner exit Juliet Seven, welcome home."

"Roger Golf Delta Zero Three Niner exit Juliet Seven," confirmed Jonny.

Poppy stretched her arms out and let out a big yawn as Jonny turned off the runway and headed back towards the hangars that they had left earlier that day.

"That was quick," she said still yawning.

"Oh, welcome back you two," said Grandpa raising his eyebrows, "landed earlier than we thought."

"Hello Grandpaaaa, were you allowed to fly the plane too?"

"No, only genuine co-pilots get to have a go."

They stopped outside the hangar and Jonny cut the engine.

"I'll park her up later," said Jonny, "I'll need to refuel her first as I'm off again tomorrow, up north for the morning."

"Never a dull day eh?" said Grandpa.

"It's all go mate."

They all got out of the plane, Poppy holding on to Lord Ted as she climbed down off the wing, and after saying goodbye and thanking Jonny once more, made their way back to the car.

"That was a brilliant day, thank you," said Poppy.

"Loved it," said Grandpa, "great fun. We are lucky to have such a good friend."

"We are," said Nanny.

"Right let's get home, I believe you two are making fairy cakes for your new neighbours Poppy. Are you staying in the treehouse tonight?"

"If that's OK?"

"Of course, but let's try and have a normal night tonight shall we," said Grandpa laughing but being fairly serious at the same time, "you can always come in if you want to but it's not going to get cold tonight."

"It will be a normal one," said Poppy, "I promise."

"Come on then, let's get back and get the oven on," said Nanny.

They drove back through the village. There were still a few white vans lining the village green but not as many as earlier in the day. Poppy could see some reporters still making recordings for their television stations but now they had a more tranquil backdrop of the village green, pond, ducks and geese rather than a bank of satellite dishes. Poppy was sure it would make the village look a lot better on the television.

They arrived home and unpacked.

"Quick showers I think to get all that sea water off then we'll get baking, make tea and catch up on the news," said Nanny. "Is all still OK in the treehouse?"

"Yes Nanny, but I'll go and check first before I have a shower."

"OK pop your bag down there and I'll do the washing later."

Poppy dropped her bag down and, with Lord Ted under her arm, went to check on the treehouse. The last time she was in there was when she saw all the activity at Jonny's barns through her binoculars, it seemed so long ago now. She climbed the stairs and opened her door. Either Nanny or the fairies had been in and tidied up and had also made her bed, everything was spick and span ready for bedtime. She returned to the house excited that she would see the fairies later along with some cakes.

"Fairies do like cake don't they?" she asked Lord Ted giving him a squeeze.

"Who doesn't?"

"True, very true."

After her shower Poppy felt a lot fresher. With the sea water and sun cream she had felt quite sticky but was now raring to go and was soon in the kitchen with her hair in a bun and sleeves rolled up making cakes under the guidance of her nanny. The best thing about making cakes of course, is scraping the bowl out. Poppy always left an extra cake mix in the bowl for such occasions. They managed to make 24 small fairy cakes. There were 12 plain and 12 with sultana's in.

"Once they've cooled down we can decorate them," said Nanny, "I thought we could make a lemon icing for the plain ones and a butter icing for the others – what do you think Poppy?"

"I think that sounds perfect."

"Me too," said Grandpa walking into the kitchen from the garage, "any left for a poor old man?"

"Of course Grandpa, we made extra."

"Perfect."

After dinner it was time for the 6 o'clock news and a catch-up of the day's progress. They sat round the television, Poppy with Lord Ted on her lap, and Grandpa found the correct channel.

This time Fiona was in the studio and gave them an update. Nothing really had changed. There were still two of the robbers at large, some of the crown jewels and some gold still missing, but the best news was that George Featherbottom was back at home at the Tower and feeling well. The screen cut to pictures of George arriving back home and waving to the cameras but no interview.

The robbery still dominated the news with stories of sightings of the Pearson brothers all over the country, more details of the tunnel with experts making their views heard, news from the queen who was feeling very relieved that George was back home and the majority of her collection had been recovered.

"I think me and Lord Ted may go and see the queen soon," said Poppy, "what do you think Grandpa?"

"Yes, I think that would be a good idea. I must give her a call actually as she would have seen where the robbers were found so she'll know we were close. I'll do that later," said Grandpa, "she'll be pleased to see you I'm sure, and Lord Ted."

"You must take some banana bread with you too Poppy," said Nanny.

"Yes I will, thank you."

Poppy sat and thought about what a unique conversation that was. No other family would be having the same conversation at all, anywhere, and yet it seemed so normal. What a magical place this was with her talking teddy bear, the coolest grandparents and fairies for neighbours. It had been the most incredible few days of her life and tonight she was going to have freshly baked cakes with the fairies; life does not get much better surely.

They continued to watch the news.

"Do you think there's anything else going on in the world at the moment other than the robbery," asked Nanny.

"Well, I'm surprised the world record win at Porthcastle Arcade hasn't been on yet," said Poppy, "surely that's newsworthy?"

Nanny and Grandpa laughed at their clever and witty granddaughter.

"Me too," said Nanny, "thought it would have been the first headline. Right come on let's get those cakes iced so they set in time for your party."

Nanny helped Poppy prepare the two types of icing. Poppy poured the lemon icing carefully over the first 12 without sultana's making sure she got as much as she could over the cakes, then took her time to spread the butter icing on the remaining cakes.

"Give them an hour to set then it'll be bedtime anyway," said Nanny, "fancy a game of Uno while we wait?"

"What's Uno?" asked Poppy.

"It's a card game – Grandpa you joining in?"

"You bet, love a game of Uno."

For the next hour or so they played Uno. It didn't take long for Poppy to pick it up and she won the second game. It was so funny watching her nanny and grandpa play, nearly thinking they had won then having to pick up more cards.

"What a great game," said Poppy.

"We'll take it on holiday with us if you'd like, be something to do in the evenings."

"Brilliant," said Poppy.

"Right, I reckon the cakes will be ready now so let's put some in a tin for you to take with you and then get washed and clean your teeth ready for bed. Mind you, you'll be eating cakes later but one night won't hurt I suppose."

Poppy was soon ready for bed. She gave her grandpa a hug and kissed him goodnight, thanking him for a wonderful day, then with Nanny carrying the cake tin and Lord Ted under her arm, she made her way to the treehouse. It was still light and quite warm out so Poppy was sure she would be warm enough during the night.

As they got to the bottom of the ladders Poppy switched on the lights.

"Do you want me to come up and read to you tonight Poppy," said Nanny stopping at the bottom.

"No, I'm OK tonight thank you Nanny."

"OK then, well you take these and have a fun night. Don't stay up too late either."

"Thank you, Nanny, and thank you for such a brilliant day."

"It's been lovely hasn't it, we're glad you had a good time. Right night night my angel," said Nanny and gave her granddaughter a big hug. Poppy squeezed her nanny as hard as she could with poor Lord Ted getting stuck in between.

"Here you go then, take the tin and have fun. Night night poppet,"

"Night night Nanny."

Poppy took the tin and climbed the ladders to her den. Nanny waited until she had reached the top and then returned to the house leaving the back door unlocked in case Poppy needed to get back in.

Poppy opened the door and switched on her bedside light and closed the curtains. She placed the tin of cakes on her desk and sat on the edge of the bed giving Lord Ted a squeeze.

"What a fantastic day Lord Ted."

"It's been great hasn't it? You've not stopped apart from your sleep home."

"I'm not too tired though. I'm looking forward to seeing the fairies tonight. I hope they'll come around?"

"Oh yes they will. I'm pretty sure they will have smelled the cakes cooking earlier."

"Great."

Poppy arranged her pillows and sat up on her bed. She picked up her book and started reading with Lord Ted snuggled in by her side.

After a while she put her book down. "So, tell me how we go and see the queen?" she asked.

"Well, the easiest way is through the crooked door in your bedroom."

"I had a feeling you might say that."

"You just have to believe that behind the door is what you want it to be."

"So, I just open the door and walk into the palace?"

"Pretty much yes."

"Right OK," said Poppy curiously, "and you're sure it works?"

"Of course, it always works if you believe."

"OK, can we do that tomorrow?"

"I'm sure that would be OK," said Lord Ted, "your grandpa was going to call the queen later and I'm pretty sure he would have told her everything, so I think she'd want to meet you too."

"We must take some of Nanny's banana bread, the queen loves banana bread."

"Yes, yes, of course we should."

Just then the bell on Poppy's bright red front door rang. Poppy carefully moved Lord Ted to one side and got up to answer the door. She walked to the top of the ladders to see if it was Nanny or Grandpa but there was no one there. She turned around and there all flying inside were the fairies. Elvina and Oona with Nixie, Jareth, Alfred, Gullveig, Sophie, Belle, Zuzana, Deri, April, Emma, and Maisy.

Poppy was so pleased to see them all and had a smile wider than her face.

"Hi guys, I'm so happy to see you, are you all OK?"

"Hi Poppy," came a response from them all with Jareth and Gullveig adding "Miss Poppy miss" on the end.

"We are all good thanks," said Elvina, "caught up on our sleep and ready for the next adventure."

"I've been so worried about you all," said Poppy.

"We're fine honest," said Deri, "we had a great time the other night."

"Yeah, we never get to do stuff like that," said Jareth.

"Yes, we do," said Gullveig.

"No, we don't," said Jareth.

"Boys!" shouted all the fairies together.

"So, what's the latest?" asked Oona.

Poppy sat back on the edge of the bed with Lord Ted as the fairies all found somewhere to sit too. Lord Ted and Poppy then proceeded to explain what had happened, what the story was, who was where, what had been found, what was missing and what the police had agreed.

"Aw we never get any credit," said Maisy.

"Really?" said Elvina, "who's going to believe what actually happened. That's a smart move by Grandpa, you know he knows what's best for us and Poppy."

"He does," said Lord Ted.

"I know," said Maisy, "but sometimes it would be nice."

"Well, I'll tell you what is nice," said Poppy as she sprang to attention. "I've made you some cakes to say thank you."

"Oh wow," was the combined response.

Poppy opened the cake tin. Inside Nanny had put a small cake knife and some serviettes so Poppy could cut the cakes into smaller pieces. She proceeded to cut each fairy cake into eight equal pieces and handed out each piece.

"There's plenty to go around," she said being just like her nanny.

The fairies ate their cake as Poppy told them about her day, flying the plane, playing on the beach and of course the massive win at Porthcastle Arcade. They all listened intently as they flew back and forth filling themselves up with as much cake as they could.

"I'm going to burst if I have anymore," said Emma, "the cake is beautiful Poppy, thank you."

"My pleasure, so what have you guys been up to?"

"Just getting to know where we are really, there are some more fairies in the woods beyond the barns where we were the other night," said Elvina, "nice bunch."

"Really?" asked Poppy.

"Yes, not sure Grandpa knows they're there, been there for a few years apparently, about 90 I think," continued Elvina.

"He's never mentioned them," said Lord Ted.

"Oh well, we've met them, told them all about you both and our adventure, they are dying to meet you one day."

"Oh, that would be nice, thank you," said Poppy.

"Other than that, just collecting teeth and being lazy for a change," said Oona.

"Well, I've been collecting teeth," said Jareth.

"No, you haven't," said Gullveig.

"Oh no! here we go again," said Poppy, laughing.

After chatting for a while longer Elvina suggested it was time to go. It was getting late, they had teeth to collect and could see Poppy was tired. Poppy was already yawning and more tired than she had first thought. Most of the cake was gone but Jareth and Gullveig were fighting over the last few pieces just as they did with Poppy's teeth. It made everyone laugh.

"Thanks ever so much for coming around tonight everyone," said Poppy, "it means a lot."

"It's been fun. Keep us up to date please and we'll see you soon Poppy," said Elvina.

"I will and thanks again."

Poppy opened the door and the fairies flew out apart from Deri who hovered in front of Poppy.

"We love you Poppy," she said then span round to join the others, slightly embarrassed but glad she had told Poppy.

"We love you too," said Poppy blushing slightly then closed the door, "ah that was nice Lord Ted."

"It was, they're great, and they look up to you. I think you may be their new queen one day."

"Really?"

"Yes, I think so."

"Wow," replied Poppy stuffing the last piece of cake in her mouth, "huuuw exthiting woodfatbee."

"Indeed," said Lord Ted, laughing.

Poppy finished her cake, cleared up placing all the serviettes and crumbs back in Nanny's tin, switched off the light and snuggled down in bed.

"What another great day, and tomorrow we might go and see the queen."

"Another great day in store then. I think the queen would love to see you too, it's a long time since I have seen her."

There was no reply from Poppy, as her head touched the pillow she fell fast asleep.

"Night night Poppy, I love you too," whispered Lord Ted and snuggled into Poppy's side.

18

Poppy woke up, yawned and stretched her arms out of her quilt nearly knocking Lord Ted out of the bed in the process. She gave him a hug.

"Morning you," she said rubbing her nose on his, "sorry about that."

"Good morning Miss Poppy miss," he laughed, "sleep well?"

"Yes, thank you, looks like another nice day," she said, "hopefully we can go and see the queen today."

Poppy looked up at the clock. It was nine-thirty already. She got out of bed, cleared up, picked up Lord Ted and the cake tin and made her way down the ladders.

She could see that all the washing from yesterday's beach trip was already hanging on the line drying as she walked into the kitchen. Nanny was standing watching the television news with a cup of tea held to her chest.

"Morning sleepy head."

"Morning Nanny,"

"Cup of tea?"

"Yes, please, anything new on the news?"

"No, nothing new, it all seems to have gone quiet, would you like some toast too?"

"Yes please, where's Grandpa?"

"He's in the garage messing about with something or other. So how was your night, cake OK?" said Nanny opening the empty cake tin, "well, it's all gone anyway."

"It was lovely thank you. Everyone turned up and they're all well. They loved the cake."

"Lovely."

"Did someone say cake?" asked Grandpa as he came through into the kitchen, "good morning Popsicle, sleep well, fun time?"

"Hi Grandpa, yes thanks, great time."

"Great stuff, and everyone OK?"

"Yes, they're all well. Elvina said there are some other fairies in Diddlesdale Woods."

"Are there?"

"Yes, been there about 90 years she said."

"Oh, wow, well I never knew that, they've kept themselves quiet. And they don't mind their new neighbours?"

"Seems all OK, she said they're looking forward to meeting us."

"OK great, well I'm sure that will happen soon enough."

"Did you manage to speak to the queen last night?" asked Poppy.

"Yes, yes I did. She is quite shaken by all the upset, but she's OK. She knows what you and Lord Ted did and is looking forward to meeting you both, but I suggested that we would do that when we come back from our break in the Lake District. I'm not sure she's up to visitors really with everything going on. Is that OK?

"Yes of course, of course it is. I'm glad she's OK," replied Poppy.

"She's going to the Tower later today too, to have a look at everything and meet all the warders that were there on the night. Now the police have finished their initial investigation she can go and see. It's been quite an ordeal. She still has quite a bit of the collection missing. I think Mary Underberry will be with her too. We can watch it later, on the news."

"OK Grandpa."

"In the meantime, we have packing to do, shopping for the holiday and the garden to get straight before we go," said Grandpa.

"And the cleaning," said Nanny buttering Poppy's toast, "boring jobs I'm afraid Poppy but needs must. You also need some proper walking boots so we can go into town while Grandpa gets on with the garden. We can do that tomorrow."

"OK Nanny, thank you, I'll clean the treehouse and my bedroom today then."

"Well, that would be a great help thank you. And we can do some more baking to take with us too."

"Great thanks Nanny."

"Anyone else for another brew?"

"Yes please," said Nanny and Poppy together.

The day passed quickly. Poppy took care dusting and cleaning her bedroom then did the same in her treehouse. Grandpa was finishing some jobs in the garage then dug over various parts of the vegetable garden and

Nanny finished some washing and ironing and started to get things ready for the holiday. Lord Ted sat in his place on his bed.

Poppy's mummy and daddy arrived with some more clothes and a few bits for her holiday and stayed for a cup of tea. Poppy showed them her bedroom and the treehouse, and Daddy said she was a very lucky girl. They sat in the garden for a while before they had to go, and Poppy told them about her adventures on the plane and the beach but didn't talk about the night she found the robbers, as obviously she had 'slept through it all'.

Before they knew it the day had passed and it was time for dinner and, by the time they had cleared away, time for the news.

"Well I'm not sure where the time's gone today Poppy," said Nanny as they sat down to watch the television, "it's been a busy one. We'll pop into town in the morning and get your boots and do a big shop."

"OK Nanny thank you. Yes, it's been very busy but fun getting ready and lovely to see Mummy and Daddy," said Poppy sitting next to Nanny with Lord Ted on her knee. She'd not seen much of Lord Ted during the day, so it was nice to have him with her.

Sophie was the newsreader this evening with the headlines saying the queen had visited the Tower of London. The screen showed pictures of the queen arriving and walking into the main entrance dressed in a matching turquoise dress and hat with her shiny black handbag draped over her arm. To her side, escorting the queen throughout her visit, was Assistant Chief Constable Mary Underberry in her full uniform and hat.

"Well they both look smart don't they," said Nanny.

Sophie then went on to explain and confirm what was still missing. A quantity of gold as well as three crowns, two robes, four rings, a sceptre and the secular and alter plates.

"None of these can be replaced of course and the queen is rightly distressed that these are still missing," said Sophie.

The screen showed pictures of all the items then cut to pictures of Raymond and Reginald Pearson who are believed to have the items and are also still missing. News from the other robbers in custody was minimal, no one was saying anything at all. After some other news the national weather picture came on.

"At last, right, let's see what next week is going to bring us." said Grandpa.

The forecast for the following week was good and that pleased Grandpa especially, mostly sunny with rain some evenings.

"Great we can get out on the boat, and I don't care if it rains every night," he laughed.

The news now cut to the regional news where Bob, the newsreader, announced a new lead in the hunt for the tractor robbers that was being followed up which sounded interesting.

"Looks like they are trying to flush them out," said Grandpa, "right who's up for a game of Ludo!"

"Yes me!" said Poppy and Nanny together, "we mustn't forget to pack Uno," said Nanny, "and Ludo too," added Poppy.

"Right what colour would you like to be Poppy?" asked Grandpa setting up the board game.

"Ask Nanny first Grandpa."

"Oh, thank you, I'll be green please," said Nanny.

"And I'll be red please Grandpa."

"Then I'll be blue."

Just then Grandpa's phone rang.

"Ooo, it's Mary Underberry," he said looking at his phone screen, "hello Mary."

There was a pause.

"Yes, we're all well thank you and you?"

Grandpa waved his hands to Nanny to finish setting up the board game.

"Yes, I was speaking to her last night, she sounded quite down about it all," continued Grandpa followed by another pause.

"Oh, did she?" said Grandpa, "that's nice of her, yes I've known her for many years."

Grandpa was obviously talking about the queen at the Tower earlier in the day and was now listening, he raised his eyes at Poppy and Nanny.

"Oh, right yes, wow, that would be, err, wonderful thanks. Yes, we'd love to, tomorrow you say?, yes no problem at all, see you both there at seven thirty, thank you. Yes, bye and thanks again."

Grandpa ended the call.

"Wow," he said looking at Poppy and Nanny, "we've been invited to dinner in the private dining room at The Greedy Duckling in the village tomorrow night."

"That's amazing, it takes months to get a table there," said a very surprised Nanny, "tomorrow?"

"Yes, I know. Mary and Jimmy Pickles-Cunningham would like to take us all for dinner in the private room."

"Gosh."

"Is that good Grandpa?"

"You bet Popsicle, what a treat," smiled Grandpa.

"I wonder how they managed to get in there. It's so long since we've been," said Nanny, "right, new walking boots and a new dress tomorrow Poppy."

"I'm not sure that's the look I'm going for Nanny," said Poppy, laughing.

They all laughed at the image of Poppy walking into a very exclusive restaurant with her new hiking boots on.

"And what did the queen say?" asked Nanny eventually.

"Just that she knew us and what Poppy and Lord Ted did."

"That's nice," said Nanny, "right let's get this game underway."

After three long games of Ludo that Nanny won, it was time to get washed and into bed. Poppy hugged her grandpa.

"Grandpa, will Lord Ted be able to join us tomorrow?"

"Abso-bloomin-lutely he will," said Grandpa kindly, "night night beautiful, sleep tight, we have a lot to do tomorrow."

"Night night Grandpa," said Poppy as she, with Lord Ted under her arm, went upstairs.

After Nanny had read her a story, Poppy was soon fast asleep with Lord Ted snuggled into her side.

"Well, well, well that's a surprise isn't it," said Nanny as she returned downstairs to sit with Grandpa, "The Greedy Duckling, no less, and in the private dining room too – very la-di-da."

"Yes, we're in there for a reason too, I didn't mention it in front of Poppy."

"Oh really?"

"Yes, the Duke and Duchess of Cambridge will join us. That's how you get a private dining room," smiled Grandpa.

"Oh, wow."

"Exactly, I think you'll need a new dress too m'lady," smiled Grandpa.

"Yes, I do, you're absolutely right old man, thank you," laughed Nanny, "Poppy adores Kate too."

"I know, that's why I didn't mention it, she'll be beside herself with excitement, so best we keep that quiet until we get there eh?"

"Yes. Oh, how exciting."

19

Poppy woke earlier than previous days and with Lord Ted sat on her shoulder, looked out of her bedroom window. She could see that the harvest had finally started. Clouds of dust filled the air as the combine harvesters did their work at the bottom of Nanny and Grandpa's garden.

"Wow look at that Lord Ted," said Poppy giving Lord Ted a squeeze, "Jonny will be busy for the next few days."

"Good morning you, yes he will."

"Sorry, good morning," smiled Poppy, "I'm going to have to leave you here today when I go into town with Nanny if that's OK?"

"Yes please, that's more than fine, I couldn't think of anything worse than going shopping."

Poppy could also see Grandpa at the bottom of the garden working in the vegetable patch. They went downstairs and saw Nanny in the kitchen.

"Good morning," said Nanny sweetly, "you're up early."

"Mornin' Nanny, what time is it?"

"It's just gone eight thirty, Grandpa will be in for a cup of tea in ... three ... two ... one... "

Grandpa burst through the door coughing.

"Keep that door shut!" said Nanny, "don't let any of that dust in."

"How did you know?" asked Poppy.

"I saw him coming up the garden," said Nanny, laughing.

Poppy laughed.

"Good grief it's dusty out there," said Grandpa.

"It'll be gone soon enough, it's a late harvest this year," said Nanny.

"Yeah, Jonny had a late planting because of all the rain earlier in the year. So, good morning Popsicle, it's early for you," said Grandpa, smiling.

"Good morning Grandpa, I was watching you out of the window earlier, you looked very busy."

"Lots to do today before our exciting night tonight and holiday tomorrow so thought I'd make an early start. Sleep well?"

"Yes, thank you."

After breakfast Poppy went upstairs to get washed and dressed and after making her bed carefully placed Lord Ted in his spot. She kissed him on the forehead and again explained that she would have to leave him there for the day, much to his relief, then went downstairs to wait for Nanny.

Poppy waited in the kitchen for Nanny and looked out of the window down the garden where Grandpa was working hard. Eventually Nanny appeared.

"You look nice Nanny."

"Why thank you, that's kind of you. I'm going to get a new dress today too."

"Oh lovely."

"You can help me choose it."

"OK, that's cool."

"Is it cool? err OK, good," Nanny smiled, "right, we need a full shop, walking boots, new dresses," then whispered, "and new shoes too but let's not mention that to Grandpa." She smiled, "OK, ready?"

"LG Nanny."

Nanny and Poppy drove into town to buy all the things they needed for their holiday and their posh night out with royalty. Nanny was very excited and dying to tell Poppy about the special hosts but knew she should wait as long as she could.

Grandpa remained at home to continue his work in the garden. After working all morning, he went inside and had some lunch, Nanny had already made him a sandwich knowing that with shoes to buy, there was no way she would be back with Poppy before lunch.

Grandpa's next job involved ladders up to the tree house. After Poppy had cleaned the inside, Grandpa had promised to brush over the outside, especially now the harvest dust had covered it, and trim back a few branches that were covering her window. He extended the ladders to the roof, over the side window and with a soft hand brush in his left back pocket and secateurs in his right, made his way up the ladders. He was not overly keen on heights but nevertheless this needed doing. He carefully dusted off where he could reach then moved down the ladders to brush the side of the treehouse and the window. Then, using the secateurs, he reached out to trim the branches and drop them to the floor.

He felt the ladders move so stopped still waiting until he had steadied himself. Then he reached out a little further to snip off the final branch but felt the ladders slide towards the right. He knew they were going to fall so frantically tried to reach back to the windowsill. As the ladders slid past the window he missed, so held on to the ladders, closed his eyes tightly and waited to hit the ground. He tensed up and braced himself for an impact. But nothing happened, he stayed still.

"I've got you old boy," came a soothing voice from below as he felt the ladders move back to the left and rest on the treehouse, "what the blazes are you doing?"

Jonny was at the bottom and saw what was happening as he walked up the garden to see his friend. He quickly ran and grabbed the ladders and using all his strength moved the ladders and his oldest friend back to where he came from.

"You OK old boy?" asked Jonny.

"Jeezo, am I glad to see you, I thought I was a goner mate," said Grandpa trembling and sweating.

"Come on down now, let's go and grab a cuppa, I only popped round to see if you wanted a lift later," said Jonny kindly.

"Are you coming too?" asked Grandpa excitedly as he started his descent.

"Yeah, that Mary Underwhatsit called me last night, said we have a royal invite at The Greedy Duckling no less, said you guys were going so thought I'd offer a lift. I am assuming the ladies will be in heels, well not Poppy maybe, so thought it would be easier."

"Mate you're a star, thank you. I'm thrilled you're coming too. Who'd have thought it eh? Us pair out with the future king and queen for a night?" laughed Grandpa as he reached the bottom. He reached out and hugged his best friend. "Thanks mate, I owe you. Come on let's get a cup of tea."

"I don't think we ever envisaged this when we were at school eh?" laughed Jonny as they walked up the garden, "anyway what were you doing up there?"

"No, I don't ever recall that conversation. I was just trimming a couple of branches like a wally. How's the harvest going?"

"Yeah the guys are on it, left 'em to it to come and rescue you," said Jonny, smiling.

They sat in the kitchen with a cup of tea and talked about the old days and laughed about all the things they got up to, old teachers, girlfriends, rugby and nights out. Grandpa had not laughed so much in ages and was crying with laughter just as Nanny and Poppy came back and walked into the kitchen loaded with bags.

"What are you two laughing about," asked Nanny smiling.

"Oh, just old times, Jonny here saved my life earlier."

"No change there then," said Nanny, "don't tell me, what I don't know won't hurt me. Hi Jonny."

"Hello you two, nice day."

"Hi Jonny," said Poppy.

"Spent a bloomin' fortune but there we go," said Nanny.

"Well it is a royal occasion," said Jonny.

The room fell silent and Grandpa looked at Nanny. Nanny looked at Grandpa, they both looked at Jonny.

"What?" he asked.

They all looked at Poppy.

"What?" she asked.

"Oops, sorry," said Jonny.

"Yeah we hadn't mentioned it yet."

"Sorry mate," said Jonny very apologetically. "I'll leave that one with you then shall I?" he continued getting up to go, with a smile on his face that he was trying to disguise, "I'll pick you up just after seven."

"Yes Jonny, thanks buddy, and thanks again for earlier."

"No worries, I'll see myself out."

"See you later."

Jonny left through the back door and Nanny and Grandpa both looked at Poppy who was standing there wondering what was going on.

"What?" she asked.

"Well, we'll be joined by a special couple tonight at dinner," said Nanny.

"Mr Johnson and his wife Sue?"

"Well yes," said Grandpa.

"Really?" asked Nanny looking at Grandpa. "Oh I see now, yes, that's brilliant. No Poppy, well yes, but also the Duke and Duchess of Cambridge."

There was a pause as they both looked at Poppy.

"What, KATE!"

"Yes."

"Really. Oh wow," said Poppy, "good job we got new dresses then," she smiled, "thank you, thank you so much."

"And new shoes too I suppose?" asked Grandpa.

"And a new tie for you Grandpa, I chose it," smiled Poppy.

"Well, we'd better have a looksie at your new things and my tie then, won't be long before we need to go."

"Will you give me a hand with the shopping?" Nanny asked Grandpa, "and you'd better go and tell Lord Ted the good news," she said to Poppy,

Poppy ran upstairs as Nanny and Grandpa went to the car to fetch the rest of the bags. She bounded into her bedroom and threw herself on the bed while grabbing and hugging Lord Ted all in one movement. She lay on her back and with her arms outstretched above her head held Lord Ted.

"Guess what!" she said so excitedly.

"You've got a new dress?"

"Yes, and the Duke and Duchess of Cambridge are coming to dinner tonight too. I love Kate, and Wills of course – a real prince and princess!"

She now brought Lord Ted down, so he sat on her chest,

"I think that's amazing Poppy."

"Yes, and you're coming too."

"Oh thank you but I have nothing to wear."

Poppy laughed at the thought of Lord Ted in a posh suit, "What about one of Grandpa's bow ties?" she asked.

"I think that would be perfect."

"Me too, you'll be the smartest bear there," she smiled and gave Lord Ted the biggest hug, "this is the best day ever," she said.

She ran back downstairs with Lord Ted and skipped into the kitchen at the same time as Nanny and Grandpa were bringing in the final bags.

"Someone looks excited," said Nanny.

"I'm so excited I'm not sure what to do first!" said Poppy jumping up and down on the spot.

"Well first you can show Grandpa his new tie, then we can have a fashion parade after I've unloaded the shopping. What do you think?"

"Perfect."

"Then we need to get packing for tomorrow as we're off in the morning and then get ready for tonight," said Nanny.

Poppy reached into the bag that Nanny pointed to and showed Grandpa his new tie. It was very colourful and not Grandpa's usual style but that didn't matter. Poppy chose it so as far as he was concerned it was the best tie in the world and he would be wearing it.

"It's perfect Poppy, thank you."

"Glad you like it Grandpa. Do you have a spare bow tie for Lord Ted to wear this evening please?"

"I have just the thing."

"Thank you."

"I thought it would go with your grey suit," said Nanny.

"Indeed, it will," said Grandpa having no idea which grey suit Nanny meant but that was fine by him.

"Right, let's get cracking," said Nanny.

Grandpa said he would put the shopping away, some in the cupboards and freezer but mainly in a box Nanny had got ready for food for their holiday, while Nanny and Poppy went upstairs to prepare for the fashion show.

Eventually Nanny shouted downstairs "Are you ready?" she asked Grandpa.

"Yep."

Grandpa sat at the table like a judge on a television show. Nanny entered the kitchen first. Nanny's new outfit was an elegant black dress with white spots that draped over her shoulders, crossed at the front with a matching thin belt in the same material. The skirt was just below her knees and flowed as she walked in. She wore black heels and a small clutch handbag.

Grandpa sat there with his mouth open. "You look stunning," he said, "just stunning."

"Thank you my darling," said Nanny, "OK Poppy your turn."

Poppy entered the kitchen, her dress matched Nanny's but in reverse, white with black spots but the same design. She had a pair of new shiny black shoes with straps over the top of her feet. Under one arm she had borrowed one of Nanny's small handbags, shiny and black to match her shoes, and under the other was Lord Ted with a big spotty black and white bow tie.

"My word Poppy, you look beautiful," said Grandpa quite taken aback at just how grown up she was becoming, "absolutely beautiful. And look at you Ted, what a smart bear. Well, you all look stunning, what a lucky man I am to take two beautiful ladies with me this evening."

"Thank you, Grandpa, I was going to wear my walking boots but decided against it," said Poppy, laughing.

"Oh yes I saw those in the box, they look good ones."

"They're lovely, thank you both, thank you for everything."

"That's our pleasure," said Nanny, "right let's get these posh things off so we don't ruin them and start to get things ready for tomorrow, Jonny and Sue will be here before we know it."

"I'll finish off outside, only got to sweep up and put the ladders away and do a quick watering. Would you like to help me Poppy?"

"Yes please."

"Well, you definitely need to get changed then," laughed Nanny, "I'll start packing."

Before long Poppy was helping Grandpa water the garden and Nanny was packing clothes for the week ahead. Grandpa then got a few things together in the garage, like walking boots, waterproofs and foldaway camping chairs ready to put in the car in the morning. By six thirty they were nearly ready for Jonny and Sue to pick them up.

The doorbell rang so Poppy, who was ready first, opened the front door to be greeted by a very smart Jonny and his very glamourous wife Sue.

"Wow don't you look beautiful," said Jonny.

"Thank you, Jonny, hello Mrs Johnson, I'm Poppy."

"Please call me Sue and yes you look beautiful."

"Thank you, so do you."

"Oh, sorry I'd forgotten you had not met Sue before Poppy. Poppy this is Sue."

Poppy shook Sue's hand just as Grandpa appeared.

"Nice tie mate," said Jonny, smiling

"Yes, Poppy chose it."

"Yes, I can see you didn't," he laughed.

"It's wonderful," said Sue digging Jonny in the ribs with her elbow.

Poppy laughed, "It's a bright one isn't it."

"You both look stunning," said Grandpa.

"Talking of stunning," said Sue just as Nanny appeared, "my word you scrub up well."

"Thank you, you too. Don't we all look the part."

They all agreed, and they certainly all agreed that Lord Ted looked very smart too.

"Just one thing before we go," asked Jonny, "how do we address them. Is it your Royal Highness, or Duke and Duchess, or sir? Any ideas?"

"Oh blimey, no idea," said Grandpa.

"I was relying on you," said Jonny.

"I think it's your Royal Highness first then Duke and Duchess or sir and ma'am as in ham," said Poppy, "I was reading about it."

"Works for me," said Grandpa, "I think they're very laid back though, let's see."

"And you bow your heads," she said looking at Grandpa and Jonny, "and we curtsy at first, not every time otherwise you'd look a bit silly," she laughed.

They all agreed and practiced their nodding and curtsies before it was time to leave. Poppy now felt quite nervous so held Lord Ted close as they made their way to Jonny's car.

They pulled up outside The Greedy Duckling. There were no more vans left on the village green now. It was quiet, just as it always had been, with the sound of the odd duck quacking or car driving carefully down Beehive Lane.

"Do you think we'll be first, or they will already be here," asked Sue.

"Oh blimey, I'd not thought of that," said Nanny.

"Well, if we are first, we should remain standing until they come in and if they are there we'll just make it up as we go along."

"Good planning Grandpa," said Poppy.

"Thanks Popsicle, I put a lot of thought into that."

They giggled together on the back seat.

"Look out for Agnes's curtains twitching Sue," said Nanny.

After lots of nervous laughter they all got out and made their way into the restaurant. They were met at the door and shown through to the private dining area by a very smartly dressed man, "Your hosts are already here," he said.

"Oh blimey, right, thanks," said Grandpa suddenly standing up a little straighter as he entered the room followed by Nanny holding Poppy's hand who had Lord Ted tucked firmly under her right arm, followed by Jonny and Sue.

20

Inside the brightly lit room Mary Underberry and the Duke and Duchess of Cambridge were standing talking with drinks in their hands. A round table, with glasses and cutlery that sparkled, was in the middle of the room, with a chandelier that dazzled and twinkled above. Poppy had not seen anything quite like it before.

As Grandpa walked in, Poppy looked out gingerly from behind him. There were lots of greetings and handshakes, head bowing and curtsies. It was all a daze for Poppy. She heard the prince mention Grandpa's tie which made her smile, and how nice it was to see Jonny again. Then it was her turn.

She found herself standing in front of the duchess. She made an elegant curtsy and looked up. The duchess was so tall and so beautiful, the most beautiful and elegant lady she had ever seen with a stunning royal blue dress. She felt as though her throat had tightened up, her mouth had become completely dry.

"And you must be Poppy," said the duchess crouching down in front of her, "I am thrilled to meet you and I love your dress."

Poppy froze and blushed, she had never been nervous in her life before but then the duchess took her hand and the nerves seemed to disappear.

"Good evening, Your Highness," she said with another curtsy just in case. "Thank you, your dress is beautiful too."

"I think I'd like you to call me Kate please," said the duchess, "and this must be Lord Ted, looking very smart too,"

Poppy turned Lord Ted to face the duchess and she took his paw.

"It's wonderful to meet you too Lord Ted," she said softly.

Lord Ted bowed his head slightly out of respect. The duchess looked a little stunned and was not overly sure what she had just seen, so assumed it was her imagination.

"Would you like to sit next to me tonight Poppy?" asked the duchess as Poppy nodded, "then you can tell me about the fairies, I believe too you see."

"Do you?" asked Poppy excitedly, "they are so magical aren't they. Grandpa told me not many people believe."

"No, that's very true, only a few but that's a good thing and very few of those have actually really seen any. Now please come and meet William."

Nanny and Grandpa were watching their remarkable granddaughter handle herself with such grace. Their faces were obviously showing how proud they were as Mary Underberry pointed out to them how wonderful she was. Poppy walked hand in hand with the duchess to the other side of the table to meet the duke, Prince William, who was deep in conversation with Jonny. He stopped talking as soon as his wife and Poppy approached, and Jonny respectfully took a step back. Poppy looked up at the very tall prince and future king.

"Now then," said William, "this is the young lady we owe a great debt too is it? It's wonderful to meet you Poppy."

Poppy let go of the Duchesses' hand and performed her best curtsy yet.

"Good evening Your Highness," she said very confidently.

"I hear from my grandmother you were very brave, our family is very grateful Poppy, thank you."

"Thank you, sir," said Poppy.

After a brief conversation Poppy then spoke to Mary.

"Is the chief inspector coming?" she asked.

"No, unfortunately he can't make it, the number you gave us for the van has grown into something quite big," she replied.

"Oh, has it?"

"Yes, I'll explain later," said Mary kindly, "isn't this all amazing though?"

"Yes, I'm very excited."

Drinks were now being served and the waiter asked Poppy what she would like to drink, knowing that wine would not be an option

"Please may I have a lemonade?" asked Poppy.

"Me too please!" asked Jonny to the waiter.

Poppy walked over to be with her nanny who was talking to the duchess. As she did so another waiter came to speak to Nanny.

"Excuse me madam," said the waiter being careful not to be disrespectful, "we were unaware a child would be joining us this evening."

"Poppy is the reason we're here," interjected the duchess in a kind voice.

"Yes, ma'am but we don't have a children's menu," replied the waiter slightly flustered but standing his ground.

"Poppy doesn't need a children's menu thank you," replied Nanny in her best voice.

"Thank you, madam, thank you," said the waiter, turning and leaving the room.

Poppy gave her nanny's hand a squeeze as if to say thank you. There was more chitchat around the room. Poppy told the duchess about her treehouse and her new neighbours and she listened intently.

"I have never actually seen any fairies myself Poppy," she said kindly, "you are very special indeed."

"Then you must come to meet them all," said Poppy, "they're feeling a bit left out to be honest, well Maisy is anyway."

"That would be delightful, we must thank them too," replied the duchess looking at Nanny.

"Yes of course you must, we would be thrilled to have you," knowing full well that it was unlikely to happen.

"Perhaps we could go to Nanny and Grandpa's house after we've finished here?" asked Poppy as if she was speaking to her best friend Sarah.

"Well, err of course you may but … " stuttered Nanny.

"We'd be delighted to," said the duchess trying to save any embarrassment on Nanny's behalf.

"Well, that's a date then," said Nanny relieved but panicking that she may have left her knickers drying on a radiator somewhere. "Of course you may, we could go for coffee after dinner?" she asked sheepishly.

"That would be wonderful, thank you," said the duchess. "I'll tell William that's what we'll be doing later," she continued, smiling.

Eventually they all sat at the table. Poppy sat between Nanny and the duchess. Next to the duchess was Grandpa, then Mary, Jonny, Prince William and Sue who sat the other side of Nanny. Lord Ted sat on a stool behind Poppy and watched her every move. A waiter came in and placed menu's in front of each guest.

Poppy picked it up and hoped, that after Nanny's conversation with the waiter, that there was something on the menu that she would like.

"Are you OK Popsicle?" came Grandpa's kind voice across the table.

"Yes, thank you Grandpa, this is just magical." They both winked at each other.

Poppy's eyes returned to the menu. She had to pick a starter, main course and dessert and there were three or four choices for each, and all sounded very grand indeed. She was never shy of trying new things but decided to stick to things she hopefully recognised so she got it right in front of all these people.

For her starter she decided on the glazed pork cheek with a bacon fat potato, which made her giggle to herself, pickled apple, and potato foam, all because it said bacon. For her main course she was going to select the pan-fried sea bass with glazed parsnip, bacon and parmesan risotto, thyme crumb and sauce again because it had bacon in the title, and for dessert the raspberry panna cotta, served up with white chocolate ganache, mini sponge pieces and lemon sorbet simply because it said chocolate but had absolutely no idea what ganache or panna cotta really was. She made a mental note to find out about all these things and learn more about food.

The room had gone a little quieter now, the lights were dimmed slightly, and a waiter entered the room to start to take the orders. It seemed he was unsure where to go first. He would normally attend to the ladies, but the future king of England was there, so he stood by him and waited patiently, praying he had got it right.

Prince William looked up from the menu "Oh, please see to the ladies first, do me last, I have no idea what I want yet," he said, laughing.

"Thank you, sir," said the waiter who was obviously more nervous than Poppy had been earlier, "Ma'am?" he said to the duchess.

"Please ask Poppy first," she said.

Poppy was sure the waiter wanted to say "Good grief will someone just make their minds up and place an order" but he remained calm, although Poppy noticed he was sweating slightly, probably hoping he wouldn't mess anything up too. He looked at Poppy unsure how to address her. *Is this a member of the royal family* he wondered but took a guess that she wasn't. He was at least hoping that Poppy would place an order.

"And for you, young lady?" he asked tentatively.

This was it; Poppy was now being looked at by everyone. Would she get it right? Would the waiter assume that she would ask for chicken nuggets or spaghetti hoops? Poppy felt the nerves come back but with as much confidence that she could muster she went for it.

"Thank you, yes, please may I have the pork cheek followed by the sea bass?"

"Certainly madam," said the waiter almost surprised that she had actually picked something off the menu but relieved that she'd nailed it.

"Thank you," said Poppy guessing, and hoping, that he would come back for the desserts later.

"Ma'am?" he asked the duchess again.

"I'll have the same as Poppy please," she said.

Poppy looked up at this beautiful lady by the side of her and felt totally at ease. Nanny and Grandpa looked at her with such admiration and Nanny squeezed her hand. The waiter went around the table and took a variety of different orders finally ending up with the prince.

"What did you order again Poppy?" asked the prince kindly.

"The pork cheek and the sea bass, sir," she said.

"Oooo nice choice. Yes, I'll have the same as Poppy please," he said to the waiter.

Wine and water were also ordered and another lemonade for Poppy and Jonny. There was more talk around the table and eventually Mary wanted to say something so got everyone's attention by tapping her glass with a small spoon.

"As you know Poppy was instrumental in the capture of the robbers and the recovery of the crown jewels..." she started.

The duchess clapped and then they all clapped. Poppy felt her face burn bright red so reached for Lord Ted who would now remain on her lap for the rest of the evening.

"But," resumed Mary, "there's more. Chief Inspector Pickles-Cunningham cannot be with us tonight. He asked me to thank you Poppy, and said you can treat him to a McDonalds instead," everyone laughed, then Mary continued. "He's leading an operation this evening to capture the very sophisticated gang of thieves who are stealing tractors and farm equipment."

"Oh wow," said Grandpa and Jonny together.

"Yes, indeed," she now looked at Poppy "the part number plate you gave us for the van Poppy, was the last piece of the puzzle. We tracked the van which led to three huge warehouses outside of Nottingham. So, not only have you saved Mr Featherbottom and recovered most of the crown jewels, you have been instrumental in solving this complex case. I cannot say much more at the moment, we'll know more in the morning, but I want to thank you."

"Oh Poppy," said Grandpa, "what a star!"

Poppy sat there dumbfounded.

"Bravo Poppy!" said the prince.

"Well done," said the duchess.

The prince stood up and raised his glass, "To Poppy!" he announced. Everyone stood up, held their glasses high and all shouted, 'Poppy!'

Nanny sat down and reached across to hug her granddaughter, "oh Poppy, that's really amazing."

"I had no idea Nanny, honestly."

"Maybe but no matter, you helped didn't you."

After the atmosphere had settled down slightly, Grandpa gained assurance from the assistant chief constable that these facts would remain in the room for the safety of his granddaughter and everyone was in full agreement. Then Poppy asked a question of Mary.

"May I ask the full number plate please?" she asked.

"Yes. It was GD03 followed by UCK, a false one of course."

"Thank you," she said as her grandpa looked at her in astonishment.

As chatting began around the table she picked up Lord Ted and hugged him, "Gerald Duck aged 3," she whispered in his ear, "you clever bear."

The waiters then entered the room with a pre-starter or an 'amuse-bouche' as one of them called it, "A little something from the chef," he announced. These tiny little mouthfuls were described as blackened shrimp avocado cucumber bites and to avoid any misunderstandings this time there were a few waiters so they would get the timings right. Poppy looked at the curled up shrimp stuck to a slice of cucumber by green avocado goo. Nanny knew that Poppy was not keen on avocado, in fact not many eight-year-olds are.

"You OK my lovely?" she asked kindly.

"Yes Nanny, thank you."

Poppy looked at it for a little while. She watched as others just picked it up with their fingers and popped it in their mouths. She did not want to make any fuss or be seen as a fussy little girl so went for it. To her surprise it was very tasty, and she enjoyed it. Again, relieved she looked up at Nanny who smiled at her and tapped her hand.

"OK?"

"Yes, thank you, I really liked that actually."

"Oh good, I'll make those more often then," said Nanny, laughing.

"No, it's OK, one's enough," smiled Poppy.

A short while later, after clearing away the small plates a group of waiters brought in the starters. They all stood around the table then, just like a synchronised swimming team, they all placed the starters on the table at the same time. A kind waitress smiled as she placed Poppy's in front of her. It was more like an artistic masterpiece than a plate of food, it looked amazing and the smell was intoxicating. Poppy waited for the duchess to pick up her cutlery, firstly out of politeness but also checking which knife and fork to pick up first as there were a lot of choices.

"Great choice Poppy," she said after the first few mouthfuls. Indeed, it was. Poppy had not tasted anything like it before. Soon there were eight clean plates left on the table and the waiters returned to collect them and pour more drinks. Poppy could not believe her amazing evening as more conversation and laughter flowed, followed by the arrival of the main courses. Again, a work of art was presented in front of Poppy and again, it was totally delicious. Eventually the waiter who originally took the orders came to take the dessert choices. Poppy stuck to her original selection of the raspberry panna cotta and to her surprise everyone else had had the same idea and all chose the same option.

The waiters were soon back, this time with a pre-dessert announced as a banana and lime custard. These were served in little bowls with a tiny spoon that she was sure were actually meant for the fairies they were so small.

"You get extra puddings here Nanny, that's something you could do more often," said Poppy laughing, much louder than she had anticipated. The table erupted in laughter.

This was a taste sensation and Poppy could have eaten a whole massive bowl but at last the puddings arrived. These were a colourful extravaganza of pink, green, yellow and white. Poppy had never seen anything so wonderful on a plate, it looked far too good to eat. It was so delicious, sweet, creamy, tangy and fruity altogether on each spoonful and the lemon sorbet was the best thing she had ever tasted.

Poppy was now quite full and although she would have been excited at the prospect of a post pudding option, she was not sure she would be able to fit it in. She had eaten everything in front of her and was now absolutely stuffed.

Discussion turned to the fairies again with the duchess. She wanted to know more, what did they actually look like? How big are they really? and would she really be able to see any of them tonight? Poppy explained as best as she could and gained Nanny's approval again to bring her new friend around to see the treehouse and hopefully the fairies. Nanny asked whether the duchess had spoken to her husband about now all retiring to their house for coffee and further discussion. She confirmed she had so Nanny decided to announce that they are now all returning home for coffee.

"Are we?" asked Grandpa astonished.

"Yes," replied Nanny.

"Oh right, excellent," he said.

"And Sue and Jonny you'll join us too I hope?" asked Nanny.

"Yes of course, thanks," said Sue delighted that the evening would continue.

Then came a quick and nervous conversation between Grandpa and Jonny as they got up from the table about paying the bill. Mary soon joined in, and to the relief of both of them she reassured them that it was all taken care of but would not be joining them later so she could get back and see how the evening's operation was going.

"Right then," said Nanny "let's go."

As they left the restaurant they could see a large black car outside with two very burly looking gentlemen in the front. The duke and duchess got into the back of that car, understanding they would follow Jonny on the short drive back to Nanny and Grandpa's house. Mary got in another car with a driver in a police uniform after saying her goodbyes.

Nanny, Grandpa, Poppy and Lord Ted got into Jonny and Sue's car.

"Oh, my lord I hope I've not left any of my knickers on the radiator in the hall," said Nanny and they all burst out laughing. "Good job we had a good clean up before we leave tomorrow," she said still laughing but nervous.

"It will be fine my love," said Grandpa, "they've seen knickers before."

"Not mine they haven't," she replied as they pulled into the driveway, "I'll run in and check if you can stall them for 30 seconds."

When they arrived, Nanny ran into the house like an Olympic sprinter followed soon after by Poppy and Lord Ted.

"Quickly straighten the cushions Poppy please," said Nanny pointing at the sitting room to Poppy as she ran into the kitchen checking all the radiators.

Poppy ran into the front room and looked at the cushions. There was nothing at all to straighten, everything looked just like a picture in a magazine, so she was sure Nanny was just anxious over nothing.

Then the Duke and Duchess of Cambridge, the future king and queen of England walked into their front room.

"Please take a seat," said Grandpa trying to be as relaxed and calm as he could be with Nanny beside him.

"What a beautiful home," said the duchess.

"Thank you ma'am," said Nanny.

"Right, coffee, tea?" asked Grandpa.

Everyone asked for a coffee so Nanny went into the kitchen with Poppy who offered to help, as Grandpa made the guests feel at home the best he could.

"Oh, I'm not sure I've got that many matching cups!" said Nanny in an unnecessary panic.

"I'll have a glass of milk and Grandpa can use the mug I gave him for Christmas then we'll be fine," said Poppy reassuringly and her nanny smiled at her knowing she was right.

"I'll go and switch the fairy lights on Nanny, so they know I'm coming up, is that OK?"

"Yes of course darling."

Poppy with Lord Ted, ran down the garden and switched the fairy lights on that lead up the ladders to her treehouse. On reaching the top she shouted up to see if anyone was at home. She opened her bright red shiny door and switched on the light making sure everything was neat and tidy.

"Hi Poppy," came a familiar voice. Poppy turned around to be confronted with a hovering and very happy Deri.

"Hi Deri, so good to see you."

"What's up?" asked Deri cheerfully but then saw that Poppy was a little anxious.

"Is everyone about?" she asked.

"Yes, I think so, why?"

"Oh good," she said relieved again for the fourth or fifth time within the last two hours, "the Duchess of Cambridge, our future queen is here and wants to say thank you and meet you all, would that be OK?"

Deri hovered still then her mouth just fell open as if she had lost all control over it.

"Is Maisy here too?" continued Poppy, "Deri?"

"Yes," said Deri resuming control over her mouth, "yes I think so, let me just check," she said slowly, "so … you're saying that the future queen is here to see us?"

"Yes, I know it's hard to believe, it's a long story."

"Oh my, oh my, oh my, this is a first ever I think."

"Yes, she's never met any fairies before. You sure you all want to do this?"

"Yeeessssssss," said Deri now flying her normal excited loops.

"OK then, all meet me back here in a few moments, you'll see us walk in then ring the bell a few moments later OK?"

"Yes, yes OK," said Deri now beside herself with excitement.

"OK I'll be back soon."

Poppy ran back into the kitchen having left the fairy lights on, just in time to help Nanny take the drinks through into the sitting room. After a few more minutes chatting, Poppy turned to the duchess.

"Would you like to come and see my treehouse?" she asked winking at the same time.

"I would love to, thank you," replied the duchess widening her eyes.

"Nanny and Grandpa built it for me with the help of Jonny."

"How lovely, show me the way," she said getting out of her seat.

"Shan't be too long Nanny," said Poppy.

"OK sweetie, have fun."

The duchess followed Poppy and Lord Ted through the kitchen "What a beautiful house," she said entering the garden. She could see ahead at the fairy lights, "how pretty, is that your treehouse?"

"Yes, it's beautiful isn't it."

"Yes very."

"Just before we go up I'd like to introduce you properly to Lord Ted, Lord Teddington of Bearshire, please."

"Yes, we were introduced at dinner."

"Well yes," said Poppy giving Lord Ted a squeeze, "but not properly."

"Good evening ma'am," said Lord Ted bowing his head.

"Oh my," said the duchess holding onto the ladder rail nearly spilling her coffee, "I thought I saw you bow your head earlier, how wonderful, err, hello."

"Lord Ted was a huge part of this whole thing, you know, catching the robbers and everything. None of this could have happened without him, he is truly magical."

"Well thank you Lord Ted, it's an honour to meet you, and thank you," said the duchess with as much composure as she could, clearly staggered by what she had just seen.

"Thank you, ma'am," said Lord Ted.

"The queen said you were an extremely special bear, but I had no idea."

"Thank you again ma'am."

"Would you like to come up now?" Poppy asked the duchess, "no one but me, Nanny and Grandpa and of course Lord Ted have been up here now it's finished."

"Yes, yes, of course. This is amazing, one of the most amazing nights ever Poppy, I am honoured, thank you."

They climbed the ladders and entered Poppy's reading den.

"Well, isn't this cosy," she said, "how wonderful Poppy. The children would love something like this. Do you sleep in here too?" she continued looking at the bed.

"Sometimes, this is where we saw the robbers from, over in the barns," replied Poppy pointing out of the window.

"How exciting."

The doorbell rang.

"That will be our guests," said Poppy, "they were quick."

"You sound surprised," chuckled Lord Ted.

The duchess sat on the end of Poppy's bed mainly because she was trembling with excitement at the prospect of meeting fairies for the very first time. She had believed for many years, even seen, she thinks, a fairy door when she was a little girl, but to now meet some would be amazing.

Poppy opened the door. There before her eyes were Elvina and Oona with Maisy, Nixie, Jareth, Alfred, Gullveig, Sophie, Belle, Zuzana, April, Emma and of course, Deri all hovering very still with their wings glowing. They were dressed in their best outfits with gold and silver shining and sparking from the fairy lights.

"Well don't you look wonderful," said Poppy.

"And you too, what a beautiful dress Poppy, I like spots," said Elvina.

"Thank you. Please come in and meet the Duchess of Cambridge."

The duchess stood up. Her long dark hair lying across the shoulders of her stunning blue dress making her look every inch the beautiful princess and future queen. Her hands were now clammy and her mouth dry, a complete role reversal from earlier in the evening. Now Poppy was the confident lead and she played her part magnificently.

"Ma'am, err Kate, these are my neighbours," said Poppy proudly. She introduced them all one by one as they hovered in and bowed their heads then settled on Poppy's desk or bookshelf, their wings dulling down as they sat.

Deri and Elvina were the last to be introduced. Deri bowed her head and then, as is her way, flew a few quick loops before sitting next to Jareth on the desk. The duchess followed Deri with her eyes and squealed out of pure delight.

Then Elvina was introduced by Poppy. "It's an honour for us all to meet you Your Highness," she said with as much confidence as she could, bowing her head. The only confident person in the room now was Poppy.

"Well, I don't know what to say," said the duchess, "thank you to Poppy for introducing you all tonight, I will never remember all your names I'm sure, but I wanted to thank you for helping Poppy and Lord Teddington recover our family's possessions and saving that poor man, Mr Featherbottom. His and our family will be forever in your debt, thank you."

"Thank you," said Maisy who was clearly star struck by the duchess, "and thank you Poppy," she said smiling, "this means a lot."

"And," continued the duchess, "this is one of the most amazing experiences of my life too," she said clasping her hands together in total delight now sitting down on the edge of Poppy's bed. Poppy sat next to her holding Lord Ted.

"See, I told you it would be," said Gullveig.

"No, you didn't," said Jareth.

"Boys!" said Poppy, "not now."

Everyone laughed, "Sorry about that," said Poppy, "they're always arguing those two."

"No, we're not," said Gullveig jokingly, and again they all erupted into laughter.

The duchess stayed for a while listening to the details of the exciting night the fairies helped Poppy and Lord Ted. She asked where they lived, where they came from, how old they were and smiled the whole way through clearly enchanted by the fairies who looked just as captivated too. Eventually, after looking at the clock, the duchess said she had to be going.

"Poppy thank you and thank you Lord Ted and you all. I've had the most astonishing evening," she said, "and Poppy, do you think, one day, that Charlotte might come and visit you? She would love to meet you, Lord Ted and of course all of you," she added looking at the fairies.

"Yes of course, and the boys too, not just Charlotte," said Poppy.

"Yes, that would be wonderful, thank you."

"We hope to see you again Your Highness," said Elvina, "thank you for spending the time to see us, it means an awful lot and this night will be legendary throughout our kingdom for hundreds of years to come I'm sure, thank you."

Poppy opened the door and the fairies flew out back to their homes. Poppy showed the duchess the fairy doors higher up in the tree and then they made their way back to the house. They could hear lots of laughter coming from the sitting room as Grandpa and Jonny recited funny stories from their past. They walked in and William looked at his wife who he could see had obviously been through a joyous experience, "Nice time?" he asked.

"Incredible," she said smiling, "absolutely incredible."

It was getting late and the duke and duchess decided it was time for them to go as they have a very long journey ahead of them. Jonny and Sue agreed it was time to go too. After goodbyes and a huge hug from the duchess they all left, and the house went quiet.

Nanny, Grandpa, Poppy and Lord Ted sat back in the sitting room in silence. Grandpa removed his tie.

"Well," he said, "beat that night if you can."

Poppy jumped and let out a scream of utter delight and fell back in the chair "KATE!" she shouted laughing and wiggling her legs in the air.

They all laughed, recited their favourite bits of the night, Poppy told them about the treehouse, and they agreed that this was probably going to be the best night out they would ever have.

Before long Poppy's dress was hanging on the front of the wardrobe in her bedroom and she was snuggled down in bed with Lord Ted and Nanny sitting by her side.

"We were so proud of you tonight Poppy," she said sweetly, "so proud."

"Thank you, Nanny, it has been the best night. I love you."

"I love you too sweetheart, lights out now as we're away tomorrow. More exciting times ahead."

"Lord Ted and I can't wait."

"Neither can we, goodnight my angel," said Nanny kissing her forehead.

"Night night Nanny."

21

Poppy woke to the, now familiar, clink of plates and cups coming from downstairs which meant breakfast was in progress, however this time it was the sound of clearing all the coffee cups from the night before.

"Morning Lord Ted," she said giving him a squeeze, "it looks like another lovely day again," she added stretching her arms and yawning.

"Good morning, what a night to remember that was," he said.

"Oh good, for a minute there I was thinking it was a dream, Kate was so lovely, wasn't she?"

"Yes, she'll be a wonderful queen I'm sure," said Lord Ted.

Poppy got up and went downstairs.

"Good morning!" she said walking into the kitchen, sitting at the table and placing Lord Ted next to her.

"Well, you're up early Popsicle," said Grandpa.

"What time is it?"

"It's nearly 8 o'clock, early for you," said Nanny, "you OK?"

"Yes, thank you Nanny, I still think it was all a dream to be honest."

"It was a wonderful night wasn't it, I think we'll be talking about it for many years to come."

"Yes, Elvina said to Kate that it will become a legend for hundreds of years for them."

"I bet," said Grandpa, "it will be, you've become a bit of a legend with them too I'm sure,"

Poppy smiled.

"We should catch the news really," said Nanny, "there may be an update on the farm machinery thieves after what Mary said last night."

"Yes, I'd forgotten all about that," said Grandpa.

As expected the headlines on the news were all about the capture of various people from around Nottingham and Leicester and further beyond including France, Poland, and Germany. Dawn raids had recovered a huge quantity of tractors and various farm machinery from different warehouses across Europe. Not much more information was available at this time.

"Well done again you two," said Grandpa to Poppy and Lord Ted, "great work. I bet that was a huge task to organise all that too. No wonder the chief inspector didn't join us last night."

The news also showed pictures of the Pearson brothers who were still on the run and a mention of the gold and crown jewels that were missing. Grandpa concentrated on the weather forecast and declared it a miracle that the sunny weather would continue for their holiday. They watched the television while eating their breakfast which is not normally the thing to do, but it was only a quick catchup, just tea and toast as there was much to do before they left for the long drive to the Lake District.

"So where are we going exactly?" asked Poppy finishing her mug of tea.

"Well," said Grandpa "we're going to a house that belongs to very good friends of ours, Billy and Kate."

"Ooo another Kate," said Poppy, laughing.

Grandpa laughed, "We've known them for years. They bought a house on the banks of Lake Windermere a while back. It needed a lot of work doing to it which they finished a couple of years ago. They let family and friends use it. We went last year and its absolutely beautiful, so we thought we'd go again. You'll love it Poppy."

"Actually by the lake?" asked Poppy.

"Yes, and we have our own boat to use too, it's called Grumpy Joe."

"And a hot tub," said Nanny, "I love it."

"Oh wow," laughed Poppy at Nanny's excitement and the name of the boat.

"Why is it called 'Grumpy Joe'?" she asked.

"I have absolutely no idea," replied Grandpa.

"I've bought you a little something Poppy, to use while we're there," said Nanny reaching across to the sideboard, "it's to help on our walks."

Nanny passed a small book to Poppy. It was about the wildlife you can find in the area, mammals, birds, flowers and plants.

"It will help us see what's about, what things are called, and we can identify the birds on the lake itself," said Nanny kindly, "I know you like to learn new things and you can show Mummy and Daddy when you get home."

"Wonderful thank you Nanny, its perfect," said Poppy thumbing through the book looking at all the colourful pages, "it's small enough to carry around too, thank you."

After clearing the breakfast things away, it was time to get ready and pack the car. Nanny had finished most of the packing, so it was simply toiletries, books, including her new wildlife book and most importantly Lord Ted and his green backpack that Poppy had to get together after her shower.

"You'll need the backpack for our walks Lord Ted," she told him as she was zipping up her clothes bag and giving him a squeeze all at the same time, "it's going to be great fun."

"Be good to get away from all the excitement of the last few days and just have some family times with Nanny and Grandpa won't it," he said.

"Yes, it will."

Poppy carefully put Lord Ted in his backpack and looped him over her shoulder then carried her quite heavy case down the stairs and put it in the hallway ready to pack in the car. Nanny was in the kitchen packing the food into the cool box.

"Well, you'll be delighted to hear that I remembered the milk," she announced to Poppy and Grandpa who both clapped in response, "however, we used most of it last night, so we need to pop into the shop on the way past and get another bottle."

"So close Nanny," said Poppy, laughing, "so close."

Packing the car was a lot easier than before without all the camping equipment, but Grandpa made sure all the walking boots were packed. He was pretty convinced that they would not need any waterproofs looking at the weather forecast but packed them anyway.

Soon they were off with Lord Ted sitting on Poppy's knee looking out of the car window. Grandpa pulled up outside the village shop for Nanny to pick up some milk.

"Want to come in with me Poppy?"

"OK," she said.

They entered the shop and moved towards the aisle leading to the milk. Who should be there but Agatha Jones from the post office, she looked up to see Nanny and Poppy and waddled towards them hurriedly, just like Gerald the duck towards his bread.

"Oh, you'll never guess what?" she said looking both ways over her shoulder, "you'll never guess who ate at The Greedy Duckling last night, you'll never guess."

"I've no idea Agatha," said Nanny enquiringly.

"Only bloomin' Kate and Wills," continued Mrs Jones gasping, her jaw wanting to hit the floor, "yes, can you believe it, here in Diddlesdale? Oh, it's all going on. Royalty here in our village. Apparently, there were a few folks, even young Charlotte too in a spotty dress, how lovely."

"Really? that's amazing, isn't it Poppy."

"Yes amazing," said Poppy, who was trying very hard not to laugh.

"Yes, amazing," continued the postmistress, "she wore a blue dress apparently, that will be the new colour this year I'm sure."

"Indeed," said Nanny picking up the milk also trying not to laugh.

"Rightio, I'm off to call Angela with the news," she continued and waddled off further down the aisle bumping into to someone else, "you'll never guess what … " Poppy heard her say to her next unsuspecting victims.

Poppy finally laughed out loud followed by Nanny, "Sshhhh," said Nanny, "she'll hear you."

"I doubt it," laughed Poppy, "look, she's in full flow now."

As soon as they got back in the car they started laughing.

"What are you two laughing at?" asked Grandpa starting the car.

"Agatha Jones and the news that royalty ate at The Greedy Duckling last night," she said rolling her eyes, "it will be all around the village by 11 o'clock."

"Apparently I'm Princess Charlotte too," added Poppy laughing.

"She loves the gossip doesn't she," said Grandpa, "I bet she calls Huw for another spectacular interview."

"Oh, bless her, she means well, but honestly she must have nothing better to talk about. Mind you, it is exciting though. Good job we're away for a week."

"Why didn't you tell her it was us Nanny?"

"Well sometimes my lovely, it's best to just agree and watch people make things up, then you realise who's trustworthy and who's not. And sometimes it's best to say nothing at all and leave them with their own imagination. It's never good to brag about anything."

"That's good to know Nanny, thank you," said Poppy realising the ways of the world can be complicated at times but always happy to learn.

162

"Right let's get going then," said Grandpa, "LG?"

"LG" said Nanny and Poppy.

The drive was going to be quite long and as Poppy hadn't had the longest sleep after all the excitement, she felt her eyes start to droop. Try as she might to fend off the sleep monster the inevitable happened and she was fast asleep before they got to the motorway.

Poppy opened her eyes just as Grandpa was driving down a long gravel driveway, the change in speed and road noise must have woken her.

"Are we here already?" she yawned.

"Well, welcome back sleepy head," said Nanny, "yes, we're here."

Poppy gave Lord Ted a squeeze, "You OK?" she asked.

"Yes thanks, you've slept well, I think you may have caught up now," he laughed.

Poppy got out of the car and with Lord Ted under her arm she followed Nanny and Grandpa into the house. It was staggering in size. As they walked in through a hallway it opened up, with huge double floor to ceiling windows looking down to the lake that shimmered bright blue in the sunlight. An open plan kitchen, seating and eating area covered the whole downstairs floor with the biggest television she had ever seen on the wall. She ran up the stairs where a long corridor had four doors along one side. These led to huge bedrooms, all with their own bathrooms, overlooking the lake. It was the most amazing house she had ever seen. She ran back downstairs to where Nanny and Grandpa had slid open the glass doors and were standing in the simple, yet beautiful, garden that stretched down to the lake and boathouse, to her left was Nanny's hot tub.

"Is this ours?" she asked excitedly.

"All week," said Grandpa, "I told you is was good didn't I?"

"It's amazing, absolutely amazing," said Poppy.

Poppy helped her grandparents unpack the car and then chose a bedroom that looked further down the lake and was directly in line with the boat house. She unpacked her bag and soon joined Nanny downstairs in the kitchen.

"Grandpa is firing up the barbeque so hamburgers tonight," said Nanny, "can you help me chop the salad please?"

Poppy helped her nanny, only too pleased to be part of another experience with her grandparents.

The week was to pass far too quickly. Each night Poppy helped her grandpa select a choice of three walks for Nanny to decide which one they would go on the next morning, from a book that they then used to guide them around the walk. They tried to choose a different type each time: some just woodland walks, others around lakes or following valleys. Poppy's new walking boots were very comfortable, so it made the walks nice and easy whatever the terrain. Grandpa tried to make sure each one ended near a pub so he could sample the local beer. Every walk lasted for about four hours; they would have been quicker, but Poppy, Lord Ted and Nanny were looking at different animals, birds, flowers and plants and checking them with her new book. Grandpa was more than happy, the days were long gone where he wanted to march quickly around hills and woodland, so he sat and watched his granddaughter learn new things as they went.

With Lord Ted on her back, together they spotted red squirrels which Grandpa had not seen in years. It was almost as if they had come out to wave at Poppy and Lord Ted. Poppy looked to see if she could see any fairy doors but if they were there, they were very well hidden and difficult to spot in the daytime. They saw red deer and sheep that were only found around The Lakes, the Herdwick Sheep which had a silver fleece that helped it stand out from other breeds. They found the entrances to badger setts and rabbit warrens and spotted many types of birds using Grandpa's binoculars including the Meadow Pit, Tree Creeper, Lapwing and Pied Wagtail. Poppy identified lots of different wildflowers including Common Knapweed, Bog Asphodel, Sundew, Butterwort and various types and colours of Milkwort. She found colourful Foxgloves and Harebells and marked them all off in her little book. Poppy absorbed all she could, even embracing the secret world of insects like the Bronze Shieldbug and took time to understand what they mean for the environment. She was captivated by colour and movement of everything she found.

Afternoons were spent either relaxing or playing in the garden or taking Grumpy Joe out on the lake. There was a speed limit so they couldn't go too fast but Poppy, with Lord Ted always by her side, drove the boat from one end of the lake to the other and back again many times, covering tens of miles. Lord Ted was not too excited by the boat but would not be without Poppy so hung on and enjoyed watching her drive and enjoy herself. With Nanny, they spotted different birds: Tufted Ducks, Coots, Pochards and Mergansers, all again marked off in the book. Then, in the early evenings, they would be in and out of the hot tub before a delicious dinner followed by either Uno, Ludo or by learning new card games. Poppy had never had so much fun, every day she was creating memories, learning new things and spending every minute she could with Lord Ted, Nanny and Grandpa.

On the last afternoon, as Poppy skilfully moored Grumpy Joe back in the boathouse for what she thought was the last time, Grandpa announced he'd booked the local restaurant with a table that looked over the lake as a treat; a nice night out to remember a fantastic holiday.

Poppy, who was now sporting a summery glow, decided she would wear her poppy-flower summer dress that Nanny had packed for her for such an occasion. After a last splash around in the hot tub with Grandpa she went to get ready. Nanny had been packing and was also getting ready but had left Poppy's dress and sandals out for her to wear. Once done she went downstairs with Lord Ted and found Grandpa watching the news, this was the first time the television had been switched on all week.

"Just thought I'd watch the news. It's like being at the cinema," he laughed.

The television was massive, and now there was a picture on, it looked even bigger. Poppy and Lord Ted sat next to Grandpa and were soon watching the news headlines.

"Good evening and welcome to the 6 o'clock news..." said the familiar voice of Fiona *"Further arrests made for the Tower of London robbery... record breaking days of sunshine for the United Kingdom... and farmers start to have their stolen machinery returned to help them with the harvests,"* she continued.

"Nip upstairs and see if Nanny is nearly ready, or ask her to put the tele on in the bedroom so she can listen would you Poppy?" asked Grandpa.

"No worries I'm here!" announced Nanny at the top of the stairs, "I thought we said no TV this... Oh, my that's a big screen, bigger than I thought," she continued as she came down the stairs.

"You look lovely Nanny."

"Thank you Poppy, I love you in that dress too," she smiled.

"...we can confirm the arrests of Raymond James Pearson and his younger brother Ronald Spencer Pearson earlier this morning just outside Aberdeen in Scotland..." The screen now showed the very large faces of the brothers and Poppy rocked back at the sight of their hard expressions that would give anyone nightmares.

"... The brothers were found in a guesthouse and had been on the run for nearly two weeks since the Tower of London Robbery. It's believed that the owners of the guesthouse have also been taken into custody. The remainder of the missing gold has been recovered from within the house but the crowns, robes, rings, sceptre and the secular and alter plates are all still missing. There have been three further arrests in London today of other suspected members of the gang. Let's go firstly to our reporter in Aberdeen, Robert McDougal and then to Huw in London."

Poppy, Lord Ted, Nanny and Grandpa watched the reporter explain what Fiona had already told them but as he did it from outside the guesthouse they wondered if they should be hearing something different. Huw then followed, standing outside the Tower of London, for no apparent reason and explained that there had been three further arrests in London.

"Why do they have to explain everything three or four times?" asked Poppy.

"Just in case you didn't hear it the second time," smiled Grandpa rolling his eyes.

Then came some good news for a change, the weather had broken all records for continuous days of sunshine and was set to continue, although there would be some welcome rain in the evenings. And then the fabulous news of the farm machinery that had been recovered being returned to the farmers to help with the harvests that were in full flow. The television showed huge lorries unloading tractors at farms across the country. Poppy felt so proud that she and Lord Ted played a small part in making that happen.

"Right then, that's a happy note to end on, let's get to the restaurant, I'm starving," said Grandpa, switching off the television.

Grandpa led them down the garden towards the boathouse.

"Are we going on the boat?" asked Poppy.

"Yes, it's just over there look," said Grandpa pointing at the grand looking white hotel across the lake, "I'm not driving all the way around there it could take us nearly an hour," he said, laughing, "plus the hotel has its own mooring."

"Wow, I've never gone to a restaurant in a boat before," said Poppy.

"Nor us," said Nanny, "very la-di-da, just another one to pop into the old memory bank."

"You want to drive Poppy?" asked Grandpa.

166

"Yes please!"

Soon enough Poppy was pulling Grumpy Joe alongside the hotel jetty like a seasoned professional as Grandpa hopped out and tied the boat up. He helped Nanny out and then Poppy, who of course was carrying Lord Ted. They made their way into the hotel entrance and through to the restaurant.

The food was wonderful and after dinner they sat in the garden looking across the lake back towards their holiday home with coffee before it was time to make their way back.

Poppy was again happy to drive. She loved the thrill of driving the boat seeing her grandparents sitting comfortably.

"I've had the most amazing holiday, thank you!" she shouted over the noise of the engine.

"We have too Poppy, thank you," shouted back Nanny, her long curly hair blowing back in the wind.

Poppy manoeuvred the boat into the boathouse for the final time and they made their way back to the house. They sat in the garden until the sun was going down and talked about their holiday, what were the best bits, favourite flowers and birds.

The next morning, they were up early. Nanny had agreed to wash all the bed linen and get it dry before they left which, in the dry breeze by the lake, would not take long. As the sheets were drying, they had breakfast and then cleaned up. Poppy cleaned her bedroom and helped downstairs and then with the washing dry, folded and put away, they packed the car and made their way back home to Diddlesdale. Poppy only had a few days left of her time with Lord Ted so was a little sad but knew she would be back soon enough. It would soon be time for school and her friends.

22

They finally arrived back in Diddlesdale late in the afternoon and after picking up a few essentials from the village shop and avoiding another encounter with Agatha Jones, Grandpa suggested dinner from the village chip shop. Poppy was delighted and Nanny relieved as she really didn't feel like cooking after such a long journey home.

Poppy helped Grandpa water the garden again, she was never quite sure why she loved it so much. Maybe it was just helping Grandpa as she knew the garden meant so much to him. Whatever the reason it always seemed like great fun. Nanny unpacked the clothes and eventually they were tucking into their fish and chips, with Grandpa having, as always, steak and kidney pie.

"Please may I sleep in the treehouse tonight?" asked Poppy.

"OK by me," said Nanny, "Grandpa?"

"Yes, fine by me too, I expect you want to catch up with a few people, right?"

"Yes, I do, thank you," said Poppy smiling.

"It's not going to be cold is it, but we'll leave the back door open again, you know, just in case," smiled Grandpa.

Poppy smiled. "I've had an amazing holiday," she said for the hundredth time, "thank you so much."

"Honestly, I think it's the best holiday I've ever had in this wonderful country of ours," said Nanny, "certainly the busiest one anyway."

"I don't think we've ever done so much have we?" said Grandpa.

"No, I'm exhausted to be honest," laughed Nanny.

"It's been amazing," said Poppy, "I'll be sad to go."

"Well, you'll be glad to be back home with Mummy and Daddy I'm sure, and with your friends at school too," said Nanny kindly, "but there are still a few days left then you'll be back for tea the following week. And you know you can come and stay any time, you even have your own bedroom, well two actually, inside and outside," she smiled, "and of course Lord Ted."

Poppy looked at her nanny and grandpa and then at Lord Ted.

"Do you think one day I could live here?" she asked.

"Well yes, when we go, this house will be your daddy's."

"But I don't want you to go," said Poppy with her bottom lip quivering.

"Well, that's not going to happen for a long time is it," said Grandpa realising that he needed to cheer things up quickly, "what do we have for pudding Nanny?"

"Trifle!" said Nanny quickly smiling at Poppy, who smiled back.

"When are you going to meet the fairies from Diddlesdale Woods?" asked Grandpa.

Poppy knew that Grandpa was trying to change the subject as quickly as he could so answered quite brightly, "I don't know actually, I'm not sure how well Elvina and the other fairies know them yet."

"Well, I bet they've told them all about meeting the future queen so I'm sure they'll know each other soon enough."

After trifle, one from the shop so not as nice as Nanny's but still delicious, Poppy and Lord Ted sat and snuggled up with Grandpa so he could look at her wildlife book and see how many birds, animals, trees and flowers she'd ticked off as seen.

"That's quite a lot isn't it? I think you've seen well over half of them."

"We'll have to go back and find the others won't we?"

"Yes, we can go back next year, I'll call Billy tomorrow and book us in, would you like that?"

"I'd love it Grandpa."

"Good, that's settled then," he said.

"What is?" asked Nanny walking in the room.

"We're going back to Billy and Kate's next year with Poppy."

"Excellent news, I reckon my legs will have just about recovered by then," she laughed.

"Thank you both," said Poppy giving her grandpa a hug.

"Right then, ready for bed please Miss Poppy," said Nanny, smiling.

Poppy went upstairs to get washed and into her pyjamas. She sat on the windowsill of her bedroom window for a while before returning downstairs.

"I don't want Nanny and Grandpa to go," she said giving Lord Ted a squeeze.

"I know," he replied knowing just how close she was to them both, "I'll always be with you though," he said trying to make her feel better.

Poppy gave Lord Ted a long cuddle and looked out of the window. She stared at her treehouse for a while knowing how incredibly lucky she was and was determined to make the best of every minute she could.

Eventually she was saying goodnight to her grandpa and making her way to the treehouse with Lord Ted and Nanny.

"Do you want me to come up with you and read?"

"No, it's OK Nanny thanks, I'll read my book and snuggle down. Hopefully I might have some visitors, you never know."

"OK poppet."

Poppy gave her nanny the longest and tightest hug she could before making her way up the ladders lit by the fairy lights.

"Night night my angel," said Nanny, "see you in the morning."

Poppy waved as her nanny returned to the house then made her way into her den. She closed the bright red door behind her and switched on the lamp by her bed remembering just how much she loved her treehouse and then noticed that her bed covers were not how she thought she had left them but thought no more of it.

She got into bed with Lord Ted snuggled into her side and opened her book. She had only got halfway down the first page when there was a tap at her window by the door, then her bell rang.

"They were quick," said Poppy happily, giving Lord Ted a squeeze and getting up to open the door.

"You always sound so surprised," he said.

"Oh Poppy, are we glad to see you!" said an exasperated Elvina with quite a few fairies behind her looking over her shoulder at Poppy and Lord Ted, "can we come in?"

"Yes, yes of course, what's up?"

All the fairies, many of whom Poppy and Lord Ted had not seen before, followed Elvina in and found a spot to sit.

"We've been waiting for you to return; it seems ages ago since you left," she said still very exasperated.

"We've only been gone a week; are you OK? Has something happened?" asked Poppy sitting back on her bed.

"No, nothing bad, well yes, well no, err, I don't know really."

"Can you be a little more specific?" asked Lord Ted.

"Well, err … " stumbled Elvina.

"YOU'RE SITTING ON THE CROWN JEWELS!" blurted out Jareth.

"WHAT!" shouted Poppy standing up very quickly as if she had had an electric shock and looking back at her bed all in one move. "What did you say?"

"Err, yes, thank you Jareth," said Elvina quite annoyed and wrinkling her nose at him. "It's a long story but yes, the remainder of the crown jewels are under your bed."

"Holy moly," said Lord Ted, "how the dickens did they get there?"

"Isabella and Delilah and their fairies found them," said Elvina, as if Poppy and Lord Ted should have realised, "in the woods."

"Who're Isabella and Delilah?"

"Yes, sorry, I need to introduce you to the fairies from Diddlesdale Woods," said Elvina very apologetically. "Guys this is Poppy and Lord Ted."

Elvina introduced them all one by one, just as Poppy had introduced all the fairies to Kate the week before.

"This is Isabella."

"Charmed Miss Poppy," she said with a curtsy. Lord Ted sniggered.

"This is Delilah."

"Your ladyship," said Delilah with a curtsy. Lord Ted laughed.

"Hold on, hold on," said Poppy, "I'm not a princess, please don't curtsy."

"But you know some," said Elvina.

"I know a lot of people and things, but I will never be a princess so please, you don't need to curtsy," she smiled.

"OK sorry, yes," said Elvina.

"So, its lovely to meet you both," said Poppy to Isabella and Delilah, "and who else have we got?"

"Hi Poppy, I'm Amy," said a fairy with long brown hair and big brown eyes, giving her a wave and salute.

"Hello Amy."

"And I'm Xander," said another fairy who had perched himself on Poppy's bookshelf, "I'm a tooth fairy."

"Nice to meet you Xander."

"I'm Nina, I'm a tooth fairy too."

"And me, I'm Zach, I'm Amy's brother."

"Hello both," replied Poppy looking around at all the fairies now introducing themselves.

"I'm Olly," said Olly standing to attention like a soldier and saluting.

"I'm Elga."

"I'm Emily."

Jareth and Gullveig both blushed and giggled. They obviously thought Elga and Emily were the most beautiful fairies they had ever seen, apart from Elvina of course.

"Well, hello all, it's lovely to meet you, what a lot of you there are, and this is Lord Ted," she said sort of holding him up slightly.

"Hi there," said Lord Ted.

"Hello," they all said together.

"Sir," added Olly.

"So, back to the crown jewels please," said Poppy quite concerned.

"Yes, sorry," said Isabella, "please let me explain … "

"Please do," said Poppy now walking towards the bed lifting the lid and mattress together. With Lord Ted they looked inside and saw a large sack that looked like it was made from woven strands of grey plastic. It was open slightly, and they could see gold and precious, coloured stones and white fur with black specs on it. They both just stared quite dumbfounded by what they could see.

"Well, about two weeks ago we watched all the commotion around the barns from the woods. It was the first time we'd seen some more fairies around here, you know Elvina and so on, and lovely they are too."

"Why thank you," said Deri.

"Get on with it," said Lord Ted still staring at the opened sack with Poppy.

"Yes, sorry," continued Isabella, "well, as all that was happening another car pulled up with two men in it, they saw what was going on, so turned around quickly and sped off."

"That must have been the Pearson brothers," said Poppy now closing the lid and turning to face the fairies. She thought she would listen first and then go back to the sack afterwards.

"Then they stopped by the side of the road and threw the sack into the woods," said Xander, "it landed at the bottom of my tree."

"Yes, quite," said Isabella "we went to see what it was and of course, at the time had no idea, so we hid it until we figured out what to do."

"I see," said Poppy.

"Then we saw some police searching in the woods yesterday morning and thought they might be looking for these."

"Then Isabella and Delilah came to see us," said Elvina, "I told them what they were, and said you'd know what to do so we brought them here to keep safe last night. It is very heavy."

"Looks like they must have dumped them as quickly as they could and made their getaway," said Lord Ted, "we need to get these returned."

"Yes, we do, but we can't just give them to the police. How suspicious would that look? 'Oh, it's OK officer, I was just keeping them in my treehouse for a while to play with … ' that would sound very strange don't you think?"

"Yes, you have a point," replied Lord Ted.

"Plus, Grandpa and Nanny said they do not want police here or us mentioned anywhere," added Poppy.

"Yes, you're right," said Lord Ted, "what are you thinking?"

"Well, I think we take them back to Kate. She's met everyone here, well not our new friends, but all the others. She would understand if we explain what has happened."

"Or we just take them back to the woods?"

"What if someone else found them or the Pearson brothers sent word to others to try and find them?"

"Well, there were some other men looking around last week," said Olly quietly.

"What? you never mentioned that," said Delilah.

"Never really thought about it until now," Olly replied quite shyly.

"So, they must have let some others know to go and pick them up then," said Lord Ted, "I think your first idea is better."

"Let's get the sack out and see what's there," said Poppy.

She placed Lord Ted on her desk next to Elvina, Oona and Deri and then opened the base of her bed again. She looked at it for a while. Grandpa had fixed a hook to the side so that the lid would stay open. She reached in to pick the sack up with both hands. It was nearly as big as her and extremely heavy; it took all her strength to lift it out and put on the floor. It landed with a bit of a clunk.

"I'm not going to be able to carry that," she said panting and sweating, "it weighs a ton."

"We will have to ask Grandpa for some help," said Lord Ted.

"Yes," she said, "how did you guys get this up here."

"We're fairies Poppy," said Deri, "we have fairy dust remember?"

"Oh right. Yes, of course. That could be an option too," said Poppy now opening the sack having no idea how fairy dust could help her really.

It seemed these priceless, incredible and historical items had just been thrown in the sack as if they were rubbish to throw in a dustbin. It saddened Poppy to see them like this after she had seen them so proudly displayed in the Tower of London only a few weeks before – so much had happened since then. She could see a crown, robes and sceptre along with the end of a sword. She wanted to get everything out but knew that would not be the best thing to do and she knew enough not to put her fingers on them. She sat on the floor next to the sack and stared for a short time, trying to think what the best thing would be to do.

"So how would the fairy dust work?" she asked eventually to the herd of fairies assembled in her den who were all waiting for her to speak, "how would it make it lighter?"

There followed a brief discussion in whispers between some of the fairies before Delilah spoke up. "Amy made a tie for the sack that made it smaller and lighter so we could bring it up here," she said, "that might help."

"Tell me more please," said Poppy.

"Err, well, I, err," stumbled Amy who was sitting on Poppy's bookshelf and seemingly quite nervous.

"It's OK Amy," said Poppy kindly, "you might just have the answer we need."

"Err, well, I err, I made a fairy dust tie and put it around the sack and then I tied a bow which made the sack just weigh the same as the sack itself. Then, when we lifted it to put under your bed, I undid the bow so it returned to normal," said Amy now a little less nervous.

"That's genius," said Lord Ted.

"She is very clever isn't she?" said Deri thinking she would like to be Amy's new best friend.

"Thank you," said Amy who was now very proud of herself.

"Yes, Amy that's brilliant but would it work for me? If I take them to Kate would it work until I undid the bow?"

"Yes, I could do it so you were the only person that could lift it and the only person to undo the bow, but I would need some strands of your hair to do that."

"Oh wow, yes, that's amazing," said Poppy, "what do you think Lord Ted?"

"I think we have a plan."

"OK, so Amy if you could do that, then tomorrow Lord Ted and I will return them to where they need to be."

"Of course," said Amy, "please may I have some of your hair, just three strands would be enough."

Poppy pulled a few single strands of hair then rubbed her head vigorously where they had come from, thinking that was a lot more painful than she expected it would be. Amy released some fairy dust and with a flash of light the sack seemed to reduce to half its size. She then wrapped Poppy's golden hair around the top and finished with a big red and gold sparkly bow which looked totally out of place on the grotty grey sack, but she wanted it to look nice for Poppy. Once done she flew back and sat next to Deri on the desk and looked very pleased with herself. She and Deri giggled like a couple of naughty school children together.

Poppy stared at the sack in disbelief. She stood up and attempted to lift the sack while at the same time wondering if they were all going to fall about laughing at this massive practical joke, 'of course fairy dust can't do that' they would all laugh. She placed her hand on the crumpled grey plastic above the pretty bow and lifted. To her astonishment the sack weighed nothing at all, and she lifted it as if it was an empty shopping bag. Her mouth fell open with the shock.

"That's amazing Amy," said Poppy, "look Lord Ted."

"That … is … incredible," he said very slowly and equally flabbergasted.

"No one else will be able to pick it up," said Amy confidently, "to them it would weigh more than a bus."

"Really?" said Poppy.

"Yes, and also no one else will be able to undo the bow either. All you have to do is just undo it as if it was your shoelaces then it will disappear, so you only have one chance to open it."

"Really?" said Poppy again totally astonished by what Amy was saying and had done, "Amy you are a genius just like Lord Ted said, thank you."

Amy now blushed. Poppy placed the sack back under her bed and closed the lid sitting back on her bed.

"And will that last until tomorrow?" she asked Amy.

"As long as you need it to," she replied now very pleased with herself.

"Thank you, Amy. So, do we use the crooked door tomorrow?" she asked Lord Ted.

"Yes, as long as you want it to be where Kate is behind the door, we will be OK," he replied.

"OK that's settled then, we will return them tomorrow."

For the next hour or so Poppy and Lord Ted listened to her new friends tell them about themselves. She found out more about Xander and Nina being tooth fairies, how Amy was trying new things with fairy dust, how shy Olly was and what Isabella and Delilah get up to with all their new friends. She found out that Jareth and Gullveig want to marry Elga and Emily and of course they argued about who was going to marry who with much laughter. Poppy told them about their holiday and more about the night they spent with the Duke and Duchess of Cambridge and promised to make more cake for the next night so she could tell them all about returning the crown jewels.

It was getting very late so Elvina, in her normal commanding but kind manner, said that they would go and that they'd see Poppy and Lord Ted the next night with a little reminder about the cake. Poppy thanked them all, especially Amy for her help, and assured them that cake would be available the following evening.

Eventually Poppy was in bed snuggled up to Lord Ted and agreed that they needed to let Grandpa and Nanny know that they will be going to see the duchess in the morning but not tell them about the crown jewels for now.

"I can't wait to see Kate tomorrow."

"She'll be pleased to see you I'm sure," said Lord Ted.

They lay in silence for a short while.

"I'm not sure how many people have slept on top of the queen's crown are you?" she laughed.

"Just us two," laughed Lord Ted in reply, "just us two."

"Night night Lord Ted."

"Night night."

23

Poppy woke quite early and noticed it was not as sunny as it had been. It had been raining through the night and grey clouds still hung over Diddlesdale. She walked out on to her small treehouse balcony to feel the slightly colder and fresher air then, after picking the sack up again to see if Amy's fairy dust still worked, which it did, she straightened her bed and returned to the house with Lord Ted.

As ever Nanny and Grandpa were sitting at the kitchen table with a cup of tea and surprised to see her so early.

"Good morning Popsicle," said Grandpa.

"Good morning," replied Poppy happy and bright as usual.

"Did you sleep well my lovely?" asked Nanny, "cup of tea?"

"Yes, thank you and yes please," she said.

"So, meet up with anyone new?" asked Grandpa while Nanny made a fresh pot of tea.

"Yes Grandpa, quite a few. They're led by Isabella and Delilah and have some very clever fairies too. Might be a wedding soon as well," she laughed.

"Oh wow! Never seen one of those before, they're very secret. Looks like they've really opened up to you. I'm thrilled," said Grandpa.

"I just hope it's not all a dream," said Poppy who had Lord Ted sitting by her side.

"I know it's not," said Nanny kindly, "right, boily eggs or a bacon sandwich?"

"Please may I have boily eggs and soldiers?"

"Of course," said Nanny, "Grandpa is best at making those," she smiled.

"Is he indeed?" laughed Grandpa getting up to start breakfast.

"And may we make some fairy cakes today please? I said I would take some tonight for the new fairies."

"Yes, we can make them after breakfast. And what else are you up to today?"

"Err, well we thought we'd go and see Kate."

There was a short silence.

"Well, how wonderful," said Nanny sort of surprised, happy and curious all on one go, "and why are you going today?"

Poppy knew that question would come so was sort of prepared "We're going to tell her about our holiday, as she asked us to." This was a bit of a fib, "and she said we were welcome at any time. We also have some gifts for the children from the fairies." Which was another fib just in case they asked what was in the sack but also true in a way, "and maybe play with the children too," she added for effect.

"Well," said Nanny slightly suspiciously, "that's lovely."

"Yes, that is lovely," said Grandpa, "I presume you're thinking of using the crooked door?"

"Yes, is that OK?"

"Yes of course as long as you have Lord Ted with you."

"Yes, thank you."

"Good, well that sounds like a very exciting day again doesn't it," said Grandpa.

"Yes, it does," said Poppy happily, hoping she'd got away with her slight fibs. She felt very uncomfortable about it but did not want to worry her grandparents or attract unnecessary attention. After all, she'd slept on the most sought after stolen items in the country, and they were actually on Nanny and Grandpa's property – somehow that just did not seem right.

After breakfast Nanny helped Poppy make some fairy cakes while Grandpa was working on something or other in his workshop. It was unexpectedly raining so being indoors for a change was the right thing to do. They made 12 lemon, 12 fruit and 12 chocolate cupcakes that would all be iced later that afternoon but before then Poppy and Lord Ted had a job to do.

Poppy got changed into a nice pair of jeans and a pink jumper with her favourite trainers and borrowed another one of Grandpa's bow ties for Lord Ted, a nice blue one today. While Nanny and Grandpa were both busy, she went to the treehouse and fetched the sack and placed it in her bedroom for when they were ready to go. They decided to leave around 2 o'clock so that everyone would have hopefully had their lunch and allow them enough time to be back for Sunday dinner. Poppy left Lord Ted on his bed and went to say goodbye to Nanny and Grandpa.

She found Nanny reading her book in the sitting room, gave her a hug and said she would see her later. After being told to be careful and to have a lovely time, she went to the garage to find her grandpa.

"I'm off to see Kate now," she told her grandpa.

"OK Popsicle, you look pretty, please be careful and be back by 5 o'clock please."

"OK Grandpa, and thank you."

"Lord Ted will guide you OK?"

"Yes, he'll be with me all the time."

"OK, have fun."

"Thank you," she said and skipped out of the garage back to the house.

Grandpa knew that with Lord Ted by her side, Poppy would be safe. But as a grandparent, it did not stop him being concerned and he would not be at ease until she returned. He remembered when he was Poppy's age and, on deciding to meet the queen with Lord Ted, just how much his own grandparents had been supportive and helpful. He wanted to be as good a grandfather as possible and allow Poppy the freedom he had, but of course the world had changed since then.

Poppy arrived back in her bedroom and gave Lord Ted a squeeze, "OK are you ready then?"

"Yes, I'm excited," said Lord Ted.

"You look very smart by the way."

"Why thank you, I'm quite liking the bow tie look, might keep it. OK you know what to do?"

"Yes, I think so."

All of a sudden Poppy felt very nervous. *What if she opened the door and it was still a wardrobe? What if she actually did not believe and only thought she believed? What would she then say to Nanny and Grandpa about the grey sack with the bright red and gold bow on it? What if this just did not work? What if it was a practical joke and Nanny and Grandpa had fallen to their knees laughing uncontrollably behind her?*

She stood in front of the crooked door, Lord Ted under one arm and the grey sack at her feet. Lord Ted could sense her apprehension.

"It's OK, close your eyes and believe. The other side of the door will be the Duchess of Cambridge."

Poppy closed her eyes. She thought of when she first looked up at the duchess, how beautiful she was, how she put her at ease and how overwhelmed she was sitting in her treehouse meeting the fairies.

Poppy opened her eyes and reached out and turned the doorknob. She peered inside. To her amazement she was looking at the grand entrance hall with high ornate ceilings of Kensington Palace. Elaborate wall coverings and a sumptuous red carpet lay before her.

"Whooooooh," she said quietly.

"You see, you do believe," whispered Lord Ted.

Poppy picked up the sack and closed the door behind her.

"Remember this door as we need to return through here, OK?" said Lord Ted.

"Yes, right OK," said Poppy looking back to see the door which said 'Private' in gold letters.

They entered the hallway and were suddenly greeted by a man in a black suit and tie. He was tall with thinning swept back hair.

"May I help you?" he asked sternly but politely in a soft Scottish accent. Poppy knew she had to be on top form and be confident.

"Yes, thank you. We're here to see the duchess please."

"I see, may I take your name and ask the reason for your visit?"

"Yes, we're here on a personal matter, I believe the duchess may be expecting us. My name is Poppy, and this is Lord Teddington of Bearshire," she said confidently using Lord Ted's full name for dramatic effect. The man's face did not change, he had obviously met many kings and queens and a lord did not make any difference to him. He looked Poppy and Lord Ted up and down.

"I see. Please follow me, may I take your, err, wee bag?"

"Oh yes, thank you," said Poppy forgetting Amy's comments about it being as heavy as a bus to anyone else, and passed it to the man.

As the man took the sack, it crashed to the floor nearly pulling him over and pulling his arm out of its socket.

"Oh, ummppff," he said.

"Oh dear, I forgot, I'm so sorry," said Poppy a little flustered.

"Nay bother," he said trying to pick it up with a huge amount of effort and grunts, "it's a wee bit heavy isn't it." As much as he tried, he could not move it an inch, it was stuck to the floor and not going anywhere.

"Please, I'm so sorry, I'll take it," said Poppy thoroughly annoyed with herself for forgetting what Amy had told her and embarrassed for the man. Poppy reached across and picked it up as if it was a feather. The man stepped back astounded by what he had just seen.

182

"It's a special girl's only bag, sorry," she said again trying to think quickly.

The man straightened his jacket and tie. He dabbed his head with a folded blue and white spotty handkerchief, ran his fingers through his hair and settled himself with a deep breath.

"I see, aye of course, right, err, follow me please."

Poppy and Lord Ted, with Poppy swinging the sack as if it were her school bag, followed the man down a long corridor. The ceilings looked so elaborate and paintings hung on the wall of the royal family's ancestors. They walked by large opulent sideboards with lavish ornaments on top and finally reached a large white door.

"Wait here a wee minute please," asked the man politely. He knocked the door and waited. Poppy heard a faint voice and the man opened the door and walked in.

"Good afternoon ma'am," she heard him say.

"A Miss Poppy and a Lord Teddington of Bearshire to see you."

"Oh, how wonderful!" came the Duchesses' voice from the room. Poppy was sure she heard her clapping too. "Please send them in Hamish."

The man, Poppy now knew to be Hamish, came out and asked Poppy to enter the room. She gave Lord Ted a squeeze "You ready?" she asked.

"Yup," whispered Lord Ted as quietly as he could, thinking that if Hamish heard a teddy bear speak, as well as just meeting what was obviously the strongest girl on the planet, he might just faint.

Poppy thanked Hamish, who bowed his head, then walked in to a grand, bright room that just seemed to be a comfortable family lounge. This was different to the corridor, beautifully decorated with comfortable furniture but not so over elaborate. A television in one corner made it feel normal. Large arched windows looked out to the gardens where Poppy could see children playing and a black cocker spaniel running around in the sunshine, now the rain had stopped.

"Please could we have some tea Hamish?" asked the duchess, who was dressed in a casual shirt and jeans but still looked every bit a princess. Her hair was tied in a ponytail, just like Poppy's and Poppy instantly felt at ease.

"Are you OK Hamish? you look a bit flustered."

"Aye ma'am, I'm fine," he said looking at the sack that Poppy had placed on the floor as if it was about to bite him, "I'll get you ya tea right away ma'am," and left the room.

"Poppy! how wonderful," said the duchess, walking over and giving Poppy a hug. "How absolutely wonderful to see you."

"Hello," said Poppy with a fine curtsy, "we're sorry we came unannounced."

"Nonsense, you're always welcome Poppy, and you Lord Ted. How lovely, please take a seat. So, tell me all about your holiday."

Lord Ted bowed his head.

Poppy sat next to the duchess with Lord Ted and proceeded to tell her all about her holiday, driving the boat, the fabulous house with a hot tub and the walks with all her newfound knowledge on animals, trees and flowers.

"Sounds amazing Poppy, what a fun time. I'd like to take the children there but it's difficult as you can imagine."

"Yes, but we hardly saw anyone really, I think it would be easy to get yourself lost," she smiled

Just then there was a knock at the door and Hamish entered with a large tray with cups, a large pot of tea and slices of cake. He skirted around the sack and placed the tray expertly on a table in front of where the duchess and Poppy were sitting. Poppy's first thought was for poor Hamish who had carried what looked like the heaviest tray ever with ease but could not pick up the grey sack. No wonder he looked so strangely at it.

"I took the liberty of bringing some cake for the wee children too, ma'am," he said kindly.

"Thank you, Hamish, that is most thoughtful," replied the duchess.

Hamish bowed his head, turned and left the room just as the happy black dog ran into the room straight towards Poppy.

"This is Lupo, he's our dog, mad as a hatter."

"Hello boy," said Poppy patting his head as Lupo wagged his tail.

"I'll go and get the children for you to meet, then you can give me an update on all the fairies," said the duchess standing up.

"Err, just before you do, excuse me, I need to show you something, please," she said nervously

"Oh, OK," replied the duchess sitting back down. She could see Poppy was a little anxious, "are you OK?"

"Yes, thank you, it's just, well, I need to return these," she got up and fetched the sack and placed it at her feet. Lupo sniffed at the sack.

The duchess looked at the shabby grey plastic sack and the outlandish bow with a puzzled gaze.

"You're aware that the Pearson brothers were captured a few days ago?" started Poppy

The duchess nodded.

"Well, it seems they dumped the crown jewels they had in Diddlesdale Woods that night. They turned up late and saw what was happening and left quickly."

"OK," said the duchess.

"Yes, well, what I am about to say would not have made sense to anyone else, and as you know, Nanny and Grandpa did not want any police around. You now know the fairies so it will make sense to you."

"OK," said the duchess again slower this time.

"There are more fairies in the woods, and they hid the sack. Other men came to search for it soon after but would never be able to find them, and nor could the police. Isabella, the lead fairy, then told Elvina, who you've met … "

"Yes, she was lovely," interrupted the duchess.

"Yes, she is, anyway they hid them in my tree house when we were on holiday. And here they are, I wanted to return them to you because you'd understand."

"Oh, err, wow, OK," stumbled the duchess, "it's a small sack though and not very much in it by the looks of it."

"Yes, it does look that way, try and pick it up," said Poppy nodding towards the sack.

The duchess reached across to pick the sack up. She could not move it and it nearly pulled her over as she tried, going slightly red in the face as she did so. She sat back and looked at Poppy and let out a deep breath.

"But you just carried it over here?" she said quite startled.

Poppy reached out with her left hand and picked up the sack easily and the duchess's jaw dropped towards the floor.

"It's amazing isn't it?" said Poppy who then explained what Amy had done and that only she can move it. She also explained the incident with Hamish which is why he seemed so flustered earlier.

"Once I undo this bow it will return to normal," she said finally.

"Wow," said the duchess, "I'm not sure what to say."

"I'll move it over to the corner of the room then we can open it there because once I open it, it will be very heavy to move again with what's inside it," said Poppy quite authoritatively.

185

She got up with Lord Ted under her arm, picked up the sack and walked to the opposite corner of the room; the duchess and Lupo followed. Poppy placed the sack down and hoped that it would work, and she would not look foolish.

"I just thought it would be best to do this with you on your own if that's OK?"

"Yes of course Poppy," said the duchess now quite intrigued by what she was seeing.

Poppy gritted her teeth, took a deep breath and pulled the bow. The bow simply disappeared into thin air just as Amy said it would and the bag instantly doubled in size with a small jump.

"Wow!" said the duchess as Lupo barked.

Poppy smiled with relief and gave Lord Ted a squeeze. Inside she was saying, 'Wow' too.

"Holy moly," said Lord Ted.

The sack was now open at the top just as Poppy and Lord Ted had first seen it. The duchess looked in and saw the remaining missing crown jewels.

"I think, well hope, it's all there; we have not touched any of it just in case the police need to do anything," said Poppy.

"Quite," said the duchess, "yes, good idea."

They just stared and looked at it for a short while.

"Well, I'm not sure what to do really," said the duchess eventually.

"If I may suggest ma'am," said Lord Ted.

"Yes, please do," replied the duchess.

"Well, I think we need to inform the assistant chief constable first. I suggest that we say someone left it on your doorstep, or words to that effect."

"OK makes sense, and the second thing?"

"I think we should let Her Majesty know you've found her party hat and clothes."

They all laughed at Lord Ted's description.

"Right then," said the duchess trying to shuffle the bag further into the corner, "let me cover this up with a blanket – Poppy please could you pass me one off the settee?"

"Yes, of course," said Poppy and went to fetch a tartan blanket that was draped over the back of the chair she'd been sitting in.

"This is incredible Poppy, thank you, and you Lord Ted. William's grandmother will be thrilled they're back. I'll make the calls now."

"Thank you for being so understanding," said Poppy, "I was a little scared."

"Nothing to be scared about at all. Right, tea and cake and I'll call in the children."

"Yes, thank you, I'm looking forward to meeting them all."

24

Poppy was excited at the thought of meeting the princes and a princess who were nearer to her own age although she was not sure how she would explain this to her friends at school; maybe she would leave that for now. The duchess poured the tea and told Poppy to help herself to a slice of cake while she went to fetch the children from the garden. Moments later she returned followed by Prince George, Prince Louis and Princess Charlotte. Poppy stood up ready to greet them.

"Poppy, this is George, Charlotte and Louis."

Poppy did a small and respectful curtsy "Hello," she said.

George blushed and went a little shy at the beautiful girl standing in front of him and just sort of waved. Louis waved too but Charlotte on the other hand was bright and bubbly. A little younger than Poppy she was obviously excited to meet another girl, only having two brothers.

"Hi Poppy!" she said, "Mummy has told us all about you and that you know fairies. Mummy said she has met them too?"

"Yes, that's true, your mummy met them not so long ago."

"Please can I see them?" she asked sweetly.

"Yes of course you can."

"Do you have them with you?"

"Ah, no, I wish I had. You would have to come to my nanny and grandpa's house to see them."

"Mummy, can we? Can we please?" asked Charlotte.

"Yes of course we can darling. That would be OK wouldn't it Poppy?"

Poppy nodded as the duchess continued, "I will sort it out with Poppy's nanny when we can go," she said.

"Poppy let's play in the garden," said Charlotte.

Poppy looked at the duchess as if to ask permission.

"Yes, please do Poppy, enjoy the sun. I have a couple of phone calls to make."

"OK great, thank you," said Poppy picking up Lord Ted remembering not to leave him out of her sight, otherwise she might not get back.

"You can leave Lord Ted here if you'd like," said the duchess.

"No, it's OK, thank you. I'll keep him with me," said Poppy very respectfully.

"Yes, OK, I understand," replied the duchess as Charlotte grabbed Poppy's other hand and they ran out into the garden followed by George, who was still a little shy, Louis, who was struggling to keep up and Lupo.

The gardens were just stunning. Much of them are normally open to the public but not that day, they had the freedom of the whole place which was split into different types of garden. The recent robbery at the Tower had meant the closing of royal palaces for three or four weeks for their safety, and the children were going to make the most of it before they reopened. For the next hour or so, the children and Lupo ran from garden to garden with George finally starting to speak. He told Poppy all about the sunken garden made in the memory of Diana, his grandma, full of beautiful white flowers of all sizes and descriptions. Then they decided to play hide and seek in the walled garden with Charlotte and Louis, who was much younger so stayed with his sister, winning the quickest. They laughed and ran around in the sunshine. Poppy was thrilled to play with some children her own age and the princess and princes were happy to have a new friend too.

Eventually they sat on a bench outside the windows of the lounge, slightly out of breath. Lupo sat in front of George and placed his chin on George's knee.

"Can we be proper friends do you think Poppy?" asked George who was the same age as Poppy, "and see each other more?"

"I'd like that," said Poppy.

"And me too Poppy?" asked Charlotte.

"I would love that too," said Poppy who had held on to Lord Ted all the time.

"Is that your bear?" asked George.

"Yes, well sort of, he belongs to my grandpa. His name is Lord Ted, Lord Teddington of Bearshire."

"He is a very nice-looking bear," said Louis, "can I be your friend too?"

"Yes, I hoped you say that," said Poppy kindly and Louis blushed a little.

"So, what are the fairies like?" asked Charlotte.

Poppy explained about when she first met them at Meadow Island, how they'd saved her from the geese and why they'd moved into her oak tree at Nanny and Grandpa's house. She told them their names, what they did, about fairy dust and what they looked like. She told them about when their mother had met them too.

The children listened intently and hung on her every word.

She took care not to mention the fact that they had rescued their great grandmother's crown jewels and trapped a gang of robbers, nor did she tell them that Lord Ted or some of the animals could talk. That, she thought, might be a little too much at this stage. It looked like their mother hadn't said anything either so she left it that way.

In the meantime, the duchess had been making some phone calls. Firstly, to Mary Underberry who agreed to come and see her later that day and check the contents with the Crown Jeweller, making sure all the missing items were accounted for. She also said they may well bring in a team for fingerprint analysis but would let her know. Then to the queen to let her know what had happened.

The queen would usually be at her Balmoral home in Scotland at this time of year, but because of the robbery had remained at the palace.

"Children!" came a call from the window from the duchess.

The all stood up and returned to the lounge.

George entered first, followed by Louis and then Charlotte with Poppy and Lord Ted by her side.

"Grandmama!" said Louis running to greet his great grandmother across the room. Poppy looked up and froze. Her tummy churned over and over as George and Charlotte also ran over to hug their great grandmother, Queen Elizabeth.

The duchess could see that Poppy had frozen on the spot and kindly walked over to hold her free hand. She walked with her towards the queen.

"Poppy, I'd like you to meet William's grandmother, the queen."

Poppy let go of the duchess's hand and performed the best curtsy she had ever done, bearing in mind she had only been doing them for just over a week.

"Your Majesty," she said quite weakly with a dry mouth.

"Hello Poppy," said Queen Elizabeth, "I am so pleased to meet you, my family owe you a great debt."

"Thank you ma'am," said Poppy.

"Children, please can you all go and get washed ready for tea while Grandmama speaks to Poppy?" said the duchess.

The children looked at their mother in disgust. George wanted to point out that Poppy was their friend, not their great-grandmothers, but they knew that if this was the wish of their mother for the queen they should do exactly what was needed.

George and Louis bowed their heads slightly and Charlotte did a small curtsy to the queen and left the room.

"Please, let's sit for a while," said the queen. Poppy waited until the queen had elegantly sat down in a chair and then sat on the end of the settee next to her. With all her might she wanted to get this right and do and say all the right things that she had been taught about manners and respect; if ever there was a time to get it right, it was now.

"And Lord Teddington, how lovely to see you again."

Poppy gave him a squeeze.

"Your Majesty," said Lord Ted bowing his head towards the queen as the duchess sat next to Poppy.

Just then there was a knock at the door and Hamish entered with some fresh tea.

"I am afraid ma'am that I've not brought any banana bread with me," said Poppy smiling but wondering if she should speak out of turn, knowing that she should wait until she is spoken to before she spoke really.

"Oh, you are definitely your grandfather's granddaughter," said the queen, laughing, which helped Poppy relax a little.

Hamish stopped, bowed his head and placed the tray on the small table in front of them. He then stood up, bowed his head again and left the room without uttering a single word.

"Tea Poppy?" asked the duchess.

"Yes please, thank you."

"So, Poppy, please tell me, how are your grandparents?" asked the queen, "I am looking forward to seeing them again."

"They're very well, thank you ma'am, they'll be sad they missed you today."

"Well hopefully we will be able to see them soon. Now then, this frightful mess all happened at the bottom of your grandpa's beautiful garden I understand. Please, tell me all about it, it sounds like something from a film. Kate told me the fairies and Lord Teddington were instrumental in the evening's activity."

Poppy wanted to ask, "So you've been to Nanny and Grandpa's house then?" but was too afraid to ask her question and her grandpa had never mentioned it.

"Yes ma'am, the fairies and Lord Teddington," Poppy took care to use his full name as that's what the queen had used, "were wonderful."

Poppy then explained, in the finest detail, all the happenings at the barn that night with the full moon, the part Lord Ted played and how brave the fairies had been, how Elvina had protected George Featherbottom and to meeting the police the next day. She also took care to mention Jonny Johnson.

"Ah yes, Mr Johnson," interjected the queen, "I have met him a few times and of course, watched him in the final. Very nice man, very tall but very nice."

"Yes, he is ma'am. He let me fly his plane before we went on holiday too," said Poppy.

"Did he? How exciting," she repeated, "and how did you manage to bring the rest of the missing jewels here today?"

Poppy explained why she had visited today and how the rest of queen's jewels had come into her possession and the wonderful work by Amy.

"That is fascinating," said the queen, "and you saw this too Kate?" she asked the duchess.

"Yes ma'am, I could not pick it up no matter how hard I tried but Poppy picked it up as if it were a handbag."

"Well Poppy, I am forever in your debt, you and Lord Teddington were very brave. Please pass on my sincere thanks to Elvina and all her fairies, they have been outstanding."

"I will ma'am, thank you, they'll be very excited to hear that, especially Maisy. May I ask how Mr Featherbottom is ma'am?"

"He is very well, thank you, and he has no idea what happened in the barn and why the men could not get to him. I understand it made them very anxious indeed but now I know why."

"Yes, I expect it did ma'am," said Poppy laughing, "they would never believe it if you told them."

"Indeed," said the queen.

Just then the door opened, and the children entered the room. The queens face lit up as her three great grandchildren came running across the room with big smiles on their faces. The queen asked Poppy about her holiday and agreed the Lake District was a beautiful place and how, as a child, they used to visit there without anyone knowing.

Time was moving on and Poppy looked up at a very tall and fine grandfather clock; she could see that it was very nearly 5 o'clock. The duchess saw that Poppy was looking a little anxious at the time and knowing that Poppy would not want to appear rude, asked her what time she should be back home.

Poppy was thankful. "Grandpa said I was to be home by 5 o'clock ma'am."

"Well, you should be getting back Poppy," said the queen kindly, "as must I, I did not realise that was the time," she continued now getting out of her chair. As she stood up so did the duchess and all the children, who were sitting on the floor by their great grandmother's chair. Poppy realising that must be the right thing to do, also stood up.

"I'll get Hamish to see you to your car ma'am," said the duchess.

"Poppy, it has been wonderful meeting you and of course Lord Teddington," said the queen offering her hand to her. Poppy was not overly sure what to do but took her hand and completed another perfect curtsy.

"Thank you, Your Majesty," she replied on the way back up from her curtsy looking the queen straight in the eye.

"The pleasure was all mine," said the queen. The queen then gave her three great grandchildren hugs, thanked the duchess for the call and the tea just as Hamish came to escort her to her car.

After she left the room Poppy flopped back into the settee holding Lord Ted close to her.

"How did I do ma'am?" she asked the duchess with a sigh.

"Perfectly Poppy," she said laughing.

"Phew," she laughed with George, Charlotte and Louis looking at her wondering what all the fuss was about, "right I better be getting back please."

"Yes of course," said the duchess.

"Will you come back to see us soon Poppy?" asked George.

"I would love to, thank you."

"And can we come and visit you with the fairies?" asked Charlotte.

"I would love that too, maybe the next holidays?"

"I'll speak to your nanny Poppy," said the duchess.

Poppy stood up and gave the duchess a big hug and thanked her for everything. Charlotte also gave Poppy a big hug. George however held her hand and bowed his head. It took Poppy by surprise as she thought it should be the other way around but smiled.

"I hope to see you soon Poppy," said the prince.

"Me too," said Poppy.

They stood, still holding hands, and looked into each other's eyes for a few seconds. Louis was not sure what to do so just hid behind his mother's legs and waved.

"I've had a lovely afternoon, thank you."

"Us too Poppy and thanks again for the, err… gifts. I'll walk you out," said the duchess, "do you know where you are going?"

"Yes ma'am, thank you."

The duchess walked towards the door and opened it for Poppy. She left the room and walked a little way down the corridor. Looking back at the lounge door she saw the three children and their mother who waved and Lupo wagging his tail. Poppy waved back then continued until she reached the entrance hall and gave Lord Ted a squeeze.

"Back through that door Poppy," he said.

"Yes, OK."

She looked back again and could see everyone still by the lounge door waving. She waved again and made her way to the door marked 'Private'. She knew she could not hesitate; she had to open it and hope she would walk back into her bedroom. As she approached, she focussed on her bedroom, her own bedroom at Nanny and Grandpa's. In the distance she could hear the duchess shout "No, not that door!"

She turned the handle and walked in.

The duchess ran down the corridor knowing that Poppy had gone into the wrong room. She got to the door which was the private office for the estate. She opened the door and saw the staff working at their desks who all stood up as soon as she came in.

"Did a young girl with her teddy bear just walk in?" she asked slightly out of breath from running.

"No ma'am," said one of the young ladies from behind her desk looking at the duchess as if she had gone a bit strange.

Poppy was sat on the end of her bed, in her bedroom, at Nanny and Grandpa's house in Diddlesdale.

"Well, wasn't that amazing Lord Ted," she said giving Lord Ted a squeeze.

"Brilliant, and back in time for Sunday dinner," said Lord Ted.

They went downstairs and entered the kitchen where Nanny and Grandpa were about to serve up dinner.

"Perfect timing Poppy, I was just about to give you a shout," said Nanny, "fun time?"

"Wonderful Nanny, absolutely wonderful," she said, "and I have something to tell you."

"Well let's have dinner first, then you can tell us all about it. I iced the cakes for you earlier, so they'll be ready for you this evening."

"Thank you Nanny."

They sat down to dinner, roast beef, crispy roast potatoes, fresh vegetables from the garden and beef gravy. And for pudding; hot apple pie and custard. *Could today get any better* thought Poppy.

As they started to clear up Poppy began to explain the day's events starting with the fact the missing crown jewels had been in her treehouse. Nanny and Grandpa stopped what they were doing and sat at the table to listen to Poppy. For the third time that day she explained how the jewels had been found and the expertise of Amy with the sack.

"Well Poppy, why didn't you tell us?" asked Nanny.

"I wanted to, but I also didn't want to worry you. I know we don't want to attract attention with the police and would find it hard to explain how they got there, and with Kate meeting the fairies it made sense. Once we saw what Amy could do, it seemed the right thing to do. I am very sorry for not telling you the full truth, but I didn't lie."

"That's OK," said Grandpa kindly, "we understand but you can trust us you know. Now then, tell us more about what Amy did."

Poppy went through it in great detail with her nanny and grandpa hanging on every word she said.

"Amazing," said Grandpa, "it's wonderful how closely they interact with you. It's very special."

Poppy explained what happened earlier in the day starting with the crooked door and how nervous she felt. They laughed at poor Hamish trying to carry the sack. Then how she had met Kate, met the children and played in the garden and finally getting to meet the queen.

"Oh Poppy, I am so thrilled for you," said Nanny, "how absolutely wonderful."

"Isn't she lovely?" continued Poppy, "the first thing she asked was how you both were. Has she been here?"

"Yes, a couple of times," said Grandpa.

"George, Charlotte and Louis want to come here too."

"That would be OK Poppy," said Nanny.

"George is so lovely," said Poppy slightly blushing.

Nanny smiled at her knowingly.

"So, what happens now?" asked Grandpa.

"Mary Underberry is going to Kensington Palace tonight with the Crown Jeweller to make sure it's all there. I didn't touch anything, so I'm not sure if it's all there anyway, I hope it is."

"You mean you didn't try the crown and robe on?" laughed Grandpa.

"Grandpaaaaaa!" responded Poppy, laughing.

After Poppy had explained all she could and answered all Nanny and Grandpa's questions it was time to get ready for bed. Secretly Poppy was absolutely exhausted but knew she had to meet all the fairies before she went to sleep. She had promised she would tell them all about returning the crown jewels and of course, they were expecting cake.

Poppy returned to the kitchen where Nanny had put all the cakes in a large tin ready to take to the treehouse. Cake before bedtime was something that Poppy thought she could get used to. Grandpa was watching the television waiting for the news to see if there was any mention of the crown jewels so Poppy went to sit next to him, although it was getting late.

There was no mention of it in the headlines. The news focussed more on the return of farm equipment, the harvest and the grateful farmers. It was nice to have some good news for a change.

Poppy wished her grandparents goodnight and with Lord Ted tucked under her arm, and carrying the quite heavy cake tin, made her way down to the tree house. She switched on the fairy lights and made her way up the stairs and was surprised to see Deri waiting for her. Deri was sitting on the balustrade and was really pleased to see Poppy.

"Hi Poppy," she said with her happy smile.

"Hi Deri, what are you doing here?"

"I'm on cake watch, I was hoping you'd arrive when it was my turn."

"Cake watch?"

"Ha ha, yes, we've been taking it in turns to watch out for you so we could let all the others know when you were here. We're excited to hear what happened, oh, and cake obviously."

"You are funny," said Poppy opening her bright red shiny door, "you can let the others know now."

"OK, be back in a minute or two."

Poppy placed the cake tin on her desk and opened the lid. Inside, just as before, Nanny had put some serviettes and a cake knife so she could cut the cakes into smaller pieces for the 22 fairies she now knew. She had left the door open and soon heard the familiar voice of Elvina.

"Please can we come in?"

Poppy turned around to see all the fairies, the glow of all their wings when they were hovering together was mesmerising and beautiful.

"Yes, of course you can."

"Thank you," said Elvina as they all swept by and found somewhere to sit.

As Poppy had the cake knife in her hand it seemed the right time to ask if anyone, by any chance, might want some cake.

"Me, me, me!" came the excited response from all the fairies together with, "Sir, miss please," from Olly.

"OK, so we have chocolate, lemon or fruit?"

"CHOKLIT!" came the overwhelming response, apart from Olly who very shyly added "Lemon please miss." Olly was so shy that Poppy cut him a piece first and took it over to him. He blushed but was very pleased that he was first.

On her way back she looked at Jareth and Gullveig sitting next to their new girlfriends Elga and Emily.

"You two are very quiet for a change," she laughed.

"Thank you Miss Poppy," said Jareth.

"They don't argue anymore miss," said Elga.

"Yes we do," said Gullveig and Emily poked him in the ribs, and everyone started laughing.

Eventually when everyone had their chocolate cake, Olly had seconds of lemon cake and Poppy her favourite fruit cake, Poppy and Lord Ted explained what happened at Kensington Palace. The fairies fell about laughing when Lord Ted told them about poor Hamish and loved hearing about the princes and the princess.

"They'd all like to come and meet you too; that would be nice wouldn't it?"

"Yes, it would, I think Prince George might like you Poppy," said the very wise Elvina.

"He was very nice," said Poppy blushing slightly, "but the best thing was Amy's work," she continued very quickly trying to change the subject, "it was brilliant Amy thank you."

"And when will we know if all of the crown jewels have been found, or if there are any missing?" asked Isabella.

"Hopefully soon," said Poppy, "the Crown Jeweller, the man who cares for them, was checking tonight."

Poppy then went on to the meeting with the queen herself. The fairies listened intently as Poppy explained how grateful the queen was as she had explained everything in detail to her and the part all the fairies played, not only the night they caught the robbers but the recovery of the remaining crown jewels.

"Thank you Poppy," said Maisy, "it means so much that she knows what we've done, thank you."

"And I have something to tell you too now," said Elvina "when are you going home?"

"Next week as I have to go back to school," said Poppy sadly.

"Oh, oh dear," said Elvina forlornly.

"Why, what's up?"

"Well, in 13 days' time it will be the Harvest Moon and, well we thought you and Lord Ted would like to join us?"

"Yes, we'd love to, but I'll be back at school."

"Thirteen days' time will be a Saturday," said Lord Ted.

"Oh, will it? Then yes, yes of course. I'll speak to Nanny and Grandpa."

"Good, good, because Alfred and I are getting married," said Elvina almost far too quickly and quietly to be understood.

"Excuse me?" said Poppy wide eyed.

"Yes, we're getting married."

"OH Wow!" shouted Poppy jumping to her feet, "REALLY?"

"Yes."

"Oh, that's amazing, yes, yes of course we'd like to come, we'd be honoured, congratulations."

"We've been dating for 73 years now so I suppose it's about time," said Alfred, laughing.

"Yes, well, I suppose it is, how wonderful."

"Congratulations to you both," said Lord Ted.

"I'm so excited, thank you for asking us," said Poppy almost jumping up and down on the spot.

"Humans don't usually get invited to fairy weddings, but we thought it would be different with you and Lord Ted," said Elvina.

"Thank you," said Lord Ted thinking he was a human too.

"And we'd like to invite Nanny and Grandpa too, if that's OK?"

"Yes, they'd be delighted to come. Oh Elvina, how exciting."

"Yes, I am very excited too, aren't we Alfred."

"Yes dear," said Alfred cynically and that made everyone laugh.

After everyone had calmed down and Poppy had got her breath back, she sat down and put Lord Ted on her knee.

"So where will the wedding be held?" asked Lord Ted.

"Good question, we're not sure. If we're inviting you all we couldn't have it in the trees," said Elvina who was glowing with pride at being a bride.

"We could have it in Grandpa's garden," said Lord Ted.

"Good idea," added Poppy.

"Do you think he would do that?" asked Elvina.

"Yes of course he would, you know that," said Lord Ted, "we're far enough away from any other houses for it still to be very private."

"Yes, but we would never assume anything."

"I'll ask him, but we all know the answer will be yes don't we," said Poppy, "so what happens exactly, you know, is it the same as human weddings? I've only ever been to one wedding before; I was a bridesmaid."

"Well, the most senior fairy of the closest herd tells us we're married, which is Isabella."

"It is and I am so excited," said Isabella shaking, screwing up her little face and clenching her fists.

"Then we have food and dance as it's a full moon."

"Lovely," said Poppy.

"What if it rains?" asked Nina, "we won't have any cover in the garden."

"Grandpa has one of those gazebo things I think, I'll ask him; he's always checking what the weather will be doing so he'll know what to do but I'm sure it won't rain for such a special occasion. We could get some nice chairs for us and a bench for you, Grandpa could put lots of fairy lights around and Nanny could make a cake," said Poppy not knowing if they would but was sure it would be OK if she asked nicely.

"We don't want you to go to any trouble," said Alfred.

"It's the least we can do," said Poppy, "we should try and make it as special as we can."

"That's nice, thank you, so would you like to bring George?" asked Elvina winking.

"Really!" said Poppy excitedly but then blushed slightly, "err, well, ahem, I suppose I could ask – but then Charlotte and Louis would want to come, and I'm sure Kate would not want to miss out, so I'm not sure. That's a lot of people at a secret fairy wedding."

"Elvina and I have talked about it and we've asked Isabella and Delilah too. We'd be really happy for them to all come," said Alfred commandingly, "the royal family at a fairy wedding would make history and Elvina deserves the best," he added sweetly.

"Oh, that is a lovely thing to say Alfred," said Poppy.

The chit chat continued for a while longer. Poppy wanted to know what food Nanny could prepare, establishing quite quickly that it was basically cake. She asked Elvina about what she would be wearing but she couldn't say in front of Alfred, some traditions it seems, were the same. Elvina said there may be about 50 fairies in total, some coming from Meadow Island and some from nearby herds that Isabella and Delilah said they should invite, but they must keep the fact that the royal family might come a secret, otherwise there might be thousands turning up and they did not want that. All of this discussion was happening while Poppy was serving more cake.

"Do you have bridesmaids Elvina?"

"Yes, I do – Oona, Deri, Nixie, Sophie, Emma and Maisy."

Oona, Deri, Nixie, Sophie, Emma and Maisy all smiled.

"Gosh, that's a lot," said Poppy.

"And I'm making all the dresses," said Amy proudly.

"Wow, you are a talented fairy aren't you Amy?" said Poppy as Amy blushed. "What a wonderful thing to look forward to. I was a little sad as I would be going back to school but now I am very happy again."

"Thank you so much Poppy, we knew you'd like to come."

"You just try and stop us!" replied Poppy, laughing.

Eventually everyone was stuffed full of cake, but Olly politely asked for just one more piece of lemon as he seemed to be the only one eating it.

"I'll make sure there's some lemon cake just for you on the day Olly," said Poppy making Olly all embarrassed again but he loved that Poppy was looking after him.

"Right, time for Poppy's bedtime I think, it is quite late," said Elvina.

Poppy looked up at the clock to see it was almost midnight; if she was tired before, she was now exhausted. It had been a very long and exciting day and the adrenalin of all the excitement had kept her going. After the fairies had given their thanks and finally all gone Lord Ted snuggled into Poppy's side.

"Well that's a lot to look forward to. Do you think Nanny and Grandpa will be OK?"

"You know they will."

They lay in silence for a while.

"What do you think I'll be when I grow up?" she asked Lord Ted eventually.

"I think you should just be a good, kind human being," he replied, "there's a lot of opportunity and very little competition there. I think you have all the skills that are needed."

"Thank you, Lord Ted," she said giving him a loving squeeze, "as long as you are by my side I'll be OK."

"You will."

To be continued...

in the next adventures of Poppy and Lord Ted